D0065219

STRANGELETS

STRANGELETS

Michelle Gagnon

Published in the United States in 2013 by Soho Teen
an imprint of
Soho Press, Inc.
853 Broadway
New York, NY 10003

Library of Congress Cataloging-in-Publication Data

Gagnon, Michelle
Strangelets / by Michelle Gagnon.
p. cm
ISBN 978-1-61695-137-5 (alk. paper)
eISBN 978-1-61695-138-2
1. Near-death experiences—Fiction. 2. Survival—Fiction.
3. Escapes—Fiction. 4. Science fiction. I. Title.
PZ7.G1247St 2013
[Fic]—dc23 2012038333

Interior design by Janine Agro, Soho Press, Inc.

Printed in the United States of America

10 9 8 7 6 5 4 3 2 1

For the real Lisa Brown

STRANGELETS

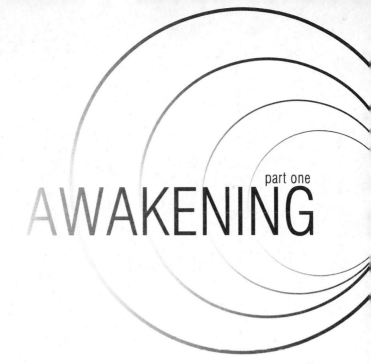

part one

AWAKENING

Palo Alto, California, USA

Sophie Page felt herself getting closer. Every inhalation drew further apart from the previous one until there were measurable gaps between them. She could almost picture the breaths strung like beads on a necklace, stretching off into the distance, growing more isolated from one another as they approached the horizon. Her heartbeat followed suit, slowing until she only felt an occasional tap against her ribcage.

It was easier than she'd expected, letting go. Sophie was vaguely aware of her parents standing on either side of the hospital bed, gripping her hands tightly as if that alone could tether her to earth. Her younger sister sobbed quietly at the foot of the bed. The whisper of sneakers on linoleum came and went as nurses flitted around like moths, doing their best to be unobtrusive.

They'd offered her a priest, but she'd turned them down. It seemed hypocritical when she hadn't been in a church in years. She'd allowed her parents to tuck Soup, the bedraggled stuffed cat she'd slept with as a child, in bed beside her. But they all knew that was more for their sakes than hers.

Sophie drew a sudden, sharp breath. She hadn't known exactly what to expect. Over the past few months, as her inevitable demise approached, she'd developed a voracious appetite for stories of near-death experiences. Apparently people saw everything from angels to a bright light to noth-ingness. Some were exotic: a Lakota chief claimed that he rose above the clouds and saw a circular hoop surrounding the world, its edges vanishing into infinity. Others were more mundane, like the Calcutta man who found himself in an office where a panel of faceless people berated him for show-ing up early, then sent him back to his body.

Sophie figured she should have *something* to look for-ward to. Anything was preferable to her present: endless rounds of chemotherapy and countless discussions with doctors who tried to explain why her lymphoma hadn't responded to treatment. A steady stream of hospital beds until she finally landed in this one, in a hospice. Would she see anything at all? The secrets of the universe revealed? A strange bureaucracy? Or just a blinding flash, then nothing?

Whatever she'd expected, it hadn't been this.

Her parents stiffened, though she could still feel their grasp. Her sister had frozen mid-sob, as if someone had snapped a photo. The walls suddenly seemed to bow out, expanding. Like the hospice room had come to life and sucked in a huge breath of air. And at the foot of her bed was . . . a circle. Not light, exactly, but not dark either. Sophie was transfixed by it. Every color imaginable whirled in a dizzying gyre. It started out small as a pinhole, rapidly increasing until it was the size of a bread loaf, then a car. As it grew, it drew the contents of the room inexorably inward. Sophie wanted to call out to her family and ask if they were seeing it too, and maybe knew what it was. But she was immobilized, heavy—and this was it, she realized. This was how she was going to die.

An overwhelming sense of calm descended on her. Sophie relaxed, letting her mind spin along with the gyre, touching lightly on memories. The time she ran away and Mom found her hiding behind the local ice cream store . . . When Nora was first brought home from the hospital and Sophie couldn't believe this tiny screaming thing was her sister . . . Dad swinging her up on his shoulders to pick apples.

Sophie didn't have any regrets, not really. It would have been nice to have lived longer: a real life, a full one. But she'd had plenty of time to come to terms with the fact that she'd never go to college. Never know what it felt like to fall in love. Never get married or have kids of her own to take apple picking and fight with and console. She was ready. The gyre reached the tips of her toes. A peculiar heat came off it, as if it were a living thing lapping at her heels. Sophie smiled one last time and closed her eyes, letting it take her.

Galway City, County Galway, Ireland

Declan Murphy tripped and nearly went flying. At the last moment he regained his footing and tore forward, feeling the hard pavement through his worn trainers.

He chanced a glance over his shoulder. The men were still after him. They looked winded—they were old, after all, probably thirty—but seemed to be closing the gap. And they looked damned pissed.

"Bloody hell," Declan muttered to himself. *All this fuss*

over a box. He tucked it more securely under his arm and kept running.

He had no idea what was inside. Based on the dogged-ness of his pursuers, it was probably more valuable than he'd thought. As Declan rounded the corner, his mind spun through possible escape routes. Usually, he'd have at least three mapped out in advance. But this had been a one-off, a job taken on a lark from a random guy in a pub. Not the sort of thing he'd usually do. Problem was, he'd had in mind to buy something nice for Katie, her birthday coming up and all. And she'd made him swear that any gift he gave her was bought, not stolen. So when the stranger offered a hundred euros up front, another hundred on delivery, Declan agreed. After all, the man said he was only claiming what was right-fully his in the first place. And it was a house job, not a bank or business. He assured Declan that the study window was never locked and no one would be home.

In and out, easy, the bloke claimed. *Quickest two hundred euros you'll ever make.*

Except, of course, there *had* been someone. Two some-ones, in fact—they'd entered the room as he was slipping back out the window. By the time Declan reached the corner they were nearly on top of him, proving to be in surprisingly good running shape for a couple of old bastards.

The house was located in Salthill, the nicer section of Gal-way. *Should've known*, he chided himself. His mum always said not to trust lads from Salthill. It was a part of town that Declan didn't know well, so he shouldn't have been surprised when he darted right and hit an alleyway that dead-ended into a solid brick wall. He'd made a right hames of it, sure enough. Either that or the fool in the pub had set him up.

Cursing, he doubled back, only to find his pursuers

blocking the entrance. Declan's eyes darted around, looking for a fire escape, a dumpster, anything. But he was surrounded on all three sides, not so much as a bin lid at hand to toss at them.

His pulse quickened as they strode toward him, clenching and releasing their fists. Still, Declan forced a cocky grin as they advanced. "Aye, you got me, then." He raised the box with both hands. "You're welcome to it."

Already got a hundred euros, after all, he told himself. More than enough to get Katie the necklace he'd had his eye on. A heart with a ruby set in the center, the color just a few shades brighter than her hair. Declan sighed. Really would have been so much easier just to lift it. She'd never have known, and there was hardly any security to speak of at Hartmann's, at least nothing he couldn't get past.

With no response from the pair, he set the box down and backed away until he reached the rear brick wall. The larger one stooped to retrieve it. He was tall with dark hair and a jutting chin. The other bloke was blond, lean, and compact. He stared at Declan, unblinking.

They whispered to each other in hard, low voices. It was a different language; Russian, maybe? They had that Slavic look, as if no matter how much they ate they'd still be hungry.

Declan swallowed. "All good then, eh?" he managed.

The taller one handed the box to his mate. He opened it without taking his eyes off Declan, checked inside, then nodded brusquely. He strode out of the alley without looking back.

The taller one watched him leave, then turned. Something in his eyes struck Declan to the core, a sort of tired resignation. With slow-motion horror, Declan watched the Russian reach under his T-shirt and pull a pistol from the waistband of his jeans. Declan raised both hands. "Hold up, mate," he said. "I mean to tell no one, if that's worrying you . . ."

The Russian glanced back over his shoulder, clearly checking for witnesses.

Turning, he raised the gun to shoulder height. Time seemed to slow. The attacker's eyes looked bored, sleepy. Somehow that made it even worse, like at the end of the day he'd barely remember this. Declan pictured him sitting down to supper, telling the wife, *Aye, I went to the bank and the Tesco, got a pint . . . something else . . . oh, nearly forgot about shooting that seventeen-year-old lad in the head.*

Declan felt his knees start to go, everything inside him rapidly turning to liquid. Katie's face flashed through his mind, her eyes sparkling, light glinting off her teeth as she laughed.

But all he could see was the dark barrel of the gun, the Russian's jaws working a piece of gum as he aimed . . .

The gunman's eyes suddenly widened. As he reared back, the gun fired. Declan ducked, terrified, hands instinctively protecting his head. Tiny shards of brick rained down on his skull.

A miss. Declan had a chance.

"Jay-sus, please," he pleaded frantically. "I swear on my mother's life . . ."

But the bloke didn't seem to have heard him. He was backing away, both hands raised as if warding something off. He looked terrified, his face curiously illuminated . . .

Declan frowned. Crazy bastard was acting as if a monster had appeared behind him; he swiveled around to make sure one hadn't. He blinked. There was an enormous hole in the wall below where the bullet had struck: a swirling, glowing whirlpool. In a brick wall.

Panic was suddenly replaced by something else . . . Wonder?

Relief? It reminded him of those stories they told in church, of true miracles . . . Reverently, Declan reached toward the colors with both hands—

Something yanked hard from the other side, dragging him into the vortex.

Rafah, Gaza Strip, Palestinian Territories

Anat Erez pulled her hair back in a tight knot and covered it with a black cap. She checked over her shoulder, scanning the line of olive trees silhouetted at the top of the hill. It was hard to suppress the feeling that she'd been followed. Then again, a certain sensible paranoia was healthy.

A single light flickered in the window of the house in front of her. It was little more than a hut: single-story cinderblock construction, no porch. A far cry from the three-bedroom house she'd spent the last eighteen years sharing with her family in Tel Aviv. *But it was just a way station,* Anat reminded herself. She'd only be inside for a few minutes anyway.

A cloudless night would have been better, but there wasn't enough time to wait. Another few weeks and Egypt would likely have completed their subterranean barrier. Plus she was due to report back for military service in two days, and escape from the base was virtually impossible. No, this was her last chance to get away. Anat drew a deep breath and approached the door.

She knocked twice, waited a beat, then rapped again. After a long pause, it creaked open soundlessly. A tiny, wizened woman blinked up at her. Her hair and face were wrapped in a traditional hijab, her body shrouded in the flowing black robe favored by the Bedouin. The top of her head barely reached Anat's chest. Without a word she turned and vanished into the depths of the house.

Anat followed, trying to exude confidence even though she was terrified. They passed through a darkened kitchen, the air heavy with the tang of lamb and spices. Anat's stomach growled. She'd been too nervous to eat much at dinner; instead she'd spent the meal covertly gazing at each member of her family, committing their faces to memory. She'd already accepted the fact that she'd probably never see them again.

That was the past, she reminded herself. Now, after months of planning, she was here. Anat gulped hard and followed the woman into the next room. The small space was lit by a candle set in a wall niche. Even in the flickering half-light, Anat could see that the rug was rich and plush in comparison to the starkness of its surroundings. The old woman kicked at it with her heel, exposing the edge of a trapdoor. She jerked her arm at the floor.

Anat bent over and rolled away the rug. The trapdoor was bigger than she'd expected, roughly four by four feet. A large metal latch was set into the wood on one end. At another harsh gesture from the woman, Anat bent double and hauled it open, grunting with the effort.

A flight of cracked concrete stairs descended into the darkness. Anat set her foot down, gauging her weight against the top step as she drew a flashlight out of her backpack's side pouch. The woman tugged at her arm, frowning.

"What's the problem?" Anat asked in halting Arabic. She cursed herself for not mastering the language; it would have been a good idea for all sorts of reasons.

The woman's hands flew as she spoke, agitation on her face.

Anat didn't recognize the dialect but gathered that there was some question about payment. "I already paid the fee," she stammered, hoping she was using the correct term. "By smuggling, last month."

The woman shook her head firmly.

Anat's lips pursed together. She'd been afraid something like this might happen. She'd arranged to cover the cost of her passage into Egypt by smuggling cartons of cigarettes across the border. Not guns, or any sort of weapons—she'd insisted on that. Khalid, the smuggler she'd dealt with, had scoffed at her but Anat refused to budge. There was no way she was bringing anything into Gaza that would then be used against Israel.

She'd paid for tonight's journey by making three separate trips between Gaza and Tel Aviv. Israelis were rarely harassed in transit. But their documents were noted, and tonight Anat didn't want to leave a trail for anyone to follow. Hence the necessity of a departure underground. The tunnels between Egypt and the Gaza Strip had served as a conduit for everything from food and medicine to rockets and mortars over the years. Anat repressed a twinge at the thought that she was entering a passage built by Hamas militants intent on the destruction of her people. If she'd finished her military training, there was a good chance she would have faced some of the very artillery that had been shipped through here.

No matter. That part of her life was over. This tunnel would lead her to Egypt, and to Hazim. At the thought, she reflexively twisted the gold band on her right index finger. Not a proper wedding ring, not yet. But soon, she'd have another ring to add to it.

As Anat's eyes refocused on the woman before her, she felt a twinge of annoyance. She'd expected Khalid to escort her through the tunnel. Typical of him to change the plan without consulting her. Was this old crone a relation? His mother, maybe? *No matter*, she reminded herself. It was a tunnel, after all, one way in and one way out; she hardly needed a smuggler to show her the way. Anat had come this far. Nothing was going to stop her now—especially not a dwarfish woman who looked like she could barely stand unassisted. At the thought, her stomach settled somewhat.

"I already paid," Anat said firmly in Hebrew. "And now I'm going."

Yanking free her arm, she clambered down the stairs. There was a muttered grumble behind her, then the trapdoor slammed shut—smothering her in pitch blackness. Anat's throat caught. She fumbled for the flashlight, emitting a gasp of relief when it flared to life.

The beam illuminated the remainder of the stairwell. At the bottom, a narrow dirt passage vanished into shadowy abyss. It smelled dank and oppressive, like that Byzantine crypt she'd visited on a field trip to Jerusalem, in happier times . . .

Anat swallowed again. She'd never liked close, dark spaces and was acutely aware of the press of earth overhead. There were frequent news reports about tunnels like these collapsing. Old Israeli cynics called them "wormholes," claiming they offered a theoretical passage to some alternate universe (Egypt certainly qualified). Get stuck in one and you'd vanish in time, like a rat Palestinian smuggler or a bit of stardust.

At the bottom of the stairs Anat waved the beam over rough-hewn walls. At least this tunnel appeared well constructed, despite its size. She had to tilt her head to keep from brushing the ceiling. This was one of the few times that her height worked against her. If she jutted out her elbows, they'd scrape the walls on either side of her. She swallowed down the claustrophobia and pressed onward.

To distract herself, Anat tried to picture the underground barrier that the Egyptian army was building somewhere close by. The bomb-proof steel wall extended along the border for more than ten kilometers and plunged eighteen meters below the surface. Once it was completed, this type of escape would no longer be possible. Anat tried to take comfort from that. She couldn't have afforded to wait, right?

Anat had no idea how far this tunnel went, or where exactly it would emerge. She'd heard that some were nearly 800 meters long. That was all right. Even stooped and stumbling, she could walk that in less than twenty minutes. Steeling herself, she picked up the pace. A street map of Rafah, Egypt was tucked in her backpack. But she didn't need it; she'd memorized the fastest route from the tunnel exit to the small hotel where she was meeting Hazim.

That is, if the tunnel ended where she thought it might. Khalid had been a little vague about the exact spot, or what she could expect to find there.

Something shimmered up ahead, just past the beam of her flashlight. Anat's heart leapt into her throat. The air was suddenly thick with a pungent smell that reminded her of burning plastic. Khalid had also promised that she wouldn't encounter anyone else. The last thing she needed was to run into real smugglers.

Trembling slightly, Anat raised the flashlight beam. She frowned. The tunnel ahead had vanished, the dirt floor dropping into darkness. Had a section of the floor collapsed, maybe?

"*Kus emek*," she muttered.

Her eyes widened as more of the floor slid into the void. Its advance picked up speed under her flashlight, like a fishing line being reeled in. Anat took a step back, then another.

Seized by panic, she turned and sprinted back toward the trap door, the flashlight jerking crazily over the rough dirt. Her breath came in tight gasps. Her chest burned. The straps of her backpack slipped from her shoulders, but there was no time to retrieve it. She'd move faster without it anyway.

She'd nearly reached the stairs when she had the disconcerting sensation of being sucked backward. Anat fought to grab hold of something, clawing at the dirt with her nails. But she was drawn inexorably toward the encroaching void. *I should have known better than to trust a smuggler*, she thought. With that, the force swallowed her whole.

CHAPTER TWO

The Hospital

Sophie opened her eyes and frowned. Weird. She was still in a hospital bed. Of course, in most near-death experience stories, people woke up just like this. She hadn't expected to be one of them, though. She really thought she'd *died*. But then, she'd always joked that spending eternity in a hospital was her idea of hell. Wouldn't it be ironic if she turned out to be right?

Her wry smile faded to a frown as she took in her surroundings. If she was still alive, they must have moved her. This wasn't the hospice room where she'd spent the last few weeks of her life. The fake ficus tree in the corner was gone. The cheap TV had been swapped out for a swanky flat screen. And instead of being hooked up to numerous beeping machines—via needles and sticky pads and probes—she was attached to nothing. At least, nowhere she could feel. Even weirder, she still wore her own pajamas—anywhere but a hospice would have insisted on an official gown. *Why had they moved her?*

The window curtains were drawn; it must be nighttime, even though the overhead lights weren't muted the way they usually were. Which also explained why her family was gone.

Still, it was kind of strange for them to head home when she was at death's door, after barely leaving her alone for weeks. Maybe something in her condition had changed. But she couldn't have improved that much, right? Unless they'd suddenly developed a cure for her rare brand of terminal lymphoma that afternoon . . .

She scoffed. The doctors had made it pretty clear that nothing short of a miracle would buy her even a few more months. And Sophie wasn't a big believer in miracles.

She felt alive enough, though: groggy and thirsty and irritated. Sophie sighed.

She was ready to be gone. She'd felt *relief* as that void had swallowed her whole. But she must have been dreaming, right?

Great. The last thing she wanted was to face more interminable weeks with her family hovering around maintaining a deathwatch.

Well, since she was apparently stuck here, she might as well try to get some real sleep. And for that, she'd need painkillers; after months of morphine, it was tough to sleep without it. But the stand that usually held the drip with its "magic button" was gone; the machine let her dose herself as needed and turned off automatically when she tried to take too much. She knew that from experience, having tried a couple of times to mess with it. She'd always found that fail-safe measure annoying; why not just let her make the decision? That way she could have spared her family weeks of *their* lives.

Well, a nurse should be able to get the drip set up in a couple of minutes, max. Sighing, Sophie fumbled around for the call button with her right hand. No sign of it. She tried with her left; sometimes the newer, more incompetent RNs moved it to the wrong side during sponge baths. Not there either. Crap. There was no way she was going to be able to sleep with fluorescent lights glaring down on her, it was like trying to nod off on the surface of the sun.

"Damn it," she muttered. "I can't believe they forgot to turn off the lights—"

Sophie yelped as the room abruptly plunged into darkness.

In the wake of the glare, it took a minute for her eyes to adjust. Not pitch black, she realized; there was a faint glowing seam around the circumference of the room at ankle height and another at waist level, casting the space in a watery blue glow. Sophie experienced the disarming sensation of having been suddenly submerged.

"Weird," she said out loud. She'd spent a serious chunk of the years since her diagnosis in various hospital rooms. None had been this fancy. And as far as she'd seen, no one had entered the room to dim the lights. Something occurred to her. It was ridiculous, but maybe . . .

"Lights!" Sophie called, feeling silly.

She flinched as the lights flared back to life. "Dim lights?" she tried. Sure enough, they faded to a pleasant half-glow. She almost laughed.

"Wow," she muttered. Wherever she was, it was pretty over the top. Dad's health insurance had balked at covering the hospice costs, so how could they afford this place? She'd really love to ask someone. She groped among the blankets for the call button again, then peered over both sides of the bed.

A strange realization struck her. Slowly, Sophie drew back up to a seated position and held her hands in front of her face, examining them.

It had been at least a week since she'd managed to move so much as a finger. She'd grown accustomed to the slightest motion sending waves of pain through her, tortuous jolts that were only diminished by the steady pump of morphine. But not only was the IV drip gone, there was no scar where it had been attached. And *nothing* hurt. She almost felt like she'd never been ill. Suddenly, Sophie wasn't tired anymore. If anything, she felt like jumping out of bed and turning somersaults down the hall.

But it would probably be a good idea to clear that with a nurse first.

Sophie took a deep breath, then called out, "Hello? Anyone?"

No response.

Here goes nothing. One at a time, she eased her legs off the bed. Wiggled her toes, then rolled her ankles. So far, so good. She lowered her feet to the floor, clutching the bed rail in case her legs buckled. She hadn't walked in over a month. Her legs felt weak, wobbly, but they held up. She took one shuffling step forward, then another. Inch by inch, she made her way across the room.

By the time she reached the door, Sophie was panting, and her legs shook. She'd never exactly been an athlete, but this was pathetic, like being a toddler again. She clung to the handle and leaned against the wall, catching her breath. Summoning her last reserves of strength, she pulled the door open.

More weirdness: the corridor was dark and empty. Sophie braced herself against the frame and squinted in either direction. There was nothing but a long line of doors, no nurses' station in sight. What kind of hospital was this? Besides being *a)* poorly lit and *b)* negligent about monitoring critical patients? She would have expected to find at least a couple of nurses hanging around, maybe a doctor on rounds or a security guard.

"Hello?" she called out again tentatively. "Anyone here?"

From somewhere behind the walls she heard a muffled exclamation, followed by the quick pounding of feet on linoleum. The door beside her suddenly flew open. A tall girl darted out, whirled, and spotted her. She was nearly six foot, and older than Sophie, maybe seventeen or eighteen. Wild black curls tumbled past her shoulders in waves. She didn't look sick, and wasn't wearing a hospital gown or pajamas. Instead she was dressed head-to-toe in a long-sleeved black shirt, pants, and combat boots.

Spotting Sophie, her dark eyes narrowed. The girl lunged forward and jabbed a finger into her chest, barking something in an accusing tone. Sophie shied back. She wasn't sure what language the girl was speaking, but it wasn't English. "I'm sorry, I don't understand you," she said meekly, holding up her hands.

The girl made a face and spat, "American?"

"Yes?"

The girl glared up and down the hall, as if someone who could understand her might be lurking in the shadows. She turned back to Sophie. "Let me out," she hissed in menacing, heavily accented English. "I promise I won't say a word. If the tunnel was built by the CIA, then we're on the same side."

Sophie blinked, thinking, *I've accidentally been transferred to a psych ward.* "Why don't we try to find a nurse," she said in a soothing voice, hoping that the girl wasn't dangerous. "I'm sure they'll help us sort this all out."

The girl erupted in a rapid-fire stream of what sounded like invectives and stalked back to her room, throwing Sophie a final glare before vanishing inside.

"Great," Sophie muttered. So much for finding the people in charge. She would gladly have traded the fancy room for a competent staff. She considered checking the adjoining wing for a nurses' station, or maybe trying to see if there were any sane patients in the other rooms. But a wave of exhaustion swept over her.

With effort, Sophie managed to stumble back into her room. She collapsed on top of the bed, then flopped over and closed her eyes. The fatigue was like an anchor dragging her down. She gratefully succumbed to it. If this was a nightmare, fine. If not: also fine. After all, her family would probably be there when she woke up. They'd be able to explain what was going on.

Declan tried the door again. It was proving to be a beast. Ever since he'd woken up in this sodding hospital, he'd been working at the lock. He'd rarely encountered a bolt he couldn't master given enough time and effort but was almost ready to declare this one a lost cause.

Well, at least he hadn't been shot. Declan wasn't sure what had landed him here, but there wasn't a scratch on him.

As he squinted at the smooth metallic bolt, he puzzled over what had happened. Hard to say what had come over him, reaching out for that light. Simple survival instinct? It had felt like more as he was doing it. Like he'd been chosen for something, and had no choice but to accept.

Silly bloody nonsense, he told himself. He'd passed out, and for some reason the Russian had fled. Someone had probably stumbled across him unconscious and brought him here. As to his door being locked, and no nurses popping in to check on him . . . no matter. He was alive, he wasn't hurt, and soon as this bloody latch gave, he was gone.

Last time he'd ever take a gig from a stranger, that was for sure. He'd whiled away more than a few hours wondering what inside that feckin' box had been worth killing for. No knowing now, chalk it up to a life lesson and call it a day.

He wrestled again with the pin. Fortunately, his pick kit had still been in his pocket when he came to. All his clothes were still on, in fact: jeans, a Pogues T-shirt, and trainers. A bit strange for a hospital, but he was grateful for it. He'd hate to have to walk the streets of Galway with his arse hanging out once he broke free.

He thought of his mum. After the necklace, he'd have a few euros left to buy her something, too. Maybe that nice electric kettle she'd had her eye on. She'd like that.

Click. The door handle turned.

Declan cast a last glance around the room. Bloody strange place this was. He'd opened the curtains only to discover a solid cement wall—why put in a window, then seal it off completely? Probably built by Poles, they'd taken over all the construction jobs.

He stepped out into a dimly lit hallway.

It looked like a standard hospital. More doors like his on the same side of the hall: three to the right that ended in a wall, another two on his left that met a hook in the corridor.

"Hallo?" Declan called out, stepping forward. Funny, a small voice inside screamed for him to stay in the room where at least he knew what to expect. The Russian might be here too. *But then again, he might not,* he told himself. And there was only one way to find out.

Declan let the door latch shut behind him. He strode confidently down the corridor, repressing a nervous inclination to hum. First sign of a guard, he'd turn and head back the other way. Maybe they'd locked him in because they knew about the box. He'd been careful not to carry ID, but you never knew. Best not to take any chances. *Right, then. Keep your head down, find the way out, and disappear.* Declan turned at the hook and stopped dead.

Halfway down the hallway was a small folding table, set smack in the center. Two lads sat at it drinking from bottles of water. They both looked up, startled.

No one spoke for a minute. Declan sized them up quickly. Too young to be guards, and they weren't in uniform, either. The blond one looked tall, even seated. He had the wide shoulders of a rugby player, a solid nose, blue eyes—the kind of fella girls always went for. He was clad head-to-toe in Gore-Tex and wore leather walking boots. The other was small, thin, either Paki or Indian with dark brown eyes and hair. Hard to say what he was dressed for, his oversized shorts and T-shirt looked straight out of a rag bin. He wore a shabby pair of sandals on dirty feet.

Declan broke out his best grin and walked over to them. "Howyas," he said. "Wondering if you could direct me out of this kip."

"Out?" The blond kid snorted and gave him a good once over. He had a thick accent, German or maybe Austrian. "There is no out."

"Must be, mate," Declan said reasonably. He directed his attention toward the Paki, who was regarding him curiously. "If there's a way in, there's a way out, aye?"

The smaller boy hesitated. "We've tried all day. Nico is correct. There is no way out."

Declan frowned, wondering if they were having him on. He said, "Maybe I'll just take a look myself, then."

The blond, Nico, shrugged and drank some water. "If you like."

They watched as he sidled past and continued down the hall. It hooked right and ended at a set of double doors. Declan looked them over, then stepped closer. Oddest set of doors he'd ever seen—no handle visible, no lock to pick. He gave one side a push, testing it. Nothing. He tried again, pressing harder, then leaned against it with all his body weight.

The door didn't budge. He did the same on the other side, and finally stopped, panting and sweating.

A low chuckle behind him. He turned to discover both boys standing where the hallway hooked, watching him. The Paki looked sympathetic, but Nico was smirking. "We told you," he said.

Declan ignored him. He ran his fingers all the way around the perimeter of the door. There was a tiny slit, it seemed nearly airtight. Still . . .

"We find something long and thin, we can run it along the seam, see? Maybe work it open that way."

"We've already looked," the Paki said. "There is nothing here but water." He held out a bottle. "Would you care for some?"

Declan resisted the urge to smack it away; the kid was just being sociable, after all. "Thanks, but no."

"My name is Zain," the Paki said.

"Declan." He glanced around. On the plus side, no security in sight. But maybe they didn't need it, with doors like this. He pulled out his mobile; bloody Vodafone, the network never worked when you needed it to. "Any of you got a signal?"

"No," Nico said, an edge to his voice. "Don't you think we would have tried that already?"

"I don't have a phone," Zain said apologetically.

"So there's no one else about?"

The two boys looked at each other. "No one," Nico said grudgingly. "We checked every room."

"Except the one you were in," Zain added. "That door was locked."

"Didn't hear me calling out, though?"

They both shrugged and shook their heads. "The rooms must be sound-proofed," Zain said.

"That's odd, isn't it?" Declan mused, looking down the hall. A plain white linoleum floor, white walls, a white tile ceiling. Long, thin fluorescent bulbs cast them all in a greenish glow. It smelled oddly musty, lacking the overpowering ammonia stench of most hospitals. "No nurses or docs?"

"We told you, no one," Nico grunted. "We've sat there for hours, waiting."

"So you're ill, then?" Declan asked. They looked chipper enough, even though the Paki could use a sandwich.

They exchanged another look. Clearly he'd arrived late to this particular party.

"We were discussing that when you came out of your room," Zain finally answered. "Comparing notes, so to speak. I am from in New Delhi. I was in my room, studying. Everything started shaking, and suddenly, the wall, it just . . . it was not there anymore. It felt like an earthquake. Almost."

"An earthquake, eh?" Declan furrowed his brow. He hadn't felt anything like that. And there was no way they'd transport quake victims from New Delhi to Galway—wouldn't make any sense at all. Maybe this one *was* a bit soft in the head. He turned to the blond and asked, "What about you?"

"I was hiking," Nico said, examining his hands. "In the United States."

Definitely mad, the lot of them, Declan thought. Brilliant. He'd been stuck in a bloody nuthouse. Best to humor them until someone who wasn't completely crackers showed up. He nodded as if that all made perfect sense. "Of course. Declan Murphy, from Galway," he said, extending a hand.

"Ireland?" As Zain shook, his voice was suffused with pleasure. "I have always wanted to see Ireland."

"It's grand. And you, then," he said pointedly to Nico. "German?"

"Swiss," Nico answered after a brief hesitation. He reached out to shake, too, but with a hint of reluctance. "Nico Bruder."

"Swiss? Why were you hiking in the States?"

"My father is American. I was there on a visit." The question seemed to make him uncomfortable.

"Sure, sure." Where they thought they were from was irrelevant. Declan turned back to eye the doors. Hard to tell how thick they were; working together, they might be able to simply smash their way out. The blond lad looked strong. Perhaps they could take the legs off the card table, use that as a kind of battering ram . . . 'course, then he'd be releasing a couple of mental cases on the streets of Galway. *Although that wouldn't be entirely his fault*, he reminded himself. They had left him alone in here with them. For once he would have been delighted to encounter a guard in the flesh.

Following his eyes, Zain said, "We've already tried voice commands, since those worked with the lights."

"The lights?" Declan asked, puzzled.

"Did you not realize they respond to voice commands? Here, I'll show you. Lights!"

The hall abruptly went pitch black. Declan yelped with surprise.

"Lights on!" Zain exclaimed, and the fluorescent bulbs overhead sprang back to life.

"Neat trick," Declan said, recovering.

"Yes," Zain said. "But with the doors, I've tried variations on the word 'open' in as many languages as I know. So far—"

"No way out," Nico said grimly.

"We could try pushing," Declan suggested.

Nico scoffed. "We already spent an hour. The doors are sealed, they don't give an inch."

"But it was just the two of you then," Declan argued. "Maybe with all three of us—"

"It won't work," Nico snapped.

"Maybe later, then," Declan said, thinking that it was probably best not to antagonize the crazy man. Anyway, it had taken him nearly an hour to open that hospital door; he was feeling fairly parched himself. A little rest wouldn't kill him. Nodding toward the folding chairs he said, "Shall we take a load off and see if we can get this sorted? Don't suppose they left us a deck of cards . . ."

Anat was seething. She'd been trapped here for what felt like an eternity. She'd spent hours stalking the three narrow hallways, shaped like the letter "π": the one her room was on, another that ran a few meters to another hall, then a final one that dead-ended into a set of impenetrable doors.

There were five rooms identical to hers, each with a window that looked out on a cement wall and a tiny bathroom with a toilet and shower. All of them were empty.

She'd started to despair, and found herself compulsively touching her gold ring. Over and over she wondered what Hazim must be thinking. He'd been so worried that she'd back out at the last minute, afraid to risk the border crossing. When she hadn't shown up at the hotel at the agreed time, had he simply gone on without her? Or was he still there, waiting for her?

Mostly Anat raged at whoever had captured her. She'd addressed long diatribes to the walls, cursing them for wrongfully imprisoning her. The worst part was that she wasn't even sure who to blame. Hamas? Her own people? Maybe she hadn't been as careful as she thought, and her smuggling activities had been noted. Maybe this was just a precursor to torture, and they were softening her up before sending in the experts.

The isolation was driving her mad. Anat would even have welcomed the reappearance of that awful old woman from the border shack.

Then, finally, she heard a voice. She rushed into the corridor, only to discover an American girl. She was weak and sickly looking, wearing an absurd nightgown with a smiley face on it. And she pretended to have no idea what Anat was talking about.

Americans. I should have known, Anat thought disdainfully. They had their hands in everything, ostensibly helping Israel while covertly arming their enemies. They'd probably sent a teenage girl hoping that Anat would bare her soul, grateful for the company. Well, they were mistaken. She had no intention of revealing anything, especially not to an American.

Fortunately, they seemed to have gathered that quickly. The girl disappeared back into her room, and the hallway fell silent again.

Anat sat on the edge of her bed, brooding. After stalking back to her room, she'd scoured every inch of the walls and floors. The other girl had emerged from a previously empty room, so there had to be another access point to it. Unfortunately, as far as she could tell, her room had no such hidden entrance.

Anat had heard terrible stories about the types of punishment meted out to traitors—that had been part of her military training, a clear warning against defying the state. *But I'm not a traitor*, Anat thought angrily. Smuggling cartons of cigarettes across the border hardly warranted this kind of penalty.

She got to her feet again, unable to remain still. It was time she had some answers. Maybe the American girl was still around, and she could force her to talk. Or maybe they'd send someone else to try and break her. She'd prefer to meet any threat head-on; she was tired of sitting around doing nothing.

Anat set her jaw and marched to the door, throwing it open. She turned left. She was stomping toward the American's room when a soft voice called out behind her.

Anat spun around—a tiny Asian girl was standing in the middle of the hallway. The girl was a full head shorter than her and looked young. She was dressed in an oversized polyester shirt and pants that had been double-cuffed at the bottom. Her hair was dark and thick and ended crisply just above her shoulders. She repeated whatever she'd said and took a step forward.

Anat's eyes narrowed. What were they trying now? The American hadn't worked, so they sent a Chinese girl instead? She opened her mouth to say something in rebuke, but the girl's expression stopped her. She appeared genuinely terrified, tears streamed down her cheeks. *A trick?* Anat wondered. But she wavered—there seemed to be something terribly sincere in the girl's confusion and terror. And, she realized suddenly, deep down it mirrored her own feelings.

The girl was staring at her. Anat managed a thin smile, and said, "Who are you?" in Hebrew.

The girl looked at her, puzzled. She said something again. What language was she speaking? Chinese? Japanese? Korean? Anat sighed, then switched back to the language she'd been forced to learn in school. "Who are you?" she asked in English.

The girl's eyes lit up. "My name is Yosh Mori," she said haltingly. "Where am I?"

"Anat Erez," she answered. "And I don't know."

They regarded each other for a minute. Anat was forced to acknowledge that the girl certainly didn't seem to be a threat. She was so tiny that even with proper combat training, Anat held a solid advantage in size and strength. She gestured toward her room and asked, "Would you like to come in?"

The girl looked relieved. She nodded and answered, "Yes, if you please."

Anat walked in and held the door for her. Yosh paused on the threshold as if expecting a trap. Seeing that the room was clear, she warily stepped inside.

Anat motioned to the only chair in the room. She settled down on her bed, oddly self-conscious about the rumpled state of it.

The girl's eyes panned the hospital room, finally settling back on Anat. She'd perched on the edge of the chair, feet crossed neatly at the ankles, hands clasped on her lap. Anat was reminded of a bird on the verge of taking flight. Neither of them seemed to know where to begin.

"What has happened?" Yosh finally asked.

"I don't know," Anat admitted. "Where are you from?"

"Kyoto," Yosh said.

"Kyoto, Japan?" Anat's mind spun. Americans were one thing, but what possible interest could the Japanese have in her? Chinese, maybe, but Japanese?

"Yes, Kyoto is in Japan." Yosh's brow furrowed.

"I know where Kyoto is," Anat said testily, although in truth she couldn't have picked it out on a map. "And you just got here?"

"Yes, I . . . was there an accident?" she asked, looking around. "Are we no longer in Japan?"

"I don't know where we are," Anat admitted. "But I've never been to Japan. I am from Israel."

"Israel?"

"Yes. Now tell me exactly what you remember."

Yosh nervously rubbed her fingers together. "I was walking to school." She spoke so quietly, Anat had to lean forward to hear her. "About to cross the street. But halfway across . . ." She muttered to herself in what must have been Japanese, then turned her palms hands up apologetically.

"There was a darkness?" Anat guessed. "Black, like the night?"

Yosh looked relieved. "Yes, black. But there were also . . . things . . . inside it. And then . . ." She looked around again. "I woke up in a room like this one. But you do not know where we are?"

"No, I don't," Anat said, puzzling it over. The girl seemed to be telling the truth. She considered herself to be an excellent judge of liars, and Yosh wasn't exhibiting any of the classic signs: avoiding eye contact, or tilting her head. All of the other rooms had been empty not long before, however. So where had she come from? "But—"

A siren started to wail. Yosh winced and covered her ears. Anat jumped off the bed and lunged toward the corridor. What was going on? Was this more of their games?

The hallway was empty, the lighting still dim. Anat marched through the connecting passage to check: the doors remained locked. She almost tripped over Yosh when she turned back, the girl was right at her heels.

"What is happening?" she cried, tugging urgently on Anat's arm.

Anat shook her off. She went back to the American's door and shoved it open.

The girl was sitting up in bed, blearily blinking her eyes. Anat stormed the bed and grabbed the girl's shoulders, shaking her. "Tell us what this is!"

"Let go of me," the girl mumbled, trying futilely to extricate herself from Anat's grasp.

"I will hurt you if you don't tell us," Anat warned. Behind her, Yosh gasped. The American barely seemed to notice. Her eyes rolled back in her head and she went limp.

Anat growled and released her grip. The girl dropped back on the pillows. "Come on," she said, making her way back to the hall without checking to see if Yosh followed.

"But she seems hurt. Shouldn't we . . ."

Ignoring her, Anat trotted back to the exit doors. They had to open somehow. There was a way out, she just had to find it.

She ran her hands across them. Even though she'd already done it dozens of times since awakening here, she might have missed something. There must be some sort of secret latch, a way to get it open.

Yosh was standing slightly back, her eyes wide.

"Help me!" Anat snapped.

Yosh tentatively stepped forward, then brushed her fingers across the door, as if afraid it would bite. After a minute, she shook her head. "It is locked," she said with finality.

Anat was about to chastise her for giving up, even though she could sense the futility of their efforts. But before she got a chance to speak, the alarm abruptly ceased.

A second later, the doors silently swung open.

CHAPTER THREE

Whatever Declan had expected to find on the other side of the doors, it definitely hadn't been this. Two girls stood there, looking every bit as startled as he felt: a swarthy one who was tall and fierce-looking, dressed head-to-toe in black, and a small Asian girl in rummage-store clothing. Of course, he was part of a fairly odd bunch, too.

They all stared at each other for a moment.

"Hallo," he said to break the silence. "Is this the way out, then?"

The taller girl stepped forward, crossing the threshold. *Stunning*, Declan thought, *but scary*. Her demeanor reminded him of a rhino debating whether or not to charge. As she advanced with a murderous look in her eye, the boys stepped back in unison.

"No," the Japanese girl said quietly. "We thought this was the way."

The taller girl threw her a sharp look. "Quiet, Yosh."

"But—"

"I said, be quiet!" She turned back to them, her eyes narrowing. "We want to leave."

"Shocking, that," Declan laughed. "Something we have in common, then." He stepped past her and extended a hand to the Japanese girl. "Pleased to make your acquaintance. Declan Murphy."

Yosh shook hands, then turned to the other two boys. Zain's mouth opened and closed several times without producing a word. The Swiss boy interceded, saying "Nico Bruder," with a brusque nod. "And this is Zain."

"Enough!" the tall girl growled. "How do we get out?"

And here's the rest of the asylum, Declan thought. Out loud he said, "We were hoping you could tell us. Not this way, I'm guessing?"

The tall girl's eyes narrowed. "You know it isn't."

"I know nothing of the sort," Declan said. "Was stuck in a shite room for hours, until I finally broke out and met these lads. Then while we're sitting around gabbing, a siren goes off and the doors finally pop open."

"It's true," Zain piped up. "There are just three hallways and six hospital rooms over here. No exits."

"And there are only the three of you?"

"Yes," Nico chimed in. "Are you two alone?"

"Alone, but able to defend ourselves," she declared.

At that, Declan had to laugh. "That's just brilliant. We're stuck here, no way out on either side, and you're worried about us? Do we strike you as a dangerous lot?"

That seemed to give her pause. She looked them over again slowly, her eyes hesitating on Zain in his ragged shorts and threadbare T-shirt. *You could blow the lad over with a good breath*, Declan thought, following her gaze. In a brawl, even little Yosh could probably best him.

"Well, you better not try anything," she muttered.

"I'll bear that in mind," Declan said dryly.

"Do you have phones? There were none in our rooms."

"Yes, but mine isn't working," Nico said. "And Declan isn't getting a signal either. How about you?"

"I lost mine," the tall girl grumbled.

"No phone." The Asian girl shook her head. "And . . . there's another girl. I think . . ." her eyes darted to the taller girl. "I think she might be hurt."

"Hurt how?" Declan asked, his eyes narrowing. Yosh seemed scared of the bigger girl. He reached into his pocket and tucked the longest pick between his fingers. It wasn't sharp, but in the past it had worked better than knuckles alone in a fight. It would be ironic if he survived getting shot at, only to end up fighting these loons.

"She seems ill," the tall girl acknowledged. "Although she might be faking."

"Why would she be faking?" Zain asked, puzzled.

She jerked a thumb back over her shoulder. "Third door down. Go see if you like. I'm going to make sure you're telling the truth." She pushed past them, stopping dead at the sight of the card table. After a beat, she stalked off down the hall.

"Lovely girl," Declan murmured. "Just the sort you want to bring home to mum." He turned to Yosh and grinned. "You seem sane enough, though."

Yosh flushed and lowered her eyes. "I think Anat is just frightened."

"Ah, so you managed to get a name out of her. Clever girl. Well, let's have a look at this other one."

Yosh led them down the hall. The setup mirrored their own: two longer halls linked by a short one, with six doors total. The door to the third room was ajar, the rest were closed.

The three boys exchanged a look behind Yosh's back. In silent acknowledgement, Zain and Nico split off to opposite ends of the hall and started opening doors, checking rooms. Declan was relieved to see they'd been thinking along the same lines; all this was damned strange, and he for one didn't care to be trapped in a hospital room when the next surprise showed up. Best to make sure the girls were telling the truth about them all being empty. And no offense to the fairer sex, but there must be a way out somewhere over here—there certainly wasn't one on their side. The girls probably just hadn't found it yet.

Declan paused on the threshold, then stepped into the room. Yosh had gone straight to the bed and stood beside it, wringing her hands.

A girl with dark blond hair lay on it. She looked dead asleep, the covers pulled up to her waist. Pretty, Declan noted, but pale and sickly looking, with dark circles under her eyes. Not as striking as Anat, but she had a kind of classic beauty, fragile-looking as a doll. Around his age, seventeen or so, wearing an old nightgown. Her chest rose and fell shallowly, her hands lay palms up on the blankets. From the looks of things, this girl actually belonged in a hospital. He scanned her room—identical to the one he'd awoken in.

"Any idea what's wrong with her?" Declan asked, reflexively lowering his voice as he approached the bed.

Yosh hesitated, then said, "I think she had a seizure."

"I did nothing to her."

Declan glanced up. The tall girl, Anat, stood in the doorway. Zain and Nico peered over her shoulder. Judging by her tone and the way Yosh was avoiding his eyes, she was lying.

Declan raised his eyebrows and said, "Found her like this, then? 'Cause Yosh here was saying something about a seizure."

"A seizure, yes," Anat said. "That's what it was." She looked at Yosh. "These boys are telling the truth. No way out on their side, either."

"Satisfied?" Nico said with a snort.

"Now I am," she retorted. "You checked here too, yes?"

"Of course."

Warily, they sized one another up. "Israeli?" Nico finally asked.

"Yes."

"Already started military training?"

"Yes."

"Can you say anything but yes?" Nico asked bluntly.

Unexpectedly, she laughed. "I'm very good at saying no, too."

"Not surprising." Nico grinned.

Declan watched the exchange with interest—kindred spirits, apparently. Charming. Maybe later they could grab a pint and swap stories about beating the piss out of people on a lark.

"Is she all right?" Zain asked, approaching the bed.

"I think so." Declan tried to sound reassuring. "Probably just recovering from a fit. My mate Michael used to have those sometimes, always slept like the dead after one."

"What do we do now?" Yosh asked.

"We leave her," Anat said, stepping into the room.

"Leave her? You're going somewhere, then?" Declan demanded.

Anat waved a hand impatiently. "There must be a way out."

"Hang on," Declan said. "She might wake in a bit—"

"Anat is right, we need to go," Nico said. "There's no

food here, nothing but water. There are enough of us now to break a hole through a wall. We'll take shifts."

"I don't know," Yosh said in a small voice. "It seems . . ."

"Good idea," Anat said approvingly. "We'll look for a weak spot between the support beams." She bent down and examined the bedrail. "If we can get these off, they should be strong enough to punch through. I will get the one from my room."

"And we leave her alone here, with no food?" Zain said. "That seems cruel."

"She'll see the hole," Anat pointed out. "It will be easy for her to follow us." She gazed at each of them. "You'd rather stay here and starve?"

Declan had to acknowledge that she had a point. And he for one was eager to get back to Katie and his mum. It wasn't as if he owed the girl in the bed anything, after all, and surely someone official would be by soon. They'd undoubtedly help her. "All right, then," he said reluctantly. "We start on a wall. By the time we break through, hopefully she'll have rejoined the living."

This was getting old fast, Sophie thought, opening her eyes. She'd spent more time awake on her deathbed. Maybe she really had ended up in hell—because whatever this place was, it clearly qualified for bizarro-land. Apparently her hospital room had been slated for remodeling while she was zonked out, because there were giant holes punched along two walls and the air was thick with plaster. Inhaling some of it, Sophie's nose wrinkled and she sneezed. From beyond her open door, she heard distant thumps and grunts.

Signs of human life. That was a relief. At this point she'd be thrilled to see anyone aside from that crazy girl from down the hall. Sophie had a vague memory of being shaken forcefully. *They should really do something about the security around here*, she thought. "Um, hello?" she called out. Maybe the nurses had finally returned. She couldn't imagine where they'd all gone earlier; maybe they had one of those walking clubs. Her favorite nurse at the hospice, Betsy, used to go on about how they circled the hospice twenty times on their lunch break. They must've screwed up and forgotten to leave someone behind.

At the thought of Betsy chugging along briskly in her hot pink scrubs and shiny white sneakers, Sophie felt a pang. She really wasn't in the mood to start over with a new crew of nurses.

A head suddenly popped around her doorframe. "Oh good, you're up. About bloody time, too."

Sophie carefully eased up onto her elbows and examined him. Not a nurse, or anyone official-looking; just a teenage boy with a brogue. Plaster streaked his thick brown hair, and there was a smudge of white beneath his bright blue eyes. *Maybe someone from the contractor's crew?*

"Uh, hi. Could you find a nurse for me?" she asked politely.

"Would that I could, but it's just us."

"What do you mean?" Sophie asked, puzzled. "Just who?"

"Buncha feckin' lunatics, to be honest," he confided in a low voice, approaching her bed. "You look to be truly ill, though."

"Well, yeah. Usually the patients on the oncology ward aren't the healthiest."

He stopped at the foot of her bed. She frowned; the only people allowed in her room were doctors, nurses, and immediate family. Yet this construction guy was acting like it was totally normal to hang out with a patient. Man, this was a weird hospital. She almost never complained about her stays, even when they served the same meal three days in a row. But this was pushing it.

"Cancer, is it?" He looked interested. "Still got all your hair, though."

Sophie ran a hand through it self-consciously; her hair felt oily and stringy. For the past week she'd told them not to bother washing it. Why stay clean when she was just going into a coffin anyway? Of course, she hadn't anticipated receiving new visitors—especially not a teenage boy who was kind of cute, even if he was pushy. "I stopped chemo awhile ago."

"Yeah? Feeling better then?"

"A little," Sophie said. Which was true. Not quite as energetic as the last time she woke up, but all things considered she felt pretty good.

"Excellent." He nodded at her. "You'll come with us, then, if we find a way out. No luck so far, but we're still at it."

"Come with you?" Sophie asked, puzzled. "Where?" She wanted to add that he probably wasn't qualified to discharge patients, but that seemed rude. She gazed past him toward the doorway, wishing for a nurse to show up and hustle him out.

He caught her expression and said, "Right, you're probably a bit confused. You haven't been out of this room yet?"

"I barely made it to the hallway."

"Long story short, then," he said. "This looks like a hospital, 'cept it has no exits. No nurses or doctors, either. And no food, which is a damned shame since I'm feckin' starving. Declan Murphy, by the way." He extended a hand.

Bewildered, Sophie shook, then said, "Wait, what? This isn't a hospital?" *He's nuts too*, she thought. Even though it was fancy, this was definitely a hospital: convertible bed, check. Uncomfortable furniture, check. Tacky curtains and bad art, check. Aside from the lack of equipment, it was a model hospital room, and she should know; at this point, she was kind of an expert.

"Madness, right?" He grinned at her. "We're not sure what it is. And here's where it really goes sideways. We all come from different places. You're American, yeah?"

Sophie hesitated but couldn't see any harm in answering. "From California."

"Los Angeles?" His face brightened.

"Palo Alto. Kind of near San Francisco," she explained, seeing the blank expression on his face.

"Ah, I hear that's a lovely town. I'm from Galway," he said. "Nico is Swiss, Zain Indian. Anat is from Israel, and Yosh is from—"

"Let me guess, Japan."

Declan nodded. "Right. First, I thought they were having me on, that I'd ended up in an asylum somehow."

"Me, too," Sophie admitted. *Could he be telling the truth?* He didn't seem crazy, at least not like the other girl. Remembering her, she said, "I think I already met Anat."

"Bet that didn't go well. She's a charmer, sure. Anyway, we all started in different places and ended up here."

"Regular 'It's a Small World,' huh?" Sophie said, half to herself.

Declan barked a laugh. "You could say that, yeah. We've been trying to find a weak spot in the walls, but so far, no luck."

She was having a hard time wrapping her mind around what Declan was telling her. Maybe she was still trapped in some sort of nightmare? But no, he seemed real enough. And that was definitely not imaginary plaster dust filling her nasal cavity. But as far as this not being a hospital, and them being trapped inside . . . that all sounded bonkers. Still, might as well play along until someone in charge came along. "So we all come from different places, we're locked up here, you haven't seen anyone else, and there are no doors or windows. That about sums it up?"

"You forgot the part about the shite service, and no clocks," Declan said. "Plus the shower pressure is terrible."

"No shower pressure? Heck, then we definitely need to get out of here," Sophie said gravely.

Declan laughed as if she'd said the funniest thing in the world. A giggle rose in her chest, too. It felt good—she couldn't remember the last time she'd really laughed. She knew they were both overreacting to what, truth be told, hadn't been a very funny joke. Still, even though it could be chalked up to a hysterical reaction, it felt good.

"What's your name?" he asked after a minute.

"Sophie." A flush rose in her cheeks. He really was cute, and he had a great laugh.

"Right, Sophie," Declan said gravely. "It's settled, we need to get out. Of this room, at least."

"That would be a start," Sophie agreed.

"You all right to walk?"

"I think so." Sophie slid her feet out from under the covers and tugged at the hem of her nightgown, fervently wishing that she'd worn a longer one. This was an old favorite, a hand-me-down from her mom that featured a smiley face with a bullet hole in the center of its forehead. The hospice nurses had universally hated it; even her mom tried to persuade her to change out of it toward the end. But Sophie had decided a long time ago that she'd meet death on her own terms. Besides, it was the most comfortable nightgown she owned, even if it barely cleared her thighs. Declan decorously kept his eyes up while placing a hand under her elbow to steady her. "Shall we?"

In spite of herself, Sophie had to lean on him as they made their way toward the door. They'd nearly reached it when Anat appeared, blocking their way. Wielding a long piece of metal coated with dust on one end, she growled, "Nothing!"

Sophie instinctively shied back. The girl looked ready to club something, and judging by the look in her eyes, she wouldn't mind starting with Sophie.

"No luck still?" Declan asked.

"Just more cement." The girl dropped the bar, and it hit the floor with a clank. "All the walls are lined with it."

Sophie peered past her. More sloppy holes like the ones in her room dotted the hall. *Construction my ass*, she thought. They were tearing the place apart. And that must have made a lot of noise, she suddenly realized; why hadn't anyone appeared to check up on them?

Could it really be true? Were they trapped? Sophie brushed the thought away. Impossible. Odds were this was just some nutty morphine dream she was trapped in. Any minute now, she'd wake up on her deathbed. She closed her eyes and pinched her arm, wincing at the pain. She opened them to find Declan giving her an odd look.

"We've tried everywhere," Anat was saying. "There's no way out."

"Sophie, this is Anat," Declan said, patting her arm reassuringly.

"We've met," Sophie said, trying to look less scared than she felt. "Twice, if I'm not mistaken."

"Yes." Anat blinked. "Sorry. I did not understand what was happening."

"No problem," Sophie said, although the apology seemed half-hearted. "So you haven't been able to find a way out?"

"No." The girl glowered at the nearest wall. "The entire hospital is encased in cement. A crazy person built this place."

"No argument there," Declan murmured.

Sophie considered suggesting that the crazy people largely seemed to be *inside* at the moment, but she wasn't really up for another shaking, or worse. She understood why the others were so desperate to get out of here, but for her it seemed to be a moot point. Although if she got rid of them, at least she'd have some peace and quiet.

"The vents," she blurted, pointing up. "That air is coming from somewhere, right?"

They followed her finger. Anat's brow furrowed. "I can't fit in there," she said bluntly, examining the narrow metal frame. A faint gust teased her long black hair.

"No, but Yosh can. Zain too, probably. If we get them out, they can find another exit for the rest of us!" Declan exclaimed. "Brilliant!"

Unexpectedly, he planted a kiss square on her forehead. Sophie managed a wan smile in response. "All right, then. If you'll just help me back to bed . . ."

But he wasn't listening. "Nico! Zain! Yosh! C'mere, we're going to give something else a try!"

Sophie gritted her teeth. Anat glared down at her like she was something unpleasant she'd found under her shoe. Other teenagers straggled down the hall, closing in ranks behind her: Yosh, Nico, and Zain, according to Declan. They were all bleary-eyed and covered in fine white powder.

The gravity of the situation suddenly hit her. This was no dream. She was a prisoner, stuck here with a bunch of strangers; one of whom had already basically attacked her. And

Declan, cute though he was, definitely didn't seem like a choir boy. Her presence had to be some sort of mistake. Had the hospice accidentally transferred her to a juvie prison ward? The thought wasn't comforting, especially since they were in the middle of plotting a prison break.

And she'd just helped them.

"Hey," Sophie said, clearing her throat. "Maybe we should just sit tight. Someone will probably be coming soon."

Anat looked at her like she was nuts, and Declan's eyes narrowed. "I think if they were coming, they'd have popped in by now, yeah?"

"Well," Sophie said, digging for an explanation. "There might have been some sort of emergency. Maybe they got stuck outside and are trying to get in."

"Which is why we need to get out," Anat snapped.

"She has a point," Declan said. "We get out then we'll know what's what, yeah?"

Sophie couldn't come up with an argument against that, at least not without accusing them all of being psychopaths. Worse, they were staring at her like *she* was the freak. At least they weren't threatening to shove her through the vents. "Right," she said weakly. "I'm sure there's a perfectly good explanation."

Anat snorted.

Declan gestured to the vents. "So we're thinking Yosh and Zain can get up there and crawl through, maybe find a way out."

"Us?" Yosh said in a small voice. Sophie didn't blame her— nothing like having strangers volunteer you for a cramped, dangerous mission.

The tall blond boy—*Nico*, she reminded herself—looked skeptical. "Well," he said, gazing upward. "It might work."

"What if they don't come back?" Anat demanded.

"Of course we'll come back," Zain said indignantly.

"I wouldn't," Anat scoffed.

"You have my word," he said stiffly. Turning to Yosh, he offered, "Would you like to go first?"

She eyed the narrow opening nervously. "No."

"All right." Zain tugged off his shirt and turned to Nico. "Give me a hand?"

Anat paced beneath the hole where Yosh and Zain had disappeared. Occasionally they could hear rattles and clanks from above, followed by muted conversation. "It's been too long," she finally said.

"It's barely been ten minutes," Declan snorted. "Relax and take a load off, bird."

"I'm not a bird," she grumbled.

He waved a hand. "It's not an insult. Go on, then. Sit."

Anat remained standing. She found Declan's equanimity maddening. He and Nico had settled down on the floor beside each other, leaning against the wall outside Sophie's room. The American girl had gone back to bed, claiming to be tired. Anat still suspected that somehow Sophie was behind all this. Although in all honesty, she did appear to be ill. Or at least, much weaker than the rest of them.

She took another small sip from the water bottle. Hard to say if the tap water was potable—she'd guess not, since there were pallets of mineral water stacked in the hallway on the boys' side. Odd that they hadn't been given any. *But then, all of this was odd*, she reminded herself.

And despite what everyone else seemed to think, she seriously doubted that Yosh and Zain would return for them. If the situation had been reversed, she wouldn't.

Silence from above. Anat tried to picture the pathway carved by the vent: based on the clanks and groans emitted by Zain and Yosh's passage, it snaked across the hall and down to the boys' section. But did it really lead up from there? Whatever this place was, it appeared to be some sort of underground bunker. Much as she hated to admit it, the American girl was right: the vents were probably the only way out.

"What's the last thing you remember?" Declan asked suddenly.

"Me?" Anat said.

"Yes, you. I've already heard from nearly everyone else. Nico here was hiking, right?"

"With my father," Nico said, sounding bored.

"Aye. Zain was in some sort of earthquake, and Sophie was about to die of cancer. I was about to be shot," he said matter-of-factly.

"Shot? By who?" Anat asked, suddenly interested.

"Russian bastard," he said, waving dismissively. "But what I'm thinking is that we all seemed to be in some sort of danger, yeah?"

"I suppose," Anat said slowly, remembering the tunnel. They suffered from cave-ins all the time, she'd known that going in.

"So maybe we were all about to die," Declan said. "Maybe that's the link."

"And what?" She snorted. "This is hell?"

"Purgatory, more likely," Declan said.

"You're serious?" Anat said, stupefied.

"How would you explain it, then?"

"I'm Jewish. We don't believe in Purgatory."

"Which doesn't mean it can't exist, right?"

"I'm not dead," Nico said with a yawn.

"Last thing you remember is slipping on a rock in the middle of a hike, though."

"So?"

"So, maybe you went over a cliff."

"There were no cliffs."

"What about Yosh?" Anat demanded. "She was just walking to school."

"Haven't had a chance to ask her yet," Declan said. "We'll see when she returns."

"If she returns," Anat grumbled. What if he was right? What if they were, in fact, dead, and trapped somewhere? She shook it off. She didn't believe in an afterlife, that was Christian nonsense. Declan was just trying to frighten her.

"It is odd," Declan mused. "I'd always figured on going straight to hell."

"Stop talking about it," Anat said sharply. "You're wrong."

"We'll see, won't we? If Yosh and Zain come back, and it turns out those vents don't lead anywhere at all, well then . . ." He shrugged.

Anat turned her back on him and crossed her arms, refusing to listen to any more of his nonsense.

All at once, there was a groan of metal hinges from down the hall. Declan and Nico leapt to their feet. Anat was already at the hook in the corridor by the time they caught up to her.

A seam had appeared in the wall at the end of the hallway in the boys' wing; it slowly creaked open. Anat cursed silently; she should have found that when she examined the boys' side. Obviously she hadn't looked closely enough.

In spite of her irritation, a wave of profound relief swept

over her. Declan had been wrong. There was a way out. They were alive.

Yosh stood there. In addition to plaster dust, she was covered in filth and cobwebs.

And she was alone.

"Bloody well done!" Declan exclaimed. "How'd you get it open?" He walked forward and examined the door. "Brilliant," he said. "Looks like just another wall panel. Lined with concrete, too, so we wouldn't have known even if we tackled this section . . ."

Anat tuned him out; she couldn't care less about the door, as long as it stayed open. Something was off about the Japanese girl, though. She had a glazed look in her eyes, and she was clenching and releasing her fists.

"Are you all right?" Nico lay a hand on her shoulder. She didn't react. He exchanged a worried look with Anat.

"What's wrong?" Anat demanded. "Where is the Indian?"

"He has a name, you know," Declan said as he came back over to them. "Young Zain didn't get stuck in the vents, did he?"

Without responding, Yosh turned on her heel and slipped back into the darkness. They all stared after her.

"That was bloody strange," Declan muttered. "What do you think?"

"We follow her," Anat said.

"Well, yeah," Declan said. "But why does she look like she's seen a ghost?"

"Guess we'll find out," Nico said with a shrug, but his eyes were anxious when they met hers.

They hesitated a second longer, then Anat decided. "I'm following her."

"Right. Let me get Sophie, we'll be right behind you."

Declan turned back toward the girls' wing and strode down the hall.

Once he vanished around the bend, Nico turned to Anat and said, "I don't like this."

"I don't either," she replied in a low voice. "I'll watch your back if you watch mine."

"Deal." He reached out to shake her hand. She felt old calluses on his palm. Nico gave her a broad smile in spite of the circumstances, and held the grip an instant longer than necessary. Anat frowned, hoping he wasn't going to take watching her back too literally. "Let's go."

CHAPTER FOUR

"**What is this place?**" Sophie asked.

Declan didn't trust himself to answer. He'd practically carried her up five flights of stairs and was panting from the effort. The stairwell was long and narrow, made entirely of concrete with the floors marked off by numbers stenciled in black paint. There were doors to other levels at each landing, but they were all locked, and as long as the stairs kept going up he figured they needn't bother checking them. It reminded him of a car-park stairwell, except it didn't reek of piss. The air was musty and stale, though, which wasn't much of an improvement.

Yosh and Anat were well out of sight by the time he and Sophie reached the foot of the stairs. Nico offered to go last, a strange choice for him considering their slow progress. Declan got the sense that the lad was leery of turning his back on them. Under any other circumstances, Declan would've found that hilarious. But in truth, he found himself overly aware of Nico's gaze on his back.

You're being paranoid, he told himself. Nico might be a bastard, but he had no reason to hurt them.

Still, Declan did his best to keep a few risers between them during the ascent.

There still hadn't been any sign of Zain. Declan was praying that he'd be waiting up top, having just decided to stay there for some reason. There was something about the silence in that stairwell that was more frightening than anything else so far.

At the top a steel door stood agape, heavy and ominous looking. They emerged from it into an enormous room, the size of an airplane hangar. It was filled with computer equipment, huge towers, and complicated-looking panels. Silent and dark as a tomb, cast in an eerie red glow by emergency lights placed at staggered intervals. It looked like a scene straight out of an old James Bond film; Declan half-expected to find a villain in a swiveling chair stroking a cat.

"Wow," Sophie said, staring around wide-eyed. "I feel like I stumbled onto a movie set."

"Or maybe mission control?" he offered.

She issued a short laugh, but it didn't sound very sincere. He couldn't blame her. The place felt threatening, oppressive. Like there wasn't enough air, despite the large open space. Even though it was clearly some sort of high-tech facility, Declan got the sense that bad things had happened here.

After all, *something* had spooked Yosh. She was standing in the center of the room with Anat beside her. They weren't talking. Anat looked impatient: her arms were crossed over her chest and she was scowling at them. "We've been waiting five minutes."

"Sorry," Declan said. "'Course, you could always have lent a hand."

Anat tossed her curls and threw Nico a glance. Some sort of silent communication passed between them, the sight of which Declan didn't like at all.

Sophie groaned slightly, distracting him. Her forehead was slick with sweat, and she looked even paler than she had down below. She appeared on the verge of collapse. "All right, bird?" he asked with concern.

"Fine," she said faintly. "Just . . . a little dizzy."

"Hang in there, we're almost through. I think." He looked back at Anat and Yosh. "There is a way out, yeah?"

"I don't know." Anat glared at Yosh. "She won't talk, and stopped moving while we waited for you."

He stared at the girl, who gazed blankly past them as if they weren't even there. Her chest rose and fell rapidly under the thin fabric of her shirt.

"Which way?" Nico asked.

Yosh abruptly turned on her heel and led them up a narrow metal stairwell. At the top, another steel door led to a long hallway. And at the end of that, a set of double doors rimmed by daylight.

"Thank God for that," Declan muttered. "Never thought I'd be so happy to see the sun."

Yosh still didn't answer, which was starting to wreck his nerves. What was wrong with her?

As they shuffled down the hall in silence, Declan tried to get a grip on his fear. They were aboveground now. There would be food, and people. They'd all be able to get back where they belonged. He hadn't been kidding about the purgatory theory—it occurred to him when he kept striking cement while punching holes in the walls. He simply couldn't come up with another explanation for how such a random assortment of kids ended up in the same place. Maybe purgatory was like prison, with everyone segregated by age and time of death. The more he'd thought about it, the more sense it made.

But if that really was daylight up ahead . . .

Yosh stepped aside after crossing the threshold. Declan helped Sophie through the doors, both of them blinking against the glare.

It took a second for his eyes to adjust. What he saw made him gasp, "Jaysus."

"Where are we?" Sophie asked.

"This is not Israel," Anat said in a low voice. "Or Japan."

It wasn't Galway, either. Declan had pictured the doors opening onto the ambulance bay of a busy hospital: the UCHG, or Bon Secours, maybe. Instead, he found himself facing a large parking lot bordered by trees. Sections of the pavement had buckled, and cars tilted crazily on them, like polar bears clinging to sinking ice floes. Even the air smelled foreign. Declan swallowed the lump in his throat. He tried to sound reassuring as he said, "Well, at least we're not trapped in that dungeon anymore."

No one replied. As a group, they turned in a slow circle. A dense forest enveloped what remained of the parking lot and encircled the ruined building from which they'd emerged. Weeds erupted from cracks in the concrete walls, and one whole section had collapsed under the weight of a fallen tree. Heavy branches drooped low overhead. It was hot and sunny, at least thirty degrees Celsius. He immediately started to sweat.

"Where's Zain?" Declan asked, peering around. No sign of the slim Indian boy anywhere. Would he really have taken off without them? But that didn't make sense; none of this would be familiar to him either, right? He was reasonably certain India looked nothing like this.

Yosh still appeared to be in some kind of trance.

"Where are all the people?" Anat demanded. "Someone owns these cars."

"Looks like there was a big quake, yeah? Maybe they were evacuated," Declan said.

"Maybe." Sophie gazed doubtfully around the parking lot. She lowered her voice so that only he could hear and asked, "What do you think happened to Zain?"

"He might've taken off as soon as they got up here, figuring he'd be best on his own." Even as he said it, Declan doubted it. The way Zain had drawn his shoulders back and given his word, like it really meant something; he wasn't the type to abandon a wee girl and head off alone, not unless Declan had misread him entirely. Maybe Yosh was just struck dumb by the fact that they were all clearly a long way from home, no denying it now.

"But the way she's not talking, like something really scared her . . ." Sophie dropped her voice lower and said, "Zain wouldn't have done anything to . . . hurt her, right?"

In spite of everything, Declan snorted and said, "Unlikely." He considered himself an expert on spotting potential problems, human and otherwise. Even based on the short time they'd spent together, he could tell that Zain was one of the good ones.

"So, what then?"

Declan shrugged, wishing he had a better answer. It was hard to ignore the gut feeling that something was really off, and they might have been better off underground with all the exits sealed.

Anat was muttering under her breath, Hebrew from the sound of it, and probably not the nicest selection of words. She glowered at their surroundings as if personally offended by the overgrowth, then turned back to face them. "This is some sort of bullshit trick."

"Trust me, bird, we're no more delighted about it than you are."

"I told you not to call me bird," she snapped.

"And I told you it's not an insult."

"Enough fighting," Sophie said wearily. "We need to find Zain. Yosh? What happened to Zain?"

Yosh was still doing her imitation of a very small, poorly dressed statue. And Declan, for one, was finding the deaf/mute routine increasingly irritating. "You want me to shake her or something?" he offered.

"Leave her alone." Anat stepped protectively in front of her. "Obviously Zain is gone."

"But gone where?" Sophie demanded. "What if he's hurt or something?"

"We need to find help," Anat said impatiently. "Then they can look for Zain. Yes?"

"I guess," Sophie said, but she still looked apprehensive. "I'm just worried about what happened to the two of them."

Anat pressed on as if she hadn't spoken. "There must be someone around. We will find them. Unless you still think this is hell?"

"I said purgatory," Declan said. "And I'm still not entirely certain it's not."

"It's not purgatory," Nico said in a low voice. He ran a hand through matted blonde hair, gazing around with an odd expression.

"No?" Declan grunted as he settled Sophie's weight more evenly on his shoulder. "Care to venture a theory, then?"

"This is Upton, New York," Nico said. "On Long Island."

"In America? How do you know that?" Anat demanded.

"Because I know this building." He gestured behind them. "My father works here."

"Where is he, then?" Anat asked.

Nico shrugged. "I don't know. There are lots of buildings like this one."

"If you knew where we were, why the hell didn't you say so before?" Declan demanded. Seemed odd, under the circumstances; if he'd spotted the Spanish Arch or Blake's Castle when they emerged, he would've spoken up right quick. "Would've been especially helpful when we were trying to get out."

"I'd never been in the infirmary. I didn't even know it was there." He shrugged, looking slightly embarrassed. "I've never gone inside any of the buildings, except for the cafeteria. It's forbidden."

"Forbidden? Why?" Sophie asked.

"My father is a scientist working on a very important project." Nico puffed up as he continued, "A heavy ion Collider."

"And what in God's name is that?" Declan demanded. *Must be purgatory, if there's science involved*, he thought to himself. *Only subject I ever did worse in was maths.*

"It collides ions so that physicists can study the earliest forms of matter, like what was created after the Big Bang." The way Nico recited the words made them sound like something he'd memorized for school, but couldn't explain in more detail if pressed. *What a gobshite*, Declan thought, liking him even less.

"This is the second largest Collider, next to CERN in Switzerland," he continued. "That's where my parents met."

"That's weird, that we ended up here," Sophie mused. "Do you think the Collider might have something to do with it? Maybe—"

"Does it matter?" Anat interrupted. "We need to find food, and help. Who cares how we got here?"

"She has a point," Declan said in a low voice. "I'm right starved, and I'm guessing the rest of you are, too."

"I could eat," Sophie acknowledged. "But I still don't feel right about leaving without Zain."

"Maybe we'll stumble across him," Declan said, trying to sound more confident than he felt. "He probably went looking for help, yeah?"

"I guess." She didn't sound convinced, though.

"We will ask people to look for him," Anat said decisively. "Food first."

"The cafeteria should be at the other end of the compound," Nico said. "It's open twenty-four hours a day. There will be someone there."

"So we head there first," Declan said. "All in agreement on that?"

Everyone stood around looking at each other. Although moving ahead had initially been Anat's idea, even she appeared reluctant. *Bunch of bloody sheep,* Declan thought with a sigh. He squared his shoulders and tucked Sophie's arm more securely around him. "Lead us there, Nico," he said, trying to sound authoritative. "I'd kill for a bag of crisps right about now."

Sophie kept silent as Nico led them on a fifteen minute walk, occasionally stopping to check the compass on his watch. Along the way they skirted other parking lots surrounding what looked like abandoned and long-neglected buildings. All were in the same state of disrepair: the pavement in upheaval, the forest overtaking everything. They stuck to the woods, winding their way past overgrown bramble patches and enormous ferns.

The parking lot in front of the cafeteria was in the worst shape of all. Some of the cars had pitched forward into gaping potholes. The front doors of the building hung askew from rusted hinges. Broken glass speckled the piles of dead leaves on the ground.

"Big quake, eh?" Declan muttered in her ear.

Sophie didn't respond. Growing up in Northern California, she knew all about earthquakes and the level of damage they could cause. And if one had occurred on Long Island, where such a natural disaster was almost unheard of . . . sure, it would've wreaked havoc with the parking lots and buildings. But weirdly, this damage didn't look recent. There was a layer of filth and fungus over everything; fully grown trees and bushes sprouted between broken chunks of pavement.

Plus, where were all the people? Based on the number of cars around, the place should be crawling with scientists. But they had yet to encounter another living soul. Would everyone have just abandoned their cars? It was seriously bizarre.

"Nico?" she called out breathlessly.

"Yes?" he said without turning around or pausing.

"Was it all torn up like this when you were here?"

"No," he replied after a moment. "Definitely not."

"Must've been major," Declan said. "Maybe one of those tsunami things, too, like in Japan. What do you think, Yosh? Does it look like that?"

She glanced back at them, but didn't say anything. Her shoulders were slumped as she trudged along. Sophie chewed her lip. It was worrisome. What could have made her draw into herself this way? Yeah, it was weird to wake up in a strange place, this far from home, but still; the rest of them were dealing with it. Kind of. *Had Yosh witnessed something terrible?* At the thought, she felt a prickle on her spine. Sophie stopped dead and scanned the forest surrounding them; nothing. But it was hard to suppress the sense that they were being watched.

"What is it?" Declan asked, noticing.

"Nothing. Just . . . thought I heard something."

"Yeah?" He cocked his head to the side. After a second, he shook his head. "Just more bloody birds. What did it sound like?"

"I can't describe it," Sophie said. "I was probably just imagining it anyway."

"We're all brickin' it," he said gravely.

Sophie raised an eyebrow. "Brickin' it?"

"Scared shiteless," he explained with a grin. "And why not? We're in Long Island at some top-secret compound. They were probably fattening us up to feed into that Collider."

She laughed. "Probably."

"My mum always hoped I'd give myself over to science," he said, brushing a sweaty strand of dark hair out of his eyes. "She'd be happy to know I'm doing her proud."

"I'm sure." She matched his tone. "So you think Nico's in on it?"

"Without a doubt." He held out a wrist for her to steady herself on, and she took it gratefully. "Guessing they all are. Anat is security, and Yosh is here just to scare the bejesus out of us."

"And what about Zain?" she asked.

"I don't know." All the humor abruptly left his voice. "But I'm hoping he just decided to be quit of us."

"That'd be the smart move," Sophie said. Privately, she doubted Zain had done anything of the sort, and she could tell that Declan had the same misgivings. But there didn't seem to be anything they could do about it, at least not until they found someone to help them.

Part of her was still hoping this was all just a strange dream. But the scrapes on her feet from walking through the forest barefoot argued against it; you never really felt pain in nightmares. And if it was a dream, it had gone on longer than anything she could remember.

Anat was gingerly easing through a gap in the cafeteria doors, taking care not to slice herself on the shards of glass that still dangled from the metal frame.

Nico followed with Yosh at his heels.

"Shall we?" Declan helped her through the doors, carefully holding one side open so Sophie could slip through.

They were in a small anteroom. Mold mottled what had once been white walls. Straight ahead, another set of double doors was intact.

"The others must've already gone in," Sophie murmured. She wasn't sure why, but the instinct to keep her voice low was overwhelming. Which was silly—wouldn't it be better if someone heard them?

Declan opened the door. The next room was enormous, about half the length of a football field with a ceiling that soared up two full stories. Long tables were lined up in rows, and there was a serving station at the far end. Dim light filtered in from windows set fifteen feet off the ground. Most of the glass was broken, and a few tree branches reached inside like giant, grasping hands.

The other teenagers had stopped dead in the center of the room.

"So strange," Sophie said in a voice just above a whisper.

There were trays scattered across the tables, some with utensils and plates still stacked on them; but they were devoid of anything that qualified as food. The entire floor was smothered in leaves, thick enough to feel like carpeting underfoot.

Each step she took released a pungent, musty smell in the air, like the floor was composting beneath them.

"Look," Sophie said.

Declan followed her pointing finger and frowned. "What is it?"

"Some sort of animal track." There was a large impression in the matted leaves: much bigger than a human footprint, ending in what looked like four sharp claws.

"Recognize it?" Declan asked.

"Why would I recognize it?"

"You're the native, right?"

"I live on the other side of the country," Sophie said, rolling her eyes. "Besides, I've never exactly been big on the outdoors." Which was true—even before she fell ill, the longest hike she'd ever taken was to the bus stop a half-mile from her house. She'd never even been a Girl Scout, and the one and only time her family had gone "camping" was a trip to Yosemite where they stayed in a cabin with indoor plumbing.

"What about you, Nico?" Declan said. "This look familiar?"

Nico slowly shook his head. "I've never seen anything like it."

"And I'm guessing that the forest décor is new?"

Nico had a pained expression on his face. "I was just here," he mumbled. "Two days ago."

"Maybe a hurricane?" Sophie offered tentatively. "I guess that could've broken the windows. And then it flooded, washing all this stuff in?" The thought cheered her somewhat, although two days didn't seem like nearly enough time for this amount of mold to grow. But it was hot as an inferno outside, which would have sped things up . . .

"Sure, that sounds likely," Declan agreed.

"After Hurricane Sandy, I think it looked like this," Sophie said, remembering all the news stories on TV; houses that looked like they'd been abandoned for years, streets strewn with detritus. "So maybe that explains it. Everyone was probably evacuated."

"Must've been one hell of a storm," he agreed.

Anat set her hands on her hips and demanded, "Enough. Where's the food?"

"It's usually set out over there." Nico pointed toward the serving station. Unfortunately, there was nothing that resembled digestible food: just metal trays filled with the same gunk that covered the floor, a mix of dead leaves, twigs, and mold. They all stared at them for a moment, disheartened.

"If this is a cafeteria there has to be a kitchen, yes?" Anat asked.

Everyone exchanged glances. Sophie wasn't sure about the rest of them, but she had a sudden urge to go back outside and make a break for the infirmary; at least it had been clean in there. But there wasn't any food, she reminded herself as her stomach grumbled.

Anat threw up her hands in a gesture of disgust and made for the set of doors behind the serving station.

"Maybe we should go with her," Nico said hesitantly.

"Right." Declan turned to Sophie and pulled out a chair. "You'd best wait here. Rest a bit while we scrounge up a meal."

"Sure." Sophie sank down gratefully. The chair was grimy and wobbly, but after their mile-long trek it felt like a sofa. She was completely drained. Maybe food would help.

Yosh settled on a chair beside her. Declan and Nico followed Anat to the double doors. They all paused for a second, then Anat shoved the one on the right hand side open.

Darkness beyond.

"Do the honors, Nico?" Declan asked.

Still looking bewildered, Nico held the door open. Declan vanished into the dark recesses of the kitchen, with Anat and Nico following closely on his heels.

Murmurs and scuffling noises. Seconds later, Declan poked his head out. He was frowning.

"Lights are out," he said.

"That's odd," Sophie said. The lights had worked in the infirmary. Maybe the electrical grid had been damaged here. "Any sign of food?"

"Just some nasty canned goods. We're checking the walk-in next."

"Keep us posted," Sophie said faintly. Her stomach was growling like crazy; even canned food sounded delicious. She hadn't had a real meal in weeks, just fluids delivered intravenously. What she'd give for a nice juicy burger right now: Animal Style, from In-N-Out, with a double order of fries. There had been a franchise near her house, attached to a Krispy Kreme where they'd always grab a box of doughnuts for dessert. She salivated at the memory and swallowed hard; whatever they found in the kitchen, burgers and doughnuts probably wouldn't be on the menu. To distract herself, she turned to Yosh and asked, "Are you feeling better?"

Yosh nodded slightly. Her eyes seemed clearer, her body less rigid.

"Good." Sophie silently heaved a sigh of relief. She desperately wanted to know what had happened to Zain, but asking straight out might send the girl back into some sort of state, so she decided to start with easier questions. "You're from Japan?"

"Yes. Kyoto."

"Really?" Sophie perked up. "I love Kyoto. My folks took us there a few years ago. Oh my God, Nara was amazing."

"Yes, Nara," Yosh said. "Very nice."

Unless she was mistaken, a look of panic flashed across Yosh's face. But maybe that was just because her English wasn't very good. "Those deer everywhere? Crazy," Sophie said, trying again. "One of them totally attacked my sister."

"Very nice," Yosh repeated.

Sophie sighed. Definitely a language barrier.

A second later, Yosh's stomach rumbled—loud for such a tiny person—and Sophie laughed. "You're hungry too, huh?"

"Yes." Yosh smiled thinly. "Hungry."

"I know, it's taking forever." She turned back toward the kitchen door and called out, "Hey, guys! Any luck?"

The only response was a loud creak from the depths of the next room.

Suddenly, someone screamed.

Sophie leapt to her feet and ran toward the kitchen, her fatigue overcome by a burst of adrenaline. Before she got halfway there, Declan burst through the double doors. He stumbled and fell to his knees, crying, "Jaysus!"

She rushed to his side. "What happened? Are you okay?"

He was bent double, wheezing. The others spilled out behind him; they all looked green. Declan was gagging. "The smell, it's just . . ." he choked. "Lord!"

"We opened the door to the refrigerator," Anat explained. She wasn't in as bad shape as the others, but she still looked pale. "The food must all have rotted. It smells . . ."

"Bloody terrible!" Declan said.

"So there is nothing to eat?" Yosh said in a small voice.

"There are cans," Anat said. "On the shelves against the back wall. We could try those."

"But that means going back in there," Declan said.

"I'll do it." Anat set her jaw and unwound the black scarf

from around her neck. In one smooth motion she tied it around her face, leaving only her eyes exposed. *Looks like she's done that before*, Sophie thought. *Interesting.*

Anat marched back through the doors. Nico held one side open to provide light but stayed well behind it. A terrible odor filtered through, a rot unlike anything she'd ever smelled before. "Ugh," Sophie gasped. The stench was so strong it set her eyes watering. She limped to the far side of the room and collapsed in a chair. Yosh followed and sat beside her again. Sophie found herself gazing at the footprints on the floor, trying to imagine what could have made them. She'd never been to Long Island but didn't think there was much wildlife there besides deer. And they definitely weren't a hoof prints.

A minute later, Anat emerged with a half dozen large cans filling her arms. She dumped them on the nearest table. Nico let the door fall shut.

"Garbanzo beans," Declan said, reading the cans doubtfully. "Diced tomatoes, jalapeño peppers—oh, those'll be tasty."

"You're more than welcome to look yourself," Anat said icily.

"This one does not look right." Yosh held up a can of stewed peaches.

"Botulism," Sophie agreed, examining it. The entire can had bowed out in the center. "Must have been close to the expiration date."

"Shame," Declan commented. "Peaches would've been nice."

"We've got another problem," Sophie said.

"What?" Anat asked.

"No can opener."

Declan groaned. "Fantastic. Looks like we're going back in anyway."

"Someone else's turn," Anat announced.

"I'll go."

Everyone turned to Yosh, surprised. She lowered her eyes. "I don't mind smells so much. I will try to find some utensils, too."

"You're sure?" Declan asked.

She nodded, then squared her shoulders and marched toward the door. Nico pulled it open again, and she vanished inside.

Five minutes later, they were all digging into enormous cans of peaches, stewed tomatoes, and garbanzo beans at the far end of the cafeteria. Not the best meal Sophie had ever had, but it was food, and for the moment that was all that mattered. She couldn't remember having ever been so famished. They shoveled bites in quickly, the silence only broken by the clink of forks against metal.

Finally, Sophie sat back. She'd been fed through an IV for so long, her stomach must have shrunk. If she ate another bite she'd burst. She watched the others still chewing, their entire focus directed on the food before them. They were a random group of kids, that was for sure. Kind of like a post-apocalyptic model UN. The thought made her snort. Declan looked up and raised an eyebrow, and she smiled at him. He grinned back; she flushed and quickly looked away. The light sifting down from the windows was turning orange; shadows stretched long across the room.

"It's getting late," she noted.

Declan's brow furrowed as he followed her gaze. "It is," he said. "Strange that we still haven't seen a soul. How many buildings are there?"

"I don't know exactly," Nico said. "A lot. But if no one is here . . . that's strange. My father said this was the one building that's always staffed. They figure that if food and coffee are available, people won't mind working all night."

"So if the cafeteria is empty, there's a good chance the whole place is, too?" Sophie asked.

Nico shrugged. "Probably."

"How close is the nearest town?" Anat asked.

"Six or seven miles." He leaned back in his chair. "I could walk there."

"Shouldn't we should stick together?" Yosh asked.

"I vote we rest up, then get a fresh start in daylight," Declan said.

"Sleep in here?" Anat asked disdainfully. "It smells awful."

"No, back at the infirmary." Declan held up a hand to still their grumbles. "We know there are beds there, and working bathrooms, and light. We'll take food with us, then leave straightaway in the morning."

"Who made you leader?" Nico protested.

Sophie pursed her lips. Apparently the meal had restored some of his swagger.

"I can walk miles in the dark," Anat said, tossing her hair. "I've done all night marches."

"Yes, please, tell us more about your extensive military training," Declan muttered. "Apparently it didn't include grabbing an opener when there are cans about."

"You wouldn't even go back in there," Nico scoffed. Turning to Anat, he said, "I'll go with you."

"Good," she said. "We'll make better time on our own anyway."

"Hang on," Declan protested. "We need to stick together. We don't know what's going on yet. And if you leave us, we're bolloxed. You're the only one who even knows where the hell we are."

"Declan's right," Sophie said. The prospect of separating made her feel panicky; she'd seen enough horror movies to know that nothing good ever came of splitting up. And Declan was right, without Nico the rest of them would be totally clueless. At least he knew the area. "We should stay together. Even if only for the night."

Anat and Nico exchanged a look. Whatever was going on between them, they were clearly not sold on the togetherness idea. But then Anat glanced at Yosh, and Sophie could see her waffling. "There's that weird animal track, too," she reminded them. "Something big made that. And we don't have any weapons."

"That is true," Anat said slowly.

Nico shuffled his feet, looking unhappy. "So, what? We stay?"

"We stay," Anat stated. "But just until dawn. Then we go into town. Is your phone working yet?"

"None of them will work until you're a mile away from the facility," Nico said. "They block the towers as some sort of security measure."

"Lovely," Declan said. "Is that why the time is wrong, too?"

"What do you mean?" Nico asked.

Declan held up an iPhone. "Says January 1, 2000."

"What?" Nico scoffed. "That can't be right." As he checked his own, his eyes narrowed. "Mine says the same."

Sophie was too exhausted to engage in a riveting conversation about time stamps on cell phones. All she wanted was to crawl back into bed and stay there, preferably until help arrived. "Vote, then? All in favor of heading back to the infirmary, raise your hand."

Declan lifted his. She and Yosh quickly followed suit. After a pause, Anat jutted hers up. Nico glowered at them all for a beat, then nodded curtly. "Fine," he said. "Sunrise."

"Sure thing," Declan said. "And with luck, by this time tomorrow we'll all be headed home."

The return trip took longer than Anat had anticipated. Now they were burdened with large cans, and the lengthening shadows made picking their way through the forest difficult. During her mandatory military service, Anat had marched for kilometers across rough terrain. That hadn't been the worst of it, though. She'd also been forced to carry an M16 everywhere, even to the bathroom; another recruit had forgotten theirs, and the entire unit was punished, forced to hold the rifles over their heads for nearly an hour. As her arms shook from the pain and stress, Anat knew she wasn't the only one who would have preferred to turn the weapon on the imbecile who'd forgotten. He never did so again, though; a beat down after lights out made sure of that. In comparison, carrying a couple of cans through the woods was easy.

The others were having a much harder time. Nico was doing all right, but everyone else kept stumbling and falling. They'd be covered in bumps and bruises by the time they got back. On her own, Anat could have made it to the infirmary in half the time. But instinct made her stay close. Even though she barely knew these kids, she was starting to feel responsible for them—Yosh in particular. Protecting the weak had been another major facet of her training; her responsibility to fellow citizens was drilled in from day one. Soldiers swore to abide by a rigid code of conduct. Even such minor offensives as neglecting to give up a bus seat to an elderly person could result in punishment. Not that any of these kids were her fellow countrymen. *Far from it*, she thought with a snort. They were all soft, whining about missing a single meal. If anything happened, she was clearly the best equipped to handle it.

She'd be shed of them all by tomorrow anyway. Once they got within cell phone range, the others could contact their families. Shortly thereafter they'd be tucked away in their respective embassies, assisted with transportation home. But who could she call? If she contacted Hazim and tried to explain what had happened, he'd probably think she'd lost her mind, or worse, changed it. This entire situation had made joining him all but impossible; neither of them could afford a plane ticket to Egypt. And her parents would just try and compel her to return home. Plus Anat could imagine the skepticism with which the Israeli government would view her circumstances. They'd figure her for a deserter, maybe even throw her in prison. And then she'd have no hope of running away with Hazim.

Wrapped up in her thoughts, Anat tripped on a tree root and went flying. She landed hard on the can of peas clutched against her chest and grunted as the wind was knocked out of her.

"All right?" Nico asked.

"Fine," Anat said, embarrassed. She scrambled to her feet, dusting off with her free hand. She'd have a nasty bruise on her belly tomorrow, and her toes throbbed where she'd stubbed them. Anat forced herself to focus solely on the trail, pushing all other thoughts from her mind. Declan was helping Sophie along, one arm braced around her back. Watching them brought another pang.

"What's wrong?" Nico asked.

"Nothing," she muttered. "Just thinking about something."

"Something, or someone?"

She looked up at him. Nico was giving her a look she

recognized, the same one she'd been getting from men ever since she turned fifteen and developed breasts. "Yes," she said. "I was thinking of my fiancé."

"You're engaged?" he asked, sounding surprised. "To whom?"

"A Palestinian named Hazim." Saying his name out loud caused tears to well up in her eyes. Hastily, she wiped them away.

"Huh," Nico said. "Did he give you that ring you always touch?"

Anat closed her hand into a fist self-consciously; she hadn't realized she'd been doing that, and was shaken by the fact that he'd noticed. "Yes." She hesitated, then added, "I gave him one, too." She'd chosen the ring carefully, a simple interwoven band of gold and silver. It had reminded her of them, two very different people from opposing worlds, now wound together until you couldn't tell where one ended and the next began.

"But you're only eighteen, right?" Nico asked.

"So?"

"That seems young to be getting married."

"My mother was married at sixteen," Anat retorted. "Besides, we're in love."

"People usually don't get married otherwise," Nico said drily. "So why wasn't he with you?"

Anat was reluctant to tell him too much; after all, she barely knew him. But she finally admitted, "We were running away together. My family would never have let me marry him. And I was about to be assigned to active military duty."

Nico grunted.

"What?" she demanded.

"You must really love him," he said, a trace of wistfulness in his voice. "You'd be in big trouble if you got caught, right?"

"Right," she said.

"So, you decided to leave your home, and everything you knew. I can't imagine doing that."

They walked in silence for a moment. Anat unexpectedly found herself wrestling with a surge of emotions. The night she left, she'd mainly been excited about finally being with Hazim. She'd spent months dreaming about falling asleep with his arms around her. The fact that she'd never see her family again, or her friends; that she'd never sit on the beach watching the sunset, or have dinner under their orange trees in their backyard . . . that hadn't really sunk in yet.

Until now.

"My family doesn't even know about him," Anat mumbled. "We met at a retreat a year ago."

"I thought Israelis and Palestinians didn't really mix."

"That was the whole point. The retreat was all about discussing what our countries were doing to each other, and coming to some sort of understanding."

"Sounds interesting," Nico said.

Anat snorted. "It was a disaster. Everyone screamed at each other for three days straight. I finally went to a café just to get away from them all. Hazim was there, too. We started talking. And . . ." She took a deep breath. "Afterward, we kept in touch by cell phone."

"How did you see each other?"

"We only managed once. Border crossings are too dangerous." Anat flashed back on the afternoon they'd managed to share, just a few months ago. It was during one of her few leaves from training. She hadn't gone home, hadn't even informed her family that she was free. As an art history major, Hazim had received a special pass to visit the Ashdod Museum of Art, ostensibly to research a paper. But instead, he'd spent the day with her. They'd sat in a café, hidden behind a tall plant in the corner, clasping hands beneath the table. That was when they'd exchanged rings, and made plans to escape together through Egypt.

"So you've only seen him once since you met?" Nico sounded dumbfounded.

"We talked on Skype," Anat said defensively. "Besides, a year is nothing when you know you're going to spend the rest of your lives together." That was what Hazim always told her, what she knew to be true. And they'd been so close to making it happen.

"Well, maybe it wouldn't have worked out anyway."

"That's supposed to make me feel better?" She glared at him. Nico was walking with his head down, focused on the rough path in front of them.

"Sorry, I didn't mean any offense. But most marriages don't work out these days." A shadow flitted across his face. "I'm never getting married."

The American girl suddenly hissed, "Did you hear that?"

"What?" Anat demanded.

Sophie had frozen in place. She was at the rear of the group, lagging behind. Her legs were covered in scrapes, testimonials to how many times she'd fallen.

"I heard a noise, like a branch snapping behind us."

They all stopped. Anat strained her ears but couldn't hear anything except the whisper of a breeze through the leaves overhead. Regardless, she sensed a presence behind them. She'd experienced something similar during training exercises; an atavistic awareness of being hunted.

"We need to move faster," she said abruptly. "Nico, you lead. I'll bring up the rear. "

"But—" Declan started to protest.

"It's nearly dark," Anat pointed out. "And we have a half kilometer to go."

She exchanged a glance with Nico, who nodded curtly, apparently just as happy as she was to curtail their conversation. *He hadn't meant anything by that marriage comment*, she reminded herself; his parents were probably divorced. It was natural that he'd have strong feelings about it. He just didn't understand how she felt about Hazim. They were meant to be together, she'd known it the day they met.

Something about the way he carried himself echoed Hazim, though; he possessed the same easy confidence. Not that they looked anything alike. Nico was tall and broad-shouldered, muscular and fit. Handsome, although not really her type. Hazim was slim, with shoulder length dark hair and deep brown eyes—an artist, not a fighter. An inch shorter than her, though that had never really mattered.

Nico broke into a trot. Yosh hesitated, then scurried along behind him.

"Bloody hell. What is this, a marathon?" Declan grumbled.

"Big animal tracks," Anat reminded him. "And no weapons."

"I'd almost prefer to be eaten."

"Then bring up the rear," Anat said, narrowing her eyes.

He laughed, then tucked an arm around Sophie and said, "C'mon, bird. I'll give you a hand."

"This would be a lot easier if I had some shoes," Sophie replied, wincing. She was the only one among them without a pair.

"We'll check cars on our way out tomorrow, yeah?"

Declan soothed. "Probably find you a lovely pair of trainers. But for now, you can climb on my back if you want."

Sophie snorted. "No thanks. I look ridiculous enough as it is."

"True enough." He winked. "Ready to move it along, then?"

"If you insist." The American sighed, but her ears were flushed.

Anat raised an eyebrow. The two of them seemed to be getting along well. Interesting, since Declan had mentioned a girlfriend. Maybe that's why he'd insisted on returning to the infirmary for the night. Well, most men weren't as faithful as Hazim. Growing up with her father, she knew that well enough. *None of her business, anyway*, she reminded herself.

At least the two of them were moving faster now. Anat let them draw ahead, keeping her eyes peeled for something that could be used as a weapon. It didn't take long—there were plenty of branches strewn about the ground. She selected one about a meter long, with some heft and a sharp point where it had split from the tree. She shifted the can of peas, cradling it in her left arm so that her right was free to wield the stick. Nico wove quickly through the trees, doing an admirable job of finding the clearest path. She caught herself watching the way his shirt fabric stretched across his back and frowned. *Not my type*, she reminded herself. *Focus*.

Anat kept her senses attuned to their rear flank. Unfortunately, the group was making so much noise it was hard to hear anything else. The sun sank below the horizon, leaving a seam of pale blue in the east. Night was coming.

"Faster!" she called out.

"Doing what I can, Captain," Declan grumbled, but he yanked Sophie along at a trot.

The parking lot in front of the infirmary had just come into view when Anat heard the distinct *crack* of a branch breaking behind her.

She spun, scanning the forest. It was dark, impenetrable. But something was definitely there.

"What is it?" Nico called back.

"I'm not sure." Anat stayed focused on the woods.

"Help, maybe?" Sophie suggested. "Other people?"

Anat hesitated. Her gut said no. A person wouldn't have stalked them in silence. They would have shown themselves, or called out. Unless they weren't friendly, in which case she'd almost prefer to run into an animal; at least it wouldn't be armed.

Nico had stopped on the first jagged section of concrete. In a low voice he asked, "Should we wait to see what it is?"

"No. Better to meet it near the building."

"You're sure? What if it's someone coming to help?"

"Then we'll let them in. If not, we close the door."

He nodded. "Good plan."

Another *crack*, this time off to her left. The rest of them just stood there, staring helplessly into the forest. Angrily, she waved her arms at them and yelled, "Go!"

Nico broke into a run and started leaping from one concrete floe to the next. Anat dropped the can—she hated peas anyway. She gripped the stick with both hands as she swiftly moved backward, keeping her eyes on the forest the entire time. It was slow going, but she wasn't about to turn her back on a threat. She could make out distinct footfalls now, the sound of something large forcing its way through the undergrowth.

Halfway across the parking lot, she finally caught a glimpse of their pursuer: Massive shoulders. Broad, furry snout. Ears flattened back against its head. Anat's eyes widened. Even though she'd never seen one in person, she immediately recognized it. The bear growled at her, baring two rows of enormous jagged teeth.

She spun around, all thoughts of fighting gone as she screamed, "Run!"

Declan was helping Sophie manage the last few yards to the door when Anat's cry pierced the hot, stagnant air. He whipped around and spotted her bounding across the parking lot—paces ahead of an enormous, dark shape.

"Holy mother," he said. "It's a feckin' bear!"

"Oh my God," Sophie gasped.

Nico and Yosh had already reached the entrance. If he and Sophie ran, they'd be able to join them and bolt the door. But Anat . . .

The branch in her hands looked pitifully small. Even a gun probably wouldn't bring down an animal that size, at least not with a single shot. As the bear charged, its mouth fell open, tongue lolling to the side. It was impossibly fast. There was no way she'd make it.

Declan shoved Sophie forward, yelling, "Get everyone inside and close the door!"

Heart pounding, he kept his eyes on Anat. She was fifteen feet away . . . then ten . . . the bear had narrowed the gap, she could probably feel its breath on the back of her neck.

"I said run, you idiot!" she screamed as she passed him.

"Bloody ungrateful," Declan muttered. He hefted the garbanzo bean can up with both hands. Summoning all his strength, he heaved it. *Direct hit*—it smacked the bear on the snout. The animal shook its head, but barely broke stride.

Not exactly the effect he'd been hoping for—and now the bear looked pissed to boot. Declan spun on his heels and raced toward the door. He quickly caught up with Anat, whose long legs chewed up the pavement.

"That was a bad plan," Anat panted.

"Everyone's a bloody critic. Apologies for trying to save your arse."

"I don't need your help," she gasped.

"Right, you had that completely under control. You can thank me later, if . . ." The words died in his throat as he checked back over his shoulder. The bear was coming up fast, and they were still ten feet from the door. They weren't going to make it.

Declan pictured it all with awful clarity: the giant paw slashing across his back, followed by teeth clamping down on his throat. Distracted by the image, he stumbled and went sprawling. He landed hard on his chest, getting a mouthful of dirt. In desperation he flung both arms over his head.

Nothing happened.

His breath came in hard, sharp pants.

Cautiously, Declan lowered his arms.

The bear was gone.

"What the hell?" He turned to check on Anat.

"It kept running that way." She pointed past the building to where the woods continued.

"Away from us?" Declan said, perplexed. "Why?"

"I don't know." Anat shook her head. "It kept looking back, as if . . ."

"As if what?" he demanded when she didn't continue.

"Like it was being chased."

"Did you see anything behind it?"

"No." Anat chewed her lower lip. "What could be large enough to frighten a bear?"

"In Long Island? Not much, I don't think." Declan wasn't sure of that, though; maybe Nico would know.

"You guys coming in?" Sophie called. "Or are you going to hang around out there until the bear changes its mind?"

Turning, Declan saw her frame in the doorway. In the shadows behind her he made out Yosh and Nico. They'd kept the door open for him and Anat. He felt a surge of gratitude for that; he wouldn't have bet on some of his mates doing the same.

And thankfully, whatever had spooked the bear seemed to be gone.

As soon as they were inside, Sophie slammed the door shut and locked it.

"Not sure that'll be enough," Declan said. "Perhaps we should block it."

"Last time I checked, bears couldn't open doors," Sophie said, raising an eyebrow.

"No, but—"

"How do you say it . . . better safe than sorry, yes?" Anat jerked her chin toward the desks at the far end of the room. "Those look heavy. Help me stack them."

"But it was a bear," Sophie said, enunciating each word as if they were slow.

"Maybe not just a bear," Declan said. "Anat's right. Better safe than sorry."

Sophie opened her mouth again as if to protest, but the others were already heading for the desks. "Really?"

Declan stepped close to her and said, "Honestly, I'll feel much better about closing my eyes tonight if the only way in is blocked."

"Seriously?"

"Seriously. That bear was running from something. You didn't see it, though?"

She shook her head. "We didn't see anything. I wasn't really looking, though. I was kind of focused on the bear that was about to tear you apart." Hesitantly, she laid a hand on his arm. "I'm really glad you're okay."

"Me, too," Declan said. Their proximity suddenly made him uncomfortable, even though he'd technically been much closer to her the past few hours; hell, he'd basically been carrying her. But he found himself overly aware of how warm and soft her hand was. He took a step back. "I should go help with the desks."

"Yeah, sure," Sophie said. "But it's just . . . what else do you think could be out there?"

"Honestly? I haven't a clue," Declan said. "But when we leave tomorrow, I'd like to be holding something more lethal than a can of beans."

part two

FLIGHT

Sophie lie wide awake staring at the ceiling. She'd used verbal commands to dim the lights—after what happened outside, she couldn't stand the thought of a pitch black room. The look in Declan's eyes had seriously unnerved her. Up until this point, nothing seemed to faze him, but he really seemed to think that something even scarier than a bear was out there. She mentally tried to reconstruct the mysterious print they'd seen in the cafeteria; a bear could have made that, right? She was forced to admit that her familiarity with animal tracks was limited to cats and raccoons.

By unspoken accord, they'd all chosen to sleep in the same wing of the hospital, on the girls' side. After propping open the infirmary's outer door with metal bed rails to guard against accidentally locking themselves in, they'd selected rooms. Anat stuck to hers, Nico was at the end of the hall, and Yosh chose the one next door. Sophie didn't want to return to the room she'd woken up in, so Declan took it. She couldn't explain why, since all the rooms were basically identical. But part of her was afraid that if she fell asleep in there, she might wake up somewhere even stranger.

It was kind of spooky, that there had been just enough rooms in each section for the six of them. Almost like someone had planned it that way.

Of course, now there's only five of us, she reminded herself.

As if by mutual consensus, they'd stopped talking about Zain. *It was already like he'd never been there at all*, she thought guiltily. Yosh seemed to be doing better, but when Declan had gently prodded her about what happened in the vents, she shut down fast, in a way that didn't invite any other questions.

Granted, Sophie had only spent a few minutes with Zain, but he didn't seem like the type to set off on his own. Had a bear gotten him? If so, wouldn't they have seen some sign of it? And if he was attacked, how had Yosh gotten away?

Sophie sighed. This definitely wasn't helping her sleep. Maybe Yosh would be better in the morning, and they'd finally get some answers.

She ran a hand through her wet hair, trying to untangle the snarls. She hadn't been able to find a comb, even though the shower had soap and shampoo dispensers. Nasty, industrial-quality soap, but at least she'd been able to wash the grime out of the cuts on her hands and legs. She was exhausted, and her whole body ached; she felt like she'd run a marathon. Still, she found herself unable to sleep. Her head was spinning from everything that had happened, and her pulse rate had kicked up; she recognized the onset of a panic attack, and forced herself to calm down. Going over and over things in her mind would only make her crazy. She wouldn't find anything else out tonight. *Besides*, she reminded herself, *they'd been outside now*. And weird though everything was,

this was definitely the real world; no fire or brimstone anywhere. *Long Island probably wouldn't turn out to be purgatory*, Sophie thought with bemusement. Tomorrow they'd
get back in cell phone range and find out what was going
on. There was probably a perfectly reasonable explanation.
They'd all end up laughing about how paranoid they'd been.

Right?

Sophie couldn't stop picturing that strange void, the swirl
of colors reaching out for her. She wondered what had happened to her family—were they still standing around an
empty bed in Palo Alto, wondering what the hell had happened to her? How *had* she ended up here?

And since when were there bears on Long Island?

On reflection, Sophie was happy that Declan and Anat had
insisted on barricading the door. It had struck her as a silly
precaution at the time. Now she was comforted by the fact
that a few desks stood between her and whatever lurked in
the darkness.

She wished one of the others was still awake and willing
to talk. But no one seemed to want to discuss the strangeness
of their situation. As soon as they got back to the infirmary,
they'd shuffled off to their separate bedrooms. Five minutes
later, she'd heard Declan snoring next door.

Meanwhile, her stomach was churning, and she kept tasting bile in the back of her throat. She hoped all that canned
food they'd eaten was really okay. How ironic if she survived
cancer, only to die of botulism poisoning . . .

There was a quiet rap at her door—she'd left it open to
prevent getting locked in. Sophie raised her head off the pillow and saw Yosh standing on the threshold looking uncertain.

"Come on in," Sophie said, keeping her voice low. She

struggled with the bed's controls, trying to adjust it. Frustrated, she finally gave up and pushed upright, wrapping her arms around the extra pillow.

Yosh perched on the chair beside her bed. "I could not sleep," she said in a small voice.

"Me either," Sophie said. "Anyone else awake?"

Yosh shook her head. "I checked."

"Guess that makes us the sentries."

"Sentries?" Yosh looked puzzled.

"Yeah, like . . . guards who keep watch. You know, the people who warn everyone else of danger."

"Were we supposed to be sentries?" Yosh asked, wide-eyed.

"No. Although I'm kind of surprised Anat didn't suggest it. Seems like the kind of thing she'd go for," Sophie snorted. "Of course, a bear could come marching in here right now and there's not much I could do about it."

"No, there's not," Yosh said gravely. "We would be eaten."

Sophie laughed, even though Yosh hadn't sounded like she was kidding. "Yup. Although considering how I feel right now, I doubt we'd taste very good. I kind of pity the bear that would have to experience those chickpeas secondhand."

Yosh made a strange sound. She held a hand in front of her mouth. It took a second for Sophie to realize she was giggling.

"Seriously," Sophie said. "I'm totally nauseous. Aren't you?" But despite her stomachache, she started cracking up too. The two of them laughed for a full minute. "You were brave, going in after the rest of the food," she finally managed to say as she wiped away stray tears.

"But you hated the food." Yosh doubled over again.

"Oh, God, stop. I'm seriously close to puking," Sophie finally gasped.

"Sorry. Going in was not so bad. Just a smell." Yosh

hesitated, then continued. "There should not have been so many bad cans, though."

"What do you mean?"

"Almost all of them were broken. Bent," Yosh said. "Even the ones on the shelves. And the food in the refrigerator—it was very old."

"So maybe we were all knocked out by . . . whatever happened," Sophie ventured.

"Yes, but for how long? I checked the dates on the cans. They should still have been good for a long time." Yosh pulled the chair closer to the bed and said, "Declan said you were sick. With cancer."

That was annoying; she hadn't exactly wanted her illness to be public information. *Thanks a lot, Declan*, she thought as she answered, "I was dying."

"And you woke up here?"

"Unfortunately, yes," Sophie said. "Why?"

Yosh didn't respond immediately. Finally, she said, "What Declan said, about purgatory. This is a real place?"

"Ah . . ." Sophie wasn't sure what to say. She was pretty sure the Japanese practiced some form of Buddhism, but didn't know if there were any parallels between that and Christianity. *Too bad Yosh didn't want to know about near death experiences*, Sophie thought wryly. Those she could have gone on about all night. "Some people believe in it."

"Not you?"

"No. Not me," Sophie had very clear opinions about heaven and hell, in that she didn't believe in either of them.

"But what happens in purgatory?"

Sophie squirmed, fervently wishing that one of the others, preferably Declan, would wake up and join them. She was way out of her element in this conversation, yet felt obligated to answer. There was an urgency underlying Yosh's words. If possible, Sophie wanted to put her mind at ease so that at least one of them had a shot at sleeping. She dug through her memory banks, trying to recall decade-old Sunday school lessons. "Declan would know better than me, but I think it's a place where people's souls get . . . stuck."

"Stuck like glue?"

"Kind of. Stuck, in that they're not in heaven or hell. They're somewhere in the middle."

"And what unsticks them?" Yosh's eyes were shaded by her bangs, making them hard to read.

"I don't know," Sophie said. "But honestly, Yosh, I don't think this is purgatory."

"What is this place, then?"

"Long Island, according to Nico," Sophie said dryly.

"I don't think so," Yosh said quietly. "This is a bad place. A very bad place."

"Yeah?" Sophie said. Yosh's eyes were anxious. Still, she was talking; that was an improvement. "Can I ask you something, Yosh?"

Yosh inclined her head slightly but didn't respond.

"That boy, Zain. Did he . . . leave you, once you got up there?" Sophie asked hesitantly.

Yosh's face crumpled as she whispered, "Zain."

"Yes, Zain," Sophie said. The color had drained from Yosh's cheeks, but Sophie pressed forward anyway. "The thing is, if he's out there somewhere, hurt or something, we should go help him."

Yosh was already shaking her head. "He is gone."

"Gone where?"

"Just gone." Yosh lowered her eyes. "He will not come back."

"Okay." Sophie fought the urge to push harder. She got the sense that if she did, Yosh might go full-on catatonic again, and frankly she didn't have the energy to deal with that. She tried to sound reassuring as she continued, "Maybe you can explain it to me tomorrow. Right now I think we should try to get some sleep."

Yosh nodded and stood. "Good night, Sophie."

"Night."

Yosh paused on the threshold and turned back. "Sophie?"

"Yes?"

"We're already dead."

"What?" Sophie said, startled. "No, really, we're—"

"It does not matter. I will be the sentries. You sleep."

Before Sophie could respond, Yosh slipped into the corridor and disappeared. Her words hung in the stillness, a presence that seemed to suck all the air out of the room. Shaken, Sophie dropped back against the pillow and gazed up at the ceiling. She had a feeling that she wouldn't be sleeping at all.

The next day, Anat scanned the forest warily as she followed the other four kids away from the infirmary. It was hard to tell if they'd even left the grounds of the facility yet; the surrounding woods were so thick, they could be steps away from a building and not see it. Funny, she wouldn't have expected America to be this overgrown. And so green—it was like a jungle, all towering trees and dangling vines. She could easily have believed they were wending through the Amazon.

It was hot, too. She wiped sweat off her forehead with the back of her arm. A different kind of heat than she was used to: the air so thick and humid it was suffocating. She thought longingly of Tel Aviv, where even on the hottest days a cool breeze eased off the ocean. Even the training facility hadn't felt this hot, though it was stuck in the middle of the desert. And she hadn't had to worry about nasty blood-sucking insects there, either. She irritably smacked one dead on her arm.

"How much farther?" Sophie called out. The American was stumbling, feet crossing over each other. She appeared on the verge of collapse, even though they'd only gone a kilometer at most.

Nico said, "Maybe five miles. We'll be in cell phone range sooner, hopefully."

Sophie didn't say anything, although a shadow swept across her features. Declan murmured something in her ear and tucked an arm around her waist. They lurched along again.

Anat repressed the urge to groan. Five miles would take an eternity with this group. They hadn't even left the infirmary until late morning. She'd hovered impatiently as the others lingered over breakfast, chewing the canned food with what seemed to be deliberate slowness and an excessive amount of complaints. Anat wolfed down her chickpeas and peaches, barely tasting them. It was fuel, and would provide energy to reach their destination. That was all she cared about.

They'd wasted even more time arguing about whether to try and take a car. Declan claimed he could get one started, and pointed out they were unlikely to be prosecuted for auto theft. But it turned out to be a moot point. All the cars outside the infirmary rested on rims, no air in their tires. Plus, maneuvering one through the jagged, upheaved pavement to the street would be virtually impossible.

At Anat's urging they'd spent another hour cobbling together a shabby assortment of weapons. Anat found a long iron rod. Nico and Declan had pried steel bedrails loose from their frames. Even Yosh was clutching a towel rack from one of the bathrooms. Only Sophie remained unarmed, declaring herself too weak to manage.

Weak is right, Anat couldn't help but think. Granted, the girl had been ill; her exhaustion was understandable. Anat knew she should be more sympathetic, but it was hard to repress frustration. She didn't want to spend the night in these woods. Agitated, she stripped off her long-sleeved shirt and tied it around her waist. She sensed Nico's eyes trailing over her tank top and raised an eyebrow at him. He quickly turned away.

Since Nico knew the route to town, he stayed at the head of their column. Anat had volunteered to cover their rear flank, and was consequently forced to shuffle along with Sophie. Every time the girl stumbled, Anat gritted her teeth and helped her back up.

We should have left her, she thought for the millionth time. Sophie had even offered to stay, claiming she'd rest up in the infirmary while waiting for them to send help. But Declan wouldn't hear of it. After their encounter with the bear the night before, he was keen on keeping them together.

And he was right, Anat grudgingly acknowledged. Annoying as Sophie was, even Anat wouldn't have felt right about abandoning her. They'd call Nico's dad as soon as they were in mobile range, and he'd arrange for help. After that, they could all go their separate ways.

Unfortunately, no matter how far they trudged, the phones refused to cooperate.

Once again, Anat watched Nico dig his out and lift it toward the sky. He frowned and shook his head, then tucked it away. He and Declan had been checking every few minutes, but neither had gotten any signal bars yet. She'd left her iPhone back home, concerned about the potential for

tracking. Now she was wishing she'd taken the chance—
she'd give anything to be able to call home. Or better yet, to
be able to sneak a glance at her photos of Hazim.

Without warning, they emerged on a road. Two lanes separated by a faded yellow dividing line, in markedly better
shape than the parking lots.

"Which way?" Declan asked.

Nico looked relieved as he pointed left. "West. This is
Upton Road. It should lead us straight there."

Despite having to skirt a few giant potholes, the road was
much less challenging than picking their way through the forest. Anat sighed with relief as their pace picked up. Maybe
they'd make it to town by lunchtime after all.

Cars were scattered about in odd clusters, as if the drivers had pulled up to each others' windows for a chat. They
appeared long abandoned: uniformly rusty, with flat tires and
a thick film of dust coating the windows. Anat peered inside
each as they passed. All empty: no bodies inside, which was
a relief. There also wasn't any evidence of a mass evacuation;
the cars weren't packed with suitcases and camping equipment. Just discarded food wrappers, a gym bag, a stuffed dog
gazing forlornly out the rear window. But why had the cars
been left here? In the aftermath of any natural disaster, clearing the roads was a priority.

Of course, this was America and not Israel; maybe
emergency policies were different here. The American girl
might know, and Anat had almost asked her a few times.
But Sophie wore a tight, drawn look, as if just putting one
foot in front of the other required enormous concentration.
So Anat kept pace silently, puzzling it over as she fought a
growing sense of apprehension. All of this was very wrong.
The cars shouldn't look so decrepit—they made the worst

junkyard salvage in Tel Aviv look like a Rolls-Royce, and that was saying something. Everything they encountered exuded an air of disuse and abandonment, from the buildings to the cars to the roads. Could a hurricane or earthquake do that? And so quickly?

Worse yet was the silence. They were on Long Island, close to the greatest concentration of population in the United States. Yet there wasn't so much as the sound of a car radio in the distance, or far-off construction.

Declan touched her elbow, shaking her out of the reverie. "I'm going to check on something with Nico," he said in a low voice. Indicating Sophie with a tilt of his head, he said, "Keep an eye on her?"

"Of course," Anat said stiffly. "Tell Nico we need to pick up the pace."

"Not sure that's possible." Declan glanced at Sophie, who was slumped against one of the cars, her head bowed, arms crossed in front of her chest. They'd found a thin pair of scrubs back at the infirmary, which she'd immediately changed into. She was still barefoot, though, and rested gingerly on the outsides of her feet. "I was actually going to ask about stopping for lunch. She's really suffering over there."

Anat grunted. "She'll suffer less once we get there."

"Says the girl all kitted out for this stroll," he said, looking pointedly at her boots. "Sophie's feet are shredded to hell, and she hasn't walked in weeks. Have a little heart."

"So we find her some shoes."

"I've checked every car we've passed," he said. "None yet."

Anat scowled. "Fine."

She marched to Sophie and perched on the car's bumper. Bending over, she started untying her laces.

"What are you doing?" Sophie asked.

"Giving you my boots."

"But—"

"They'll be too large," Anat said. "But they are better than nothing. I will keep the socks to protect my feet."

"You're sure?" Sophie asked dubiously.

"I have tough feet," Anat said.

"Tough everything, more like," Declan said, but he was grinning.

Sophie sat down beside her and pulled the boots on. Standing, she sighed heavily and said, "God, that's so much better."

"Now, please—move faster."

"Yes, sir," Declan said with a mock salute.

"And lose the attitude," Anat said, jabbing a finger into his chest. "I am not appreciating it."

"Thank you, Anat." Sophie smiled at her, then started walking again. Declan fell in step behind her. Anat followed, trying to ignore the pricks and jabs of rough gravel through her thick socks. She'd suffered worse before.

Nico and Yosh had stopped, but Anat waved for them to continue. They stretched out in a ragged line, weaving from one side of the road to the other to avoid obstacles. She frowned. They shouldn't be so spread out, better to keep a tight formation in case a threat materialized. Her field commander would never have stood for such sloppiness. She had to bite her lip to keep from castigating them. After all, they were just a group of frightened kids; and they *were* moving, albeit slowly. Plus, so far they hadn't seen any sign of bears or anything else.

Suddenly, Nico stopped and pointed. Anat trotted to catch up. Her heart skipped a beat when she followed his gaze.

It was a house, set back from the road. The grass in front was tall and overgrown, and weeds choked the driveway. Still, it was the first they'd come across. Maybe someone would be home. Or if not, at least there might be a functioning telephone.

"No car in the driveway," Declan noted. "Maybe no one's there."

"Let's find out," Anat said, marching toward the front door.

They followed her down a flagstone path. It was bumpier than it should have been, with rocks protruding at ankle-twisting angles, but still navigable.

Anat climbed the stairs to a wraparound veranda and knocked on the front door. The porch floorboards were weathered, long strips of gray paint peeling off like shedding skin. The house appeared just as forsaken as everything else.

"No answer," Nico muttered.

She knocked again, more loudly. They waited another minute, then Declan said, "Step aside."

"What are you going to do?" Sophie asked.

"I'm getting us in." Fumbling in his left pocket, he drew out a set of narrow metal tools and went down on one knee to examine the deadbolt. "Easy."

"You're going to pick the lock?" Sophie asked dubiously. "How the hell do you know how to do that?"

Declan didn't answer. He'd already set to work, inserting the pins with his eyes half closed.

"But—" Sophie protested.

"We need to find a telephone," Anat interrupted. "A land-line. There might be one inside."

They all watched in silence. Declan was impressively adept, a minute after he started there was a click. He rose to his feet and turned the knob with a flourish, opening the door.

Sophie frowned at him. The others offered muted congratulations.

"Don't all thank me at once," Declan said peevishly.

"Nice job," Anat said, squeezing his arm as she walked past. He gave her a curt nod.

Her nose wrinkled at the stale air inside. It had apparently been a long time since anyone cracked a window. The door opened onto a dark, narrow hallway, empty save for a coat rack and small table where a vase held fake flowers. There was a staircase on her left, and farther down the hall a wide entryway. She strode toward it, figuring that was a good place to start looking for a landline. The living room was crammed with chairs, end tables, lamps, and an upright piano. *An elderly person's home*, Anat guessed; all the furniture was worn and dated, the wall-to-wall carpeting cheap but functional. She swallowed. Everything was covered in a thick film of dust, much like the insides of the cars they'd encountered.

There was a messy stack of old newspapers on the coffee table, the edges brown and curling. Framed photos lined the mantelpiece above the fireplace, many in black and white. Anat examined them: most were typical family photos where everyone posed self-consciously, special occasions like birthdays and holidays recorded for posterity. Seeing them gave her a pang—a similar array lined the windowsill at her parents' house back in Tel Aviv.

"In here!" Nico called out. "Come see what we've found!"

Anat gathered herself, then returned to the hall. It deadended in a kitchen with a worn linoleum floor, a marred wooden table in the center. Nico was standing next to the sink holding a phone in his hand. Anat snorted at the sight of it. Definitely an old person's home, the phone actually had a long cord dangling from the receiver. She hadn't seen one like that since she was a kid.

"No dial tone," he said, disheartened.

Sophie groaned and dropped into one of the kitchen chairs.

"No lights either," Declan said, flicking the switch. "So we'd best not open the refrigerator."

"The rest of the house is empty," Yosh announced, entering the room.

"There are still dishes in the drying rack." Sophie noted.

Declan opened the nearest cupboard and gave a crow of joy. "Have a look at this!"

The shelves were filled with boxes of food. Anat's mouth watered at the sight of them. After two straight meals of room-temperature peaches, garbanzo beans, peas, and diced tomatoes, anything else seemed like gourmet cuisine.

"Crackers," Declan said, taking down a box. "Canned tuna—the can looks good, it's not dented . . . oh, and, biscuits. That's just grand."

As he went through the inventory, stacking things on the counter, they all pressed forward.

"Thank God. I'm starved," Sophie said. "Let's bring it all over to the table."

Five minutes later, they were gorging themselves. Everything tasted stale, but edible. Anat had never cared for tuna fish; it always reminded her of cat food. But now she piled it on crackers, gobbling them down as quickly as she could shove them in her mouth. Everyone else did the same. Nico had crumbs on his cheek, and Declan was digging into a jar of pickles.

Finally seated, Anat sat back in her chair. "Where do you think the people are?"

"Just here, or in general?" Declan asked after a pause.

Anat shrugged.

"They must have been evacuated," Nico said.

"Not like this." Sophie shook her head. "After an

earthquake or hurricane they might condemn whole neigh-
borhoods, but there would still be repair crews, and the roads
would've been cleared, right? The street we've been walking
on looks pretty major, but we haven't seen anyone else yet.
That's really weird."

So *she's noticed too*, Anat thought.

"This is the first house we've seen," Declan remarked.
"Maybe there are people just up the road."

Anat guessed everyone was thinking the same thing:
doubtful. Whatever had happened obviously wasn't limited
to the area around the facility. What if they reached town
and found it abandoned, too? What if Nico's father was long
gone?

"It could have been . . ." Nico said, then shook his head.

"Could've been what?" Anat asked, although she already
knew what he was going to say.

"Nuclear." He kept his gaze on the warped table. "I've
seen pictures of Chernobyl, and it looks like this. People left
their houses and cars in a hurry and never went back."

Silence again. Tuna fish and crackers rose up the back of
Anat's throat; she choked them back down. Israel lived under
the constant threat of nuclear annihilation, and from a young
age she had been educated about the aftermath of a nuclear
explosion. What if the food was irradiated, and they'd been
eating poison? Or they might have been walking through an
invisible cloud of fallout this entire time.

"You had the same thing in Japan after the tsunami, right?"
Declan asked Yosh. "When all those reactors started to go?"

A look of panic flitted across her face. After a moment, she
said, "Yes. After the tsunami."

Anat frowned. Yosh was obviously lying. She exhibited
all the classic signs: tensed jaw, rapid blinking, avoiding

eye contact. But that tsunami had been huge, devastating; a bunch of nuclear power plants had basically almost melted down. Anat had heard all about it in Israel; there was no way someone who actually lived in Japan wouldn't know about it.

But Yosh didn't seem to. How was that possible?

"So what do we do now?" Sophie asked.

"We keep walking," Declan said with forced cheer.

Sophie groaned in response.

Anat abruptly pushed back from the table. "There are newspapers in the living room. Maybe they say what happened."

"I'll come with you," Nico offered.

She resisted the urge to roll her eyes. He was obviously developing a crush on her, which was ridiculous given the circumstances. All she wanted was to get back to her fiancé. But she didn't want to be rude, so she kept silent as Nico followed her down the hall.

Anat bent over the papers splayed across the table. The words were faded almost to the point of illegibility, and English wasn't her first language, which made it harder. Still, the date in the upper right hand corner was clear enough but the year was smudged: August 31st. Yesterday.

There was nothing of note on the front page, at least with regard to any sort of disaster. The usual news: Iran making trouble again; financial strain in Europe . . .

All things she already knew. Frustrated, Anat dropped the paper back onto the table.

"Nothing?" Nico asked, watching her.

"No." She plopped down on the couch and blew out a breath, aggravated. Something sharp dug into her thigh, and she pulled it out. A small book, leather. Flipping it open, she discovered tight lines of neat script.

"What's that?"

"A journal, I think," Anat said.

"You shouldn't read that, it's private," Nico said hesitantly.

Anat ignored him, absorbed. She flipped forward a few pages, then a few more. It was written in a cramped, tight scrawl. She scowled; she wasn't a big reader to begin with, letters tended to jumble up for her. Mild dyslexia, according to her teachers; fortunately, soldiers weren't expected to read much more than warning signs and weapons manuals.

"What's it say?" Nico asked, curiosity apparently overcoming his objections.

Anat shrugged and tossed it on the couch. "Who cares?"

He shrugged. "Maybe it'll tell us what happened here."

"You look, then," Anat said with a shrug. "I'm going to check out—"

A *thump* outside, followed by a piercing shriek. They both froze.

"What was that?" Nico asked in a hushed voice.

Before Anat could answer, there was a sharp cry from the opposite end of the house, followed by the sound of something heavy lumbering across the front porch.

What the hell is going on? Declan wondered. One minute they were tidying up from lunch, debating which food to take and how to carry it. The next, screams from both sides of the house, punctuated by Anat and Nico calling for help.

"Something's trying to get in!" Nico yelled, his voice strained. "We need help!"

Declan rushed down the hall, the others at his heels. The door had been forced open a slit: Anat and Nico were pushing hard against it, clearly struggling against something. A large shadow, impossibly big, was silhouetted in the curtains at the top of the door.

"What is it?" he said, stopping dead. "Another bear?"

Anat had her shoulder braced against the door, but her socks kept slipping against the floorboards.

"Nothing good," she grunted. "Help us!"

A high, keening whistle pierced the air. It raised all the gooseflesh on Declan's arms. He didn't care to meet anything that sounded like that. He angled in between them, throwing his weight against the door with his right shoulder. It closed a fraction of an inch.

"Jaysus, it's strong," he gasped. Sophie fell in beside them, pressing with the flats of both hands, but even with their combined strength the door wouldn't close.

The pressure from the other side increased. The door yawned open.

Declan yelled, "Get something to help!"

"Like what?" Nico asked, looking terrified.

"I don't care. Something!" Declan screamed. The pressure on his shoulder was intense. Sophie's head was inches from his; stray pieces of her hair brushed his cheek, tickling him.

The door cracked another inch.

"It's too strong!" Sophie hissed. "It's—"

Yosh suddenly opened her mouth and screamed. Declan cringed; it was the kind of shriek that could break glass. As it echoed through the house, the pressure ceased. He nearly slipped and dropped to the floor as the door abruptly slammed shut. Anat threw the bolt and leaned back against it, panting.

Declan peered through the upper curtains: the shadow had vanished.

"Lord," he said, turning to Anat. "What was *that*?"

She shook her head grimly. "Nothing good."

"Another bear?"

Anat cocked here head to the side. "Maybe. But I couldn't see it clearly."

"Yosh, are you all right?" Sophie asked with concern.

Declan turned. Yosh was standing in the center of the hallway. Without warning, her eyes rolled up in her head and she dropped to the floor. Sophie gasped and darted to her side.

"What's wrong with her?" Declan asked.

"I don't know. That scream, it was . . ."

"Yeah, I know," he said.

Sophie carefully drew the girl's head on to her lap and stroked the hair away from her forehead. The lass didn't look good. She was white as a sheet and her breathing was shallow. Her chest rose and fell in short pants.

"I'll get a wet cloth for her forehead," Declan offered. He had no idea if that would actually help, but it was the cure-all his mum always recommended. Feverish? Hungover? Stuck in bloody Long Island? Try a wet cloth.

Declan found one in a kitchen drawer and ran it under the tap. The backyard was silent, but as he looked out the window above the sink, he caught a flash of movement by the trees at the edge of the property. Frowning, he leaned forward for a better look, but whatever it was had vanished. He returned to the hall to find Yosh still lying in Sophie's lap, blinking absently at them.

"Here." He passed the cloth to Sophie, who gently laid it across Yosh's forehead.

"Better?" she asked.

Yosh nodded slightly.

"Good. Why don't we move you to the couch so you can lie down?" Sophie looked at Declan, then Nico.

"Right. Let's get you up, bird." Declan took hold of her under the shoulders, and Nico got her feet. Sophie supported her waist as they carried her into the living room and deposited her gingerly on the couch. Yosh was limp in his arms; he could feel the shoulder blades jutting out from her back. She really was tiny as a bird; he probably could've managed her weight all on his own without breaking a sweat. He wondered if they hadn't been feeding her enough in Japan. Maybe that's why she seemed a bit off and didn't want to talk about the tsunami. He hadn't a clue what things were like over there. He bent down beside her, concerned. "All right, then?"

Yosh didn't answer. She gazed at the ceiling. He was no doctor, but she didn't look well.

"What's wrong with her?" he asked in a low voice. "Why's she keep doing that?"

"I think she might be in shock again," Sophie said. "It should pass, we just have to give her some time and keep an eye on her."

"I thought we were leaving soon," Anat said impatiently.

"I think we should read the journal first," Nico said.

"Hang on," Declan said. "What journal?"

"This one." Nico held up a small brown leather notebook. "Anat and I found it right before we heard the scream."

"You said it was private," Anat muttered. "None of our business."

"Maybe whoever kept it wrote about what happened here." Nico swiped an arm across his damp forehead.

Declan found himself absurdly pleased by the fact that the lad's hands were shaking; the big blonde bloke was just as scared as the rest of them. Then his eyes fell on Yosh. "Best bring it in the kitchen, yeah? So we don't rattle her further."

Sophie nodded. "That's a good idea."

"First we make sure that whatever was outside is gone," Anat stated flatly.

"Right," Declan said, remembering the other scream. "How about Nico and I check the rear, and you lot take the front?"

"We are not opening that door again," Anat protested.

"Course not," he said. "You should be able to see the porch through the living room windows, yeah?"

"Probably," she conceded.

"All right, then."

Anat hefted the long iron bar she'd brought with her. In silent accord, the rest of them picked up the weapons they'd discarded upon entering the house.

Nico was hanging back, clearly waiting for him to lead the way. Frankly, Declan had no idea how he'd become the de facto leader. Hadn't Nico wanted that job? It wasn't a position that suited him. He'd never been in charge of anything, not in his entire life. He tended to go his own way, and to hell with everyone else.

They were staring at him expectantly, though, so he picked up the rail he'd pried loose from his bed this morning. It felt flimsy in his hands, pitifully inadequate against whatever had been on the other side of that door. Still, better than nothing, he supposed.

Declan tried to stride confidently back down the hall, but the whole time his insides quailed. What had been trying to get in? The kitchen, which minutes ago had felt like a refuge, now seemed like just another prison cell. He swallowed hard and went over to the rear door. A window was set in the upper portion, identical to the front door but minus the curtain. He'd barely paid it any mind earlier, distracted by the discovery of real food. Looking through it now, he saw a good-sized backyard: wildly overgrown, the grass gone to seed, hedged in by towering oak trees. Declan could easily imagine something nasty hiding behind each of them.

He went back to the window over the kitchen sink, which provided a wider view. A white cap poked up in the exact center of the yard—probably a statue of the Virgin, like the one his mum had in their garden back home. More trees, the same wild grass. Looked like years since anyone had mowed it.

There was nothing else in sight.

"It's strange," Nico said. "If anything had been here, it should have left a path through the grass."

That hadn't occurred to Declan, but he was right. The grass moved uniformly, not a blade knocked out of place. That reassured him.

"I'm going to join them in the front," he said. "You mind staying here to keep an eye out?"

"Of course," Nico said stiffly, brandishing his bedrail like a sword. Declan resisted the temptation to give him grief about it. He went back down the hall to the living room. Sophie and Anat were each positioned at a window.

"Looks clear back there," he reported.

"Clear here, too," Anat said.

"What do you think it was?" Sophie's eyes were anxious, but she looked steadier on her feet. The walk had probably done her some good. Least she had color in her cheeks again, they were browning up to nearly the same shade as her hair.

Declan glanced at Yosh; she still lay rigid on the sofa. Keeping his voice low as he stepped closer to them, he said, "Didn't sound much like a bear to me."

"Me, either," Sophie said.

"Look at this track," Anat said. "Like the one in the cafeteria." She held aside a corner of heavy brocade curtain to show him. Outside, the dust on the front porch had been scuffled. But that could have been their own doing. He scanned the rest of the yard: empty. No sign that anything had come through the grass here, either, although there were bent fronds around the path they'd taken to the front door.

"I don't see—" he started to say.

"There," Anat interrupted, jabbing at the window with her forefinger.

Pressing closer to the glass and tilting his head all the way to the side, he could just make out a strange print set off a bit from the others. Anat was right, it was similar to the one in the cafeteria: large, about twice the size of a man's foot. The bulk of it was a pad, with four long claws extending out from it.

"Another bear?" he said doubtfully. He'd had no experience whatsoever with bears. It wasn't the kind of thing you encountered much in Galway, or hell, anywhere in Ireland.

"Maybe," Sophie said, squinting at it. "But that noise it made . . . bears don't scream, do they?"

Declan was fairly certain that no bear had ever made a noise like that. The memory of it sent a shiver up his spine again.

"I do not think it was a bear," Anat said in a low voice. Her expression spooked him more than anything else; if Anat was afraid, the rest of them should be positively shitting themselves.

"What, then?"

"Maybe the journal says," Sophie offered.

"Right. Let's read it, then."

"Okay. Into the kitchen," Anat ordered. "Now."

CHAPTER SIX

It had fallen to Sophie to read the journal. She still didn't quite get why but was too exhausted to argue. The reasoning (courtesy of Anat and Nico) seemed mainly based on the fact that this was her native country and language. She'd been tempted to balk, but a look from Declan settled it.

They were spread around the kitchen table, with her at the head. Everyone's attention was focused intently on Sophie, making her feel like she was under a microscope, or worse, onstage. She'd never liked performing; during the kindergarten school play she'd spent her five minutes in an egg costume sobbing out of fear and embarrassment.

Clearing her throat self-consciously, Sophie flipped through the book. The entries were recorded in a smooth cursive, all the words exhibiting an identical slant. It made her feel slightly ashamed of her own barely legible handwriting. The author was obviously female, and probably older. The first entry was dated January 1st, so she probably started a new journal every year. Sophie pictured someone like her grandma, who had worn her long gray hair in a braid down her back and had bifocals dangling from a chain around her neck. The kind of woman who wasn't fat, exactly, just pleasantly plump. The thought brought unexpected tears to her eyes. She skimmed the first few pages.

"Read it out loud," Anat urged impatiently.

"Well, the earlier entries . . . I mean, they're just about her life, really. How much snow they were getting, that sort of thing. I guess I should start on the last day we all remember, right?"

"Around then, yes," Declan said.

"All right." Sophie flipped ahead. "August twenty-ninth, thirtieth—"

"What do you mean, August?" Nico said. "It's April sixteenth."

"What?"

"April sixteenth. Yesterday was the fifteenth," he said impatiently.

"The last day I remember was August thirty-first," Sophie said after a beat.

"Me, too," Declan chimed in. "Anyone else?"

"It's September first," Anat said firmly.

Nico looked around at them, clearly confused. "Are you joking with me?"

"Strange thing to joke about, yeah?" Declan said. "Didn't it strike you as a bit warm out for April?"

Nico blinked. "I assumed it was a heat wave." He sounded defensive, and confused.

"Wait a minute," Sophie said. "You seriously don't remember anything after April fifteenth?"

Nico didn't answer. He was staring intently at the ground, as if something in the worn linoleum might explain it.

"Sure you didn't take a blow to the head?" Declan said. "'Cause you seem to be the odd man out here."

"It's April," Nico said stubbornly.

"It does not matter." Anat waved a hand. "Let him believe what he wants. Read the journal."

"It's strange, though, isn't it?" Sophie said.

"Read," Nico commanded. His tone didn't invite further discussion.

Sophie hesitated. She felt weird about continuing as if this was no big deal. The fact that the rest of them had ended up at the facility months after Nico . . . that had to mean something, right? Had he actually been there longer? But no, he couldn't have been; there was no food. A dozen questions spun through her mind, but Declan caught her eye. Taking the hint, Sophie continued, "Let's see . . . so on August thirty-first, she writes that they were having a heat wave, and her air conditioner wasn't working—"

Anat made an exasperated noise.

"I'm getting to it," Sophie said. "August thirty-first." She hesitated. The writing here was different. The words were larger, sprawling; they took up nearly twice as much space, as if the pen had been unable to keep up with the pace of events:

Today the strangest thing happened. I was watching the news—not the usual pretty blond girl, but a man who really wasn't handsome enough to be on camera. He wasn't even wearing a suit, and was terribly flustered. He said something about sudden, unexplained mass disappearances, not just in Long Island, but everywhere.

At first I assumed it was some sort of ad for a new movie. But when the emergency broadcast system started flashing onscreen, I really did wonder . . . so of course I immediately called Kathleen to see if she'd heard anything. But she didn't answer, which was so strange—ever since she got a cell phone . . . I swear she takes it to the bathroom with her, she's so worried about missing a call.

After that I tried to drive into town, but less than a half mile down the road came upon an enormous pile-up. At least twenty cars had crashed into each other, but the drivers were nowhere in sight. I was looking in the windows, trying to decide if it would be worth going forward on foot, with the roads blocked so badly. But then I heard a child crying . . .

She was all alone, still strapped into her seat in the back of a station wagon. Completely fine, which was nothing short of miraculous; the car looked like it had been through a meat grinder. Just a beautiful little girl, her name is Megan, and she's five years old. I've tried asking what happened, but every time I do she gets terribly upset. All she keeps saying over and over is that her mommy is gone. When I push for more details, Megan says that she "went poof."

I couldn't find anyone else in their cars, and there was no question of trekking into town until I'd taken care of Megan. So I took her home, gave her cookies and milk, and put her down for a nap on the couch.

I've been calling 911 all day, but keep getting a busy signal. The non-emergency line for the Yaphank police isn't being answered, either. And no one else is home. I tried both Nancy and Dan several times but there was no answer. Not that they usually pick up when I call, but still, you'd think that if there had been a major emergency here, they'd want to make sure I was okay.

There's nothing on the television now. I flipped through every channel to check, but they're all showing the same emergency symbol. Which is frightening. It brought me right back to when we were kids and used to have those nuclear war drills. Is that what happened? If so, shouldn't they be telling us what to do? It occurred to me that even though the car accident happened hours ago, I still haven't heard any sirens.

I've spent the day wandering from room to room, trying to decide what to do. Should I take Megan down to the basement? What if there's fallout? New York is so close, if a bomb went off I should have heard or seen it. And the man on TV didn't say anything about a bomb, did he?

Why didn't he come back?

But what else could it be? The gorgeous weather outside somehow makes it even worse.

Thankfully I have plenty of food in the cupboard—Kathleen was right, that home delivery from Costco makes it so much easier. Enough for a few weeks if need be, and thankfully the power is still on.

I'm going to try to go to bed now, though I doubt I'll sleep. Maybe this will all turn out to be just a bad dream.

Sophie looked up from the book. "Did we check the basement?"

They glanced at each other.

"No," Declan said. "Didn't realize there was one."

"Where does that door go?" Nico asked, jerking his finger towards what Sophie had assumed was a pantry.

Declan stood and went to it. His hand hovered over the doorknob for a minute, then he yanked it open. A gust of musty air poured out. "Stairs going down," he reported. "Definitely a basement."

"Do you think they're still down there?" Sophie asked. Her throat felt dry from all the reading. They hadn't exactly been quiet, tromping around up here. If the owner was holed up downstairs, wouldn't she have investigated the noise?

Unless, for some reason, she couldn't.

"I will look," Anat offered, getting to her feet.

"I'll come with you," Nico said.

Anat flicked the switch by the door; nothing happened. "We'll need light."

They all scrambled. Nico found some candles in a kitchen drawer, and Declan managed to scare up a pack of matches from a bedside table upstairs. Sophie watched as they lit the candles. According to the journal, the power was on yesterday. What had happened since then? No mention of a hurricane or earthquake, either . . .

She and Declan waited at the top of the stairs while Anat and Nico slowly descended, the smell of sulfur drifting up behind them. The stairs creaked beneath their feet. Sophie tugged at her scrubs. A size too big, they hung loosely off her small frame, but she was hardly going to complain, considering what a relief it was to get out of that stupid nightgown. Her feet throbbed, hot and sweaty inside Anat's boots—she should see if there was another pair of shoes in the closet upstairs. Maybe the woman was closer to her size, and had left some behind.

Or maybe she'd never left the house at all.

Sophie fought back the thought. Reading that journal, the author stood out clearly in her mind—a nice woman who had instinctively helped someone else in a crisis. A mother whose grown children didn't call enough, who lived her all by herself. A sense of loneliness pervaded the words, as if the writer knew there was little chance anyone would ever bother reading them.

Sophie wanted the woman to be okay. She wanted to give

her a big hug and tell her that the journal did matter, that it was important, that her life was important and not to give up on it.

But who was she really feeling sorry for? Sophie's thoughts were running away with her, the way they used to when she lay in a hospital bed staring at the ceiling, pondering the unfairness of it all. The woman was probably fine. She was making a big deal out of nothing.

Murmurs from downstairs.

"Anything?" Declan called.

"No one," Anat yelled back.

The sound of stairs groaning again as they climbed back up. Anat emerged first, with cobwebs dangling from her hair. She brushed them away. "It's filthy down there," she grumbled. "Just some boxes and an empty freezer."

Sophie heaved a sigh of relief. No bodies, then. She couldn't explain why she'd had such a strong sense that the woman and girl were dead. In all likelihood, the girl had been reunited with her mother, and the older woman was staying with relatives, or her friend Kathleen. She might walk in the door any minute and completely freak out at the sight of five teenagers rummaging through her things and pilfering her food.

Anat plopped down in a kitchen chair. "Let's keep reading."

Sophie turned to the entry for September 1st. The writing was calmer here, but still not as contained as the earlier passages:

Barely slept last night. Poor Megan was tossing and turning in the guest room. Finally at 3 A.M. she crawled into bed with me, nearly gave me a heart attack! Although I have to say it was comforting to have a warm little body beside me, especially since the night was so strangely silent. Well, except for a terrible racket right before dawn. Like cats fighting, but louder and more piercing (if you can believe that).

Probably just my imagination getting the best of me after a sleepless night.

At least Megan seems better. She asked when her mommy would be back, and I told her I didn't know, then set her up with Nancy's old doll house. She seems perfectly content. Meanwhile, my nerves are so wracked I can barely eat. Still no answer anywhere, even 911 clicks over to an automatic message. The television is still blank, too, and I'm not picking anything up on the radio.

It's nearly time for lunch, and I haven't the faintest idea what to do. Why has no one else come by?

"There's nothing helpful here," Nico said, glancing out the window. Late afternoon sunlight slanted across the table. "We should get going, otherwise we won't make it to town before dark."

"How many more pages?" Anat asked.

Sophie flipped forward. "Seven."

"We have time," Anat announced decisively. "I am not going back out there," she added, lowering her voice, "until we know for certain what's waiting."

"But we're so close," Nico argued. "A few more miles and we'll be in town. My father—"

"After we finish reading," Anat snapped.

Nico grunted irritably, but Declan nodded. "Agreed. We've got some time."

"All right," Sophie said, but suddenly she didn't want to keep reading. She was sore everywhere, her feet ached, and her eyes throbbed with fatigue. She'd walked more in the past twenty-four hours than she had in the past several months. Honestly, she'd rather go upstairs and fall asleep; the rest of them could go on without her. A real bed in a real house sounded like heaven right now. Maybe the old woman and the little girl would come back, and they could all play Go Fish while Declan and the others hiked to town for help.

"Keep going," Anat ordered.

"Okay. There's a break here," Sophie said, flipping the page. "Then she starts again. Looks like it was later that same day."

"Wait, the same day? But that's today, right?"

"Maybe it's September 2nd," Sophie said doubtfully. "We might have spent a night asleep in the infirmary, right?"

Declan didn't answer, but she could tell by his eyes that this unsettled him.

"What's the date on the final entry?" Nico asked.

Sophie flipped forward again, scanning the writing for the next date. Her heart clenched a bit when she found it. "September third."

"So we lost more than a day in the infirmary?" Declan asked. "How?"

"Guess you're not sure what day it is after all," Nico grunted.

"We know it's not April fifteenth," Anat snapped.

"Apparently it's not September first, either."

"Enough. Keep reading, Sophie," Declan said.

"Fine. Finish, so we can go," Nico muttered, rocking back in his chair.

She tried to ignore his glares as she picked up where she left off:

I'd just given Megan lunch (it had been absolutely forever since I made grilled cheese sandwiches! Such a wave of nostalgia, I went right back to standing over the cast iron skillet on a snowy afternoon, making grilled cheese and tomato soup for Nancy and Dan. Amazing how a smell can bring you back . . .) Anyway, we were just sitting down to eat when I heard a car in the distance. I nearly broke my ankle getting outside, convinced that they were finally clearing the roads . . . then the engine abruptly cut out. I wasn't sure what to do. No sirens, but perhaps the police weren't using them, since the accident happened yesterday?

The sound of metal being sheared, truly awful and loud. Megan was terrified, so I got her back inside and waited on the front porch. I have to admit, part of me was tempted to go dig John's old gun out of the upstairs closet—"

"There's a gun?" Anat interrupted. "We could use a gun."

"It's not going anywhere if there is one," Declan said. "Might as well hear what happened. Now I'm dying to know."

"What are you reading?"

They looked up to find Yosh standing in the doorway. She swayed slightly on her feet, but her eyes were clear.

"Have a seat, bird." Declan leapt to his feet and guided her to the nearest chair.

"What is that?" Yosh asked as she sank into it.

"A journal," Anat said. "We found it in the living room."

A flash of something swept across Yosh's features—fear? Confusion? Sophie wondered if she was still in shock. Maybe they should insist that she stay in the living room a bit longer. "Journals are private," Yosh said with a frown.

"We think it might tell us what happened," Sophie explained. "That seems more important."

"Besides, we're already sitting in someone's kitchen eating

their food," Declan declared with forced cheer. "Practically family now anyway, aye?"

"We're wasting time," Nico grumbled. "Keep reading."

Yosh started to protest again, but Anat shushed her. Sophie continued:

Within a few minutes an enormous truck, the kind they use to plow the roads, came into view. It was picking up speed, about to pass the house entirely!!! I ran off the porch, nearly tripping and killing myself again, waving the dishcloth I still had in my hands. Fortunately, the driver saw me and stopped the car.

It turned out to be a young man, in his twenties. I'd never met him before, but he looked familiar—I've probably seen him around town. He went to Longwood, same as Nancy and Dan, but years after them, of course.

I invited him inside for a drink. At first he didn't want to come in, but then I explained about the situation with Megan. As he drank the lemonade, he fidgeted terribly. He seemed frightened to death of something, although I couldn't imagine what—it certainly couldn't have been us.

After he finished, I got him to come into the living room. He kept mumbling about getting back on the road, but when I offered him a sandwich he agreed to stay, at least for lunch. I asked again if he knew what was going on.

He got the strangest expression on his face then, and looked at Megan. I understood immediately—he didn't want to discuss it in front of the child. I bustled her into the kitchen and set her up with pencils and paper for drawing (reminding me of those boxes of crayons that Nancy loved so much, with the sharpener built into the side of the box. I wonder if I still have one stored in a closet somewhere?) The whole time I had this sense that it was all much worse than I'd imagined.

The boy—though he's hardly a boy, twenty-five at least—said his name was Ryan Adams. He's polite and seems nice enough, despite the fact that he has an enormous and somewhat frightening tattoo on his arm (I'll never understand what people are thinking these days, branding themselves like that. The young clearly have no idea what the passage of time will do to their skin). He works at the auto shop in town, as a mechanic—that was how he got the truck. It was in for repairs, and to get out of town he wanted something large to push aside the vehicles blocking the road.

But why'd you leave town? I asked. What's happened? Isn't it safe there?

It was a long time before he spoke again. He said it sounded so crazy he hardly believed it himself. He'd been working on a car, trading jokes with another mechanic. He was waiting on a punch line, and when it didn't come he turned to tease his friend about forgetting it. But his friend was gone, and on the spot where he'd been standing there was nothing but a dark, spinning spot that emitted some kind of strong pull. Ryan claimed he had to grab hold of the hood of the car and haul himself away from it hand over hand. Then as suddenly as it had appeared, the spot vanished.

He rushed out of the garage and into the street. It was around noon, and usually at that time of day Main Street is crowded with people.

But everyone was gone, he said.

What do you mean, everyone? I asked.

I searched the whole town. You're the first people I've seen since noon yesterday, he said.

It took me a minute to grasp what he'd said. No one but us? You're sure?

No people, he said, with the strangest expression on his face.

There's something else, isn't there? I asked.
Yes ma'am, he said. There is . . .

"Do we really need to hear this?" Yosh interrupted.

Her voice startled Declan; he'd become so enmeshed in the story, he'd almost forgotten where he was. Nico and Anat were mesmerized, too. But Yosh had risen from the table and was leaning against the wall closest to the hallway looking irritated—and fully awake, like her earlier spell had never happened. She had a stubborn set to her jaw.

"What, you want her to stop now?" Declan said, flabbergasted. "This is the best part."

Even Nico chimed in, "We should finish."

"Actually, if you all don't mind, I could use a break," Sophie said faintly. Anat groaned as Sophie handed the book to him. "You want to take over?"

Declan nodded. "Sure. You want some water?"

"The tap still works," Nico said. "I tried it earlier. The water tastes fine, too. Probably from a well."

Sophie got up and dug through the cupboards, producing a glass. While she filled it, Declan started reading.

At first Ryan was reluctant to say more, but I finally laid it on the line with him. Young man, I said, I'm all alone here, with a little girl whose mother went God knows where. If you know what's going on, you better tell me.

I don't know, exactly, he said. Everyone just vanished. One minute they were there, and the next . . . it's like the world emptied out. Like my mom always used to say, about the Rapture. Like that.

Ridiculous, I told myself. This must be something else.

Ryan seemed to guess my thoughts, because he suddenly

reached for my hand and squeezed it. I wasn't going to say anything, he said. I was worried you'd slow me down. But . . . he glanced toward the kitchen, where Megan was industriously drawing, then turned back. You can come with me, I guess.

Come with you where? I asked, startled. Where are you going?

Away, he said. There are creatures . . . things. He lowered his voice and said, I saw one. And it . . . was eating a man—

What kind of creature? I asked skeptically, wondering if perhaps this young man was high, or drunk.

It was in the alley by the supermarket, he said. I saw it when I was passing by in the truck. He paused again, then said, It saw me, too. Stopped and watched as I drove past. I've never seen anything like it. Has to be some sort of demon for sure.

Mmm, I said, not wanting to encourage his delusions. Already I was thinking it would be best to get him out of the house, and away from Megan. Someone else will surely come by soon. Somebody sane, with any luck.

You don't believe me, he said.

Of course I do, I said, patting his hand. It's just you've had a terrible scare.

I saw it, he said angrily. Whatever it was, I saw it.

Fine, I said. What did it look like?

The thing he described . . . honestly, I don't think I could do it justice. He claimed it was huge, seven or eight feet tall at least. Like a person, but with thicker, scaly skin (like a rhino, he claimed), and a longer head that ended in a snout. Greenish-brown fur, too, as if the scales weren't enough. And to top it all off, claws on its hands and feet.

Yosh made a small noise.

"What now?" Anat demanded.

"Why are we reading this story?"

"It's not a story, it's a journal," Sophie explained.

"Still, it does sound ridiculous," Nico scoffed.

"Shall we finish?" Declan said through gritted teeth, trying to contain his annoyance.

No one answered. Sophie examined her hands. Yosh had an odd look in her eye. If Declan didn't know better, he'd swear it was rage. For a brief flash, she'd looked like an entirely different person, and a threatening one at that. Declan hesitated, wondering whether or not to say anything about it.

"Well?" Nico demanded. "Sometime today?"

"Yeah, yeah. Calm yourself," he muttered. "All right, moving on . . ."

Poor Ryan probably spent a bit too much time in Sunday school. He witnessed something odd, and his mind chose to come up with this preposterous explanation for it.

I managed to calm him down, and convinced him that I believed him (although truly, I do not). Ryan said he'd prove it; he's certain that whatever it was, the creature will be coming for him.

When I asked how he could possibly know that, he shuddered and said he could tell from the way it looked at him. That it had "smart eyes."

I shrugged it off. He was welcome to sleep in his truck, I said, but I wasn't comfortable having him stay in the house.

Ryan declared that either way, he'd be leaving at dawn. And if I was smart, I'd take the girl and go with him.

For the rest of the day, the three of us immersed ourselves in different activities. Megan took another nap and drew some more. I kept trying the phone, at one point dialing numbers at random, waiting endlessly for someone, anyone, to pick up. Ryan sat on my couch and stared at the television, even though there had been no further news reports, and every station was set to static. We weren't even getting the emergency broadcast signals anymore.

After an early dinner, Ryan retired to his car. I nearly relented at the last minute and invited him to use the couch, but he's an odd young man, and I worry that tonight I'm so exhausted I'll fall deeply asleep. Not that I fear him harming us, exactly, but you never know with people, do you?

Anyway, I'm completely spent. Megan is already in my bed, snoring away like a little angel. I'm going to try to get some sleep.

Declan paused for a minute. The writing on the next page changed. He glanced up and met Sophie's eyes. Her hands were clasped in front of her on the table, the knuckles white. He kept reading:

September 3rd

I don't know what they are, but Ryan was right. A horrible sound woke me in the middle of the night. Megan kept sleeping, thank God, but I knew something was wrong.

I heard shouting from the front yard and went to the guest room to see what was happening.

Ryan had parked the truck a little ways away from the streetlamp, so it was hard to see. But there were shadows swarming around the truck, large ones.

He was screaming for help. I rushed back to the bedroom and grabbed John's gun box. I've never fired a gun before, not once. I prayed that it was already loaded, and wouldn't blow up in my face. I raced back to the guest room, threw open the window, and pointed it out toward the street.

Those . . . things were shaking the truck from side to side, as if trying to overturn it. Ryan's screaming had become even louder. One of them had climbed onto the hood and was trying to break through the windshield . . .

I closed my eyes—stupid, I know, but I did it without thinking—and fired the gun. When I opened them again, all of the creatures—monsters, really, because that's what they looked like—had stopped and were staring up at me. There were three of them. Their eyes reflected red, glowing the way cats' eyes do. Carnivores, I thought. That was something John used to talk about, how you could tell a carnivore by the way its eyes glowed red at night, while anything harmless would appear green . . .

They watched me for a minute, then looked at each other. It was like they were having a silent discussion, and suddenly I was gripped by terror. I didn't even know how many bullets were in the gun. What if they tried to come in the house? The doors were locked, but how long would it take them to break a window?

Then they disappeared, melting off into the night.

Ryan ran onto the porch a minute later—I nearly tumbled down the stairs in my haste to let him in. He was pale, wheezing. He slammed the door behind himself and screamed that we needed to block the windows.

We did our best, but honestly, there are so many ways in. We sat up until dawn, side by side on the couch, not speaking. I was gripping the gun so tightly I still have marks on my hands.

Before Megan woke up, we decided on a plan. Ryan is right. We must leave. His idea, which I think is a good one, is to drive out to the coast and get a boat. The truck should be able to push almost anything out of the way. Ryan says there's a gun store in Middle Island, we can get more weapons there. We should be able to find a boat in Mt. Sinai, then take it across to New London.

I'm so tired I can barely keep my eyes open, but I need to leave a record of where we went, both for Nancy and Dan and for Megan's parents. I haven't allowed myself to think about my children, and what might have happened to them. I pray that they're okay.

It feels like we're the only three people left in the world, but that can't possibly be true, can it? What could have happened? Where is everyone???

Declan paused. His mouth had gone dry, and not just from reading aloud. *Monsters*, she'd written. Was she describing the same creatures that had tried to get into the house earlier?

Weirdly, the windows weren't barricaded anymore. In fact, there wasn't any sign that someone had ever tried to block them.

"I wonder what her name was?" Sophie said in a small voice.

"Is," Anat retorted. "We don't know that she's dead. She might be in New London, with the little girl and Ryan. They might all be fine."

Declan liked the way she said *New London*, it sounded oddly musical. But deep down, he had a bad feeling that this particular story hadn't ended well.

"What does it say next?" Sophie asked.

Declan skimmed through the final page. "It's all about where they were planning on going, some naval base there. She figured the military would be able to help. And she hoped they'd be able to contact their relatives from there. She also went back to Megan's car, took the registration information, left a note, and . . . oh."

"Oh, what?" Sophie said.

"Her mother's purse was still on the front seat. Her name was Lisa Brown."

"She left her purse?" Sophie said. "That's not a good sign."

Anat shook her head. "That's not important."

"Really?" Sophie sounded offended. "Because it seems pretty damn important to me, and it definitely was to *them*."

"What happened to them doesn't matter," Anat said forcefully, looking around the table. "We need to adjust our goals."

"Our goals?" Declan asked. Damned if she didn't sound like she'd just stepped out of a war movie.

"Yes," Anat said. "Clearly we should not try to go into town."

"But—" Yosh protested.

"These . . . creatures," Anat interrupted. "They might still be there."

"So we're believing this?" Nico demanded, half standing. "This fairy tale about monsters?"

Anat met his gaze. "There is something bad out there. Maybe not monsters, but something."

"Maybe they're friendly," Yosh said in a small voice.

Declan stared at her, stupefied. "I don't think that whatever was trying to get in earlier wanted tea and a chat."

"We don't know that," Yosh mumbled, looking away.

She looked tiny sitting in the chair beside him, her feet barely grazed the linoleum. Declan felt for her, he really did. It was tempting to think that all they had to do was stroll into the nearest town and find Nico's dad. But based on what he'd just read, Anat was right. If they went out there unprepared, they might as well just carve themselves up for dinner. The terror the woman had felt coursed through her words; he'd practically been able to hear Ryan screaming and picture the dark shapes hunched around his truck.

Was that considered friendly behavior in Japan?

There was no truck outside now, though, which was probably good. Maybe they had gotten away. If Ryan had succeeded, the roads should be clear in that direction. Between the five of them, Declan figured they could handle a boat. And meeting up with the military sounded like a smart option.

Before he could voice his thoughts aloud, Sophie said, "It's getting late."

Looking out the window, he saw she was right. The shadows had lengthened across the overgrown lawn. But it should be light for awhile yet, since it was still early fall . . . wasn't it?

"We don't even know what day it is," Sophie said in a low voice, as if reading his thoughts.

"She left quickly," Declan noted. "The dishes weren't put away. You'd think . . . I mean, she seems like the type of person who would have straightened up, yeah?"

"But the windows aren't blocked anymore," Sophie mused. "I wonder why not?"

"Again, it does not matter," Anat said impatiently. "We need to focus. She probably took the gun with her, but this store she mentioned, in Middle Island—we can go there in the morning. We will take the first two working cars that we come across."

"I thought we were going to find my father," Nico said. The way he said *father* sounded German, and plaintive: how a little kid would say it.

"Where does your dad live?" Declan asked.

Nico said, "In Yaphank."

"Is that on the way?" Sophie asked.

Nico shrugged. "I don't know. I've only been here once before."

"We need a map," Anat said firmly.

They dispersed throughout the house. Ten minutes into the search, Sophie yelped in triumph—she'd found an old map on one of the shelves lining the fireplace. The paper was brittle and crumbling. On the outside, it read AAA LONG ISLAND/NEW YORK.

Carefully, she brought it into the kitchen and spread it across the table. Nico and Anat leaned over it.

"We're somewhere around here now," Nico said, pointing to the area just northeast of Yaphank. "There's the lab, right here."

Declan followed his finger. *Brookhaven National Laboratory* was marked in black, with a small ring of streets surrounding it.

"There's Middle Island," Anat said pointing at a town west of the facility. "The guns are there."

"We should try to find a phone book," Sophie suggested. "See if we can get an exact address."

"I'm going to find my father," Nico said obstinately.

Anat straightened and shook her head. "It's the wrong way. We need to head north."

"We can go to Yaphank first," Nico argued, jabbing the map with his index finger. "Then take County Road 21. It goes directly to Middle Island."

"But that's not the way they went," Anat argued. "The roads won't be clear. And Yaphank is where Ryan came from. He said it was not safe there."

All excellent points, Declan thought. There was no

guarantee that any roads would be clear past Yaphank, and this "county road" sounded ominous. He recalled a scary American movie where a school bus filled with kids broke down next to a corn field, and they were terrorized by a giant bat creature that swooped in and ate them one by one. Did they grow corn around here? Because a county road sounded like the perfect place for it.

"I'm going to my father's house first," Nico repeated obstinately, crossing his arms over his chest.

"Well, I am not going to risk taking a road that might be blocked," Anat countered.

Declan sighed. This was precisely why he never went out for group sports. "We'll have to split up, then."

They turned and stared at him.

"I thought you said that was a bad idea." Sophie's face was drawn and she looked drained, as if just sitting there was taking a toll on her. When he got a chance he should check the medicine cabinets, see if the old lady had left behind something for pain.

"I don't see any other option, do you?"

"Agreed," Anat said. "I will go to Middle Island. Whoever wants to can come with me."

"But we don't have any way of finding each other again," Sophie protested. "What if something goes wrong?"

"She's right," Declan said. "No guarantee that the mobiles will ever start working, and mine's almost dead anyway. We've no other way to contact each other."

Anat chewed her lip, clearly thinking it over. Declan was torn—in his gut, he hated the thought of splitting up. And Nico was the only one keen to head toward town. But much as he harbored a knee-jerk dislike of the kid, he couldn't let him go alone.

"We meet here," Anat finally proposed, pointing to a road that led north toward the water. "Mt. Sinai Coram Road. It leads straight to the nearest port."

"Yeah, but where and when?" Declan asked. "Probably not the best idea to just hang about a crossroads. And we don't know how long it'll take us, yeah?"

"We leave tomorrow morning at dawn." Anat ran a finger over the map to illustrate. "Twelve kilometers for us to get to Middle Island from here. We'll find the closest secure building to the crossroads and wait there. I'll mark an X on the door so you'll know we're inside if we get there first. You do the same if you arrive first."

Declan could punch a half dozen holes in that plan without straining himself, but he didn't have any better suggestions. "So who goes with whom?" he mumbled.

Anat's eyes flicked over them each in turn. "You go with Nico," she said decisively. "He'll need the help. And take Sophie, too."

Declan knew she had a thing about Sophie, although it was hard to tell whether that was due to her being weak from illness, or just because she was American. "So Yosh is with you, then."

"Yes."

"All right with you all?" he asked.

"Fine," Nico mumbled, although he clearly wasn't delighted about the fact that Anat was leaving him. Poor sod had it bad for her, that was clear. Yosh had apparently been struck mute again. She merely nodded, keeping her eyes downcast.

Declan was already regretting the decision to split up. Maybe if he'd pushed harder, they would've been able to convince Nico to try contacting his dad later. He'd much prefer to be heading north, on a road that would likely have been cleared in advance. Instead, he'd be saddled with a sick girl and a kid who might refuse to leave when they arrived at his dad's house. If they even made it that far. *Ah well*, he thought, taking in his new traveling companions. *You only live once.* And it couldn't be any more dangerous than the worst Galway had to offer, right?

"We should go through the woman's things, see if she has anything we can use," Anat said. "Sophie, check for shoes. I want my boots back. I'll go through the food and divide it up. Nico, find better weapons for us."

"I saw some tools in the basement," he said.

"Get them," Anat commanded. "And hurry. If we're going to stay here tonight, I want to secure the windows before it gets dark."

"Yes, sir," Declan muttered. At least he wouldn't be saddled with her.

"Can't sleep?"

Sophie looked up from her spot in the window seat. Declan was standing in the doorway watching her. She wondered how long he'd been there. She'd been lost in her own thoughts, wondering what the rest of her family was doing right now, if they were trying to find her. The others were settled in the master bedroom across the hall. One of them was snoring loudly—Nico, probably. They'd agreed to take turns keeping watch, just in case.

"Not really." She managed a wan smile. "I told Anat I'd take her shift. Of course, I've done nothing but sleep the past few years, so maybe I saved enough up."

He came in and settled on the window seat across from her. "Got to keep up your strength, though. How are you feeling?"

His voice was tinged with concern. Self-consciously, Sophie plucked at the chenille blanket draped over her legs. "Fine, I guess."

"Yeah? Because if you were really ill, seems like . . ."

When he didn't finish, Sophie said, "Seems like what?"

"Seems like we should try to find you some medicine. There wasn't anything in the cabinets other than some bandages. But we might pass a pharmacy tomorrow."

"I was already kind of past the point of medicine." She hesitated, then added, "Actually, I was pretty much dead."

Declan didn't speak for a minute. His eyes were shadowed, so she couldn't tell if he was looking at her or not. Finally, he sighed. "What do you think this place is?"

"If it's heaven, color me disappointed," she joked.

He laughed quietly. "Right? I was thinking the same thing."

"I don't think we're in purgatory, or hell, though," she said after a minute. "We'd know if we were, right?"

"Maybe. Tell you the truth, I didn't pay much mind in Sunday school. Now I'm wishing I had."

"No, this is definitely something else." Sophie couldn't explain how she knew that for certain, but she felt it deep down. This was the real world, just . . . different. Of course, she'd spent most of the past year cooped up in hospital beds, so maybe something dramatic had been going on outside and no one had bothered mentioning it. Although she hoped someone would have clued her in to the sudden appearance of giant clawed lizard creatures. At the thought, she let out a small laugh.

"What?"

"Just . . . do you think it's true? That whatever the old lady saw was real, and that's what tried to get into the house earlier?"

"I don't know," he admitted after a minute. "Sounds nutters, sure. But then, this is all pretty crazy, right?"

"Right," she said faintly. "Still, you'd think something like that wouldn't need to use the door."

"I know, that's been bothering me, too." He shrugged. "Guess we'll find out."

"That's a cheerful thought."

He laughed quietly, then stole a quick glance at her. "So who'd you leave behind?"

"My parents, and a little sister. Her name is Nora." Saying it out loud made her want to cry. Sophie drew her knees up to her chest and tucked her chin down on them. "What about you?"

"My mum. Dad—well, haven't seen him in ages." He paused, then said more softly, "And my girl. Katie."

She heard the catch in his throat. "I'm sorry."

"Yeah," he said brusquely. "Me, too. But we'll be seeing them all soon, right?"

"Right," Sophie said, trying not to sound skeptical. Time to change the subject. "You know what the weird thing is?"

"There's only one weird thing?" he teased.

"Well, okay, one of the many weird things. I don't think I'm sick anymore." She surprised herself by saying it, but it was true. She felt different somehow, like whatever was festering inside her had been swept away. That was something they never told you about having cancer, how it felt like there was something rotting inside you.

"Huh," he said doubtfully. "How do you know?"

"It's kind of hard to explain," Sophie said, "But I just—I know I'm really weak, and it's hard for me to keep up, but inside I feel . . . different. Like all the bad stuff is gone."

"The cancer, you mean?"

"Yeah," Sophie said. "Sounds crazy, right?"

"No crazier than anything else," he said. "And if it's true, I'm glad for you."

"Yeah, me too," Sophie said. "I just wonder how it could have happened."

"However it happened, it's a good thing, right?"

"I guess," she said. "I just can't figure out how we all got here. And what happened to everyone."

"We'll find out tomorrow," he said.

Hearing the conviction in his voice, Sophie managed to force a smile. She wished she could be so sure. "Thanks."

"For what?"

"For helping me today, and . . . just for being so nice and positive. I swear, if it wasn't for you, I think we all might've fallen apart."

He snorted. "Nah. Anat would've killed you first, most likely."

Sophie laughed out loud. He was sitting on the edge of a moonbeam that dusted his eyelashes silver. She was suddenly aware of how close they were, and of other things: her breathing had changed, and there was a strange warmth coursing beneath her skin. The sensations confused her; she felt giddy, flustered. Kind of like the rush she used to get right before fainting, but different. His eyes glowed bright blue in the light, and a small smile played across his lips. On an impulse, she leaned over and kissed him.

Declan started and she jerked away, pressing the back of her hand to her lips. "Oh my God, I'm so sorry. I don't know what came over me."

"It's all right, Sophie. I just . . . you have to understand, I like you loads, but I've got Katie, and—"

"I know," she interrupted. "And I'm really, really sorry."

Embarrassed, she got to her feet, nearly tripping over the blanket wrapped around her legs. Tugging it loose, she scrambled toward the door.

"Sophie, wait!" he called after her in a low hiss.

She paused on the threshold. "What?"

A long moment passed, then Declan said, "Sweet dreams."

"You too," she muttered as she fled the room.

CHAPTER SEVEN

Anat was pleased with their progress. Yosh wasn't very talk-
ative, but that suited her. And she didn't complain about the
pace, although at times she was clearly struggling to keep up,
short legs churning double-time to match her long strides.

The night had passed uneventfully. She'd insisted they
take turns keeping watch, although she'd caught Declan dead
asleep when she went to relieve him. It annoyed her, but fortunately they hadn't seen any sign of the "monsters" mentioned in the journal.

She'd spent her shift sharpening the end of a long stick
with a knife. She'd found it in the backyard yesterday afternoon, a section of branch that must have fallen in the last
storm. It wasn't as good as a gun but would be more useful
than the iron rod she'd lugged around yesterday, and lighter,
too. She had some experience in fighting with sticks, thanks
to her Krav Maga instruction. She felt moderately better having it, although the drawback of getting saddled with Yosh
was that she wouldn't be much help in a fight.

Unless she provided a distraction if Anat was forced to flee during an attack.

Not a nice thought, but there it was. Anat intended to survive and get back to Hazim, and nothing and no one was going to stop her.

Ryan had been true to his word; this road had definitely been cleared. Most of the cars they passed had either been totaled, or were stuck in a ditch. She was unable to find keys for the only one that was potentially drivable, and hotwiring cars wasn't one of her talents. *Declan could probably have managed it*, she thought with a pang. It had been a shame that Nico had been so insistent on finding his father. He'd tried to talk to her last night during her shift, but she'd told him in no uncertain terms to go back to bed. Part of her was relieved that she wouldn't feel his eyes on her all day.

By noon, they'd probably made it three kilometers. Not what she'd hoped for, but all things considered not bad. Anat stopped in the shade of a stand of trees by the side of the road. Yosh sank to the ground, plainly exhausted. Anat dug food out of the backpack she'd found in an upstairs closet and passed her a few stale crackers slathered with peanut butter, a handful of shriveled raisins, and a cookie.

They ate in silence. It was cooler today, the air carried a whiff of rotting leaves and something else—salt, maybe?

"How much farther?" Yosh asked.

Anat repressed a twinge of annoyance. She'd outlined the trip in its entirety last night. She'd expected Yosh to be delighted that they were taking the shorter, more direct, and likely safest route. But the girl had barely paid attention. Her gaze remained locked on the middle distance, so focused that Anat was tempted to glance over her shoulder to see if something was there. Either she was having a harder time handling the situation than the rest of them, or she was always like this. Frankly, Anat didn't really care. Her initial instinct to protect the girl had been surpassed by her urge for self-preservation.

"Another few kilometers," Anat said.

Yosh chewed glumly.

"If we find a car soon, we could be there in an hour." Anat wiped crumbs from her mouth and tucked away the rest of her lunch—although she was still hungry, rationing couldn't hurt. Who knew how long it would take the others to reach the intersection? She was prepared to wait until midday tomorrow, then she'd insist on proceeding to the coastline. It was roughly another nine kilometers to Mt. Sinai harbor, the nearest port according to the map. With any luck they'd quickly find a boat, and from there the crossing shouldn't take more than a few hours. If there had been some sort of nuclear event here, the less time they spent in the fallout, the better.

They finally encountered a battered old Volvo wagon. All four tires were still on pavement, and keys dangled from the ignition. She checked the driver's side door: unlocked.

Anat opened it and slid behind the wheel. She adjusted the seat; the driver must have been a midget, it was practically pulled up to the dashboard. The car smelled musty, and the leather seat was cracked and faded. The ashtray was pulled out and filled with spare change; aside from that there were no personal items in sight.

She said a silent prayer and turned the key. The engine ground but didn't catch. Anat tried again, gently goosing the gas pedal.

The engine turned over and roared to life. A faint smile spread across her lips. "Coming?" Anat asked, rolling down the window to let in some air.

Yosh nodded and slid into the rear passenger seat.

That was an odd choice, Anat thought, irritated. As if she was some sort of chauffeur. But Yosh could ride on the roof if she liked; all that mattered was that they'd finally found a working car. Out loud she said, "Buckle up. I'll go slowly, but the road is bad."

She carefully backed up, then shifted into drive. They progressed slowly, no more than ten kilometers per hour. Sometimes the gap between abandoned cars was so narrow she was forced to slow to a crawl to edge through; other times she had to go off the road entirely to avoid gaping potholes. Still, it was a relief to be driving for a change. Sitting in the car meant they got to rest and store up energy reserves, plus the metal shell offered a degree of protection. She'd spent much of the hike checking their rear flank, clasping her sharpened stick in a death grip. It was a relief to hold a steering wheel for a change.

Anat flicked the radio on: the sound of static filled the car. She hit the scan button, and the radio panned through every station without stopping. After three passes, she turned it off again and checked the odometer. They were making decent time. Probably another six kilometers to Middle Island. Once there, hopefully it would be relatively simple to locate the gun store. If it wasn't on the main road, they'd stop and find a telephone directory somewhere.

She'd never been somewhere so green before: leaf-laden branches dangled just above the car. Wild grass sprouted from potholes, waving gently in their wake. It was sunny, and a wisp of breeze drifted through the open windows. Her eyes were caught by a riot of red, a tree with such brilliant foliage it looked like it had just burst into flame. Long Island was pretty. She'd had no idea.

All in all, she was feeling optimistic.

That feeling vanished a second later. A familiar keening sound echoed across the road ahead. It was sharp, piercing—and answered by a matching call behind them.

Anat slowed the car.

"They're coming for us," Yosh said placidly.

Anat whirled in her seat. Yosh was sitting with her hands crossed in her lap and a funny half-smile on her face.

"What do you mean?" Anat demanded. "Who is coming for us?"

For the first time that day, Yosh appeared wide awake. "They're waiting."

"What are you talking about?" Anat spat.

Before Yosh could respond, a rock sailed out of the woods and shattered the windshield.

Anat reacted quickly, slamming on the brakes, then over-correcting as the car flew into a skid. The car veered wildly from side to side. They came within inches of vaulting off the road into a ditch, but at the last minute Anat ground the brake pedal into the floor.

They both jerked forward as the car lurched to a stop.

"What was that?" Anat demanded. "Where did it come from?"

Yosh didn't answer. Anat caught a glimpse of something in the rearview mirror: the brush lining the right side of the road was waving wildly. Something big was coming their way, fast. Gritting her teeth, Anat threw the car into reverse and slammed on the gas. They jolted back a few feet, and she shifted into Drive again. She bent low to see through the small section of windshield that remained intact.

The whole time, her gaze kept flicking to the rearview mirror. Their pursuer hadn't given up: not only could she see the path it carved through the trees, she could hear branches being crushed underfoot. Her pulse pounded in her ears, drowning out the inhuman keening noise that seemed to echo all around them. "There's no point trying to escape, Anat," Yosh said. "You should stop the car."

"Would you two just let it go?" Sophie grumbled. She was hot and tired. They'd been marching along a crumbling road for the better part of two hours, and she was already regretting the decision to leave the house. Sweat streamed down her back. She hated this kind of muggy weather. The way the trees hunched over the road made it feel like she was wading through a rainforest.

Bad enough that she'd gotten stuck with the group headed into town; but to make matters worse, Declan and Nico had been bickering nonstop. Declan was sticking by his religious explanation for all of this—namely, that they were already dead. Nico kept arguing for scientific explanations: a nuclear reactor meltdown, a dirty bomb.

She'd rarely seen two people take such an instant and extreme dislike to each other. Sophie got the feeling that if they weren't arguing about this, it would be something else, like whether or not aliens existed or if veal should be made illegal.

And Declan had barely spoken to her all morning. Not that she could blame him. She was still mortified. What had she been thinking, trying to kiss him? She'd never done anything like that before. In fact, she'd only seriously kissed a boy once, right before she found out she was sick: Brad Kagel, this guy she'd had a crush on practically forever. Of course, once her diagnosis came in, he pretty much stopped talking to her. Turned out boys weren't so into you once you lost your hair.

Sophie sighed. Declan was walking a few feet ahead of her. There was a high flush in his cheeks, due either to the weather or his irritation with Nico. Sweat had curled the dark hair at the base of his neck, and his shirt was pasted across his shoulder blades.

She forced herself to look away. *He has a girlfriend, you moron.* Besides, she could just imagine what her parents would think. He'd broken into that house in under a minute and kept bragging about his car theft skills. Classic bad boy, the type who snuck cigarettes in the school bathroom and spent every afternoon in detention. What had she been thinking?

And as far as whether or not they were in purgatory . . . honestly, Sophie could not care less anymore. If they were already dead, she really didn't understand the point of doing *anything.* And if they were alive, but stuck in some radioactive wasteland . . . well, that wasn't exactly good news either. As if reading her mind, Declan asked, "So what do you think's happened, then? If this isn't purgatory?"

"At the minute, hell has my vote," she grumbled. "It's hot enough. And you two are driving me nuts."

Nico barked a laugh. "You call it Indian summer, right?"

"We're not even sure it's September," Declan pointed out. "Could be July. Hell, it could be January. Or it could be . . ."

"Please, could you both just be quiet?" Sophie pleaded. She had a pounding headache, and this debate was making it worse. All she wanted was a functioning telephone to try and get in touch with her family. They were probably worried sick about her. She was certainly worried about them. All that stuff in the journal, about vanishing people and monsters . . . part of her wanted to dismiss it outright. After all, they knew nothing about the woman who recorded those entries. She might have been the local schizo, some crazy person who believed in alien mind control and government conspiracies. Maybe Ryan and the little girl didn't even exist—it could all have been a product of her imagination.

But based on what they'd seen so far, Long Island was deserted, save for some birds and a bear. That was harder to explain away. And something had definitely been trying to get into the house yesterday. Whether or not it was a monster with claws was up for debate. Sophie didn't want to think about it anymore. The simple act of placing one foot in front of the other still required the bulk of her concentration. And she'd already nearly finished all her water. She should have been better about rationing it, but it was so hot, and she was unbelievably thirsty. Maybe months of IV fluids had acclimated her body to more water than normal.

Declan pulled out his phone and squinted at it.

She swatted at a mosquito. "Any luck?"

"Nothing yet," he said. "Should be far enough from the blocking towers by now, yeah?"

"Yes," Nico acknowledged. "I don't know why they're not working."

"Well, my battery is almost dead," Declan said, powering off. "Best save it."

They walked another hundred feet in silence, coming up on yet another broken down car.

"What about that one?" Sophie asked wearily.

"I'll check." Declan trotted over to the driver's side and peered in. The ancient sedan's tires were flat and it was coated in rust, but unlike every other car they'd seen so far, all four tires were on the road.

"No keys, but that's not a problem," Declan said. "I can get her started."

He slid into the driver's seat and dug around under the

ignition, all while maintaining a running monologue. "Easy, with the older ones like this. No alarm, no auto shutdown. Not that an alarm would bring anyone running . . ."

Sophie leaned against the bumper and put her head in both hands, massaging her temples with her fingers. That morning, she'd helped herself to the contents of the old woman's medicine cabinet and bandaged her feet. They still throbbed, but the soft pair of socks she'd also borrowed, along with shoes that were only a size too large, had made a huge difference. For a change, she wasn't wincing in pain with every step.

"You all right?" Nico asked.

Sophie looked up. He stood in front of her, blocking the sun. "Thirsty, mostly."

He handed her his water bottle. It was still half full.

"I shouldn't, that's yours—"

"Drink," he said. "I don't mind."

Sophie took a few slugs, then handed it back reluctantly. She was parched enough to have drained the entire thing. "Thanks."

"Sure." He smiled at her. "How are you feeling?"

"Not too bad," she admitted. "Tired, though. Didn't sleep that well last night."

"Me either," he said.

"Really? I could've sworn I heard you snoring," she teased.

"The Swiss never snore," he intoned with great dignity. "You must be mistaking me for that foul Irishman."

Sophie laughed. "Really? And why don't the Swiss snore?"

"Haven't you heard? We're perfect, just like everything we build."

"I only really know about your watches and pocketknives."

"Well," he said, bending lower, "I could tell you all about—"

The car engine roared to life. "If you two are done flirting,"

Declan called in an oddly stony voice, "I believe we have somewhere to be."

Nico held out a hand to help her off the bumper. "You should take the backseat so you can stretch out."

"Thanks." Sophie limped around the car and eased in behind Declan.

Even though the leather was cracked and worn, she was so tired the seat felt like a feather bed. Sophie sighed and settled back. She caught Declan scowling at her in the rearview mirror.

"What?" she asked.

"Nothing," he muttered. "Glad to see you're enjoying yourself."

"We were just talking," Sophie said, wondering why she suddenly felt defensive.

Nico climbed into the front passenger seat and slammed the door. "Let's go."

"Of course. At your service," Declan snapped. "Please note the emergency exits to the front and rear, and know that in the event of a water landing, your seat won't be a damn bit of use to you. Oh, and if you feel the need to pray, make sure it's to science, and not God, because apparently he doesn't give a whit about you."

"Enough already," Nico groaned.

"Fasten your seatbelts, trays in the upright position, and thanks for flying Murphy air!"

Declan shifted into first gear and the car slowly rolled forward. As they gained speed, Sophie leaned back against the seat and closed her eyes, feeling the breeze on her face. There was a hint of autumn in it, an undercurrent of things rotting. The scent triggered a memory of the last family trip they'd taken. Her parents had grown up in Rhode Island, and they'd flown there for a family reunion a few weeks before her diagnosis. She'd dozed during the ride from the airport, occasionally blinking her eyes open to see a succession of farm stands, corn fields, and beach parking lots. The air smelled the same then—had it been August or September? August probably, because she didn't remember missing school. Her mother and sister were playing a dumb road trip game, license plate bingo or something like that. She'd declared herself too old and cool to participate, although in truth she'd felt too exhausted to focus on plates.

Tears pressed against her eyelids. Sophie squeezed them shut tight. She wasn't going to cry over this. Unlike everyone else, she'd already said her goodbyes. Any time spent with her family now would be a bonus.

"What the hell is that?" Declan whispered. As the car slowed, Sophie opened her eyes. Declan and Nico were leaning forward, peering at something hanging down from the trees above. It looked like an art installation, or elaborate wind chimes. There were dozens of them dangling from the trees for a few hundred yards or so, all pale and slender; some were at least six feet long, others half that size.

They were almost directly beneath the first one when she suddenly realized what they were. Sophie sucked in a deep breath.

"Jaysus," Declan gasped. "Are those—"

"They're skeletons," Nico said in a flat voice.

Anat didn't dare look back anymore. Not that she needed to, out of her peripheral vision she could see the foliage on either side of the car swaying wildly.

The voices were everywhere now. She'd never heard anything like it, a mix of high-pitched keening and screeching howls that overlapped on each other. It sounded like dozens of creatures were tearing after them through the undergrowth.

For all she knew, maybe there were.

Anat forced herself to focus on the road. She was going forty kilometers an hour. She didn't dare drive faster—she'd already nearly plunged the car into a giant pothole, and twice they'd clipped cars that hadn't been shoved far enough off the road. The car was whining under the strain, the steering wheel shuddering against her fingers as the metal tire rims scraped shrilly against the pavement.

She shot a quick glance in the rearview mirror. The deadness in Yosh's eyes was chilling. And the things she'd been saying, as if she'd expected this . . . *No*, Anat told herself, *that couldn't be true.* Maybe Yosh had been crazy to begin with, or the events of the past two days had driven her over the edge. Anat half-expected to feel something sharp pierce the back of her neck.

Another giant rock, the size of a large melon, abruptly sailed out of the air. It bounced off the hood of the car, leaving a huge dent.

Her grip tightened on the steering wheel. It would take a lot of strength to throw something so heavy that far. Suddenly her sharpened stick seemed pathetic, useless. She prayed there was enough gas in the tank to get somewhere safe. Forget the other three; they'd have to fend for themselves. They might already be dead. Waiting for them constituted too great a risk. She'd skip the gun store and head straight for the shoreline. These things couldn't possibly chase them forever, at some point they had to tire. She'd get away. *And eventually, the others would find them*, Anat reasoned. Really, they should have agreed to reconnoiter at the naval base in the first place.

"Watch out," Yosh said calmly.

The car slid into a skid as Anat spun the wheel left, narrowly avoiding another gaping pothole. They nearly flew off the road, ending up on a collision course with a pickup truck parked across the right lane. Anat cursed as she tried to avoid the vehicle.

Something slammed onto the trunk.

Anat checked the rearview mirror, expecting to see an enormous dent from another rock. Yosh still sat primly in the middle of the passenger seat, expressionless. Visible through the rear window behind her was an impossibly long pair of legs, covered in greenish-brown fur, and too tapered to belong to any bear.

IT was on the car.

Anat jammed the gas pedal to the floor. A higher screech this time, then a thump. She glanced back again: the legs were gone, and something lay in the middle of the road behind them. Her mind flashed back to her grandfather's stories about giant men made out of clay, silent assassins who came after bad little girls and boys. Golems. But whatever this thing was, it wasn't made of clay—it was hairy, the head long and thin, ending in what looked like a snout.

Just as the woman had described it in her journal.

As she watched, it got back up. A second later, it was running directly along the center divider, gaining on them fast.

Anat gritted her teeth and kept the pedal pressed flat. "Watch out for potholes," she ordered. "And let me know if it starts catching up."

Yosh glanced back, then muttered something in a foreign language.

"What?" she snapped. "Speak English."

"It might've gotten hurt, falling off the car like that."

"Gotten hurt?" Anat shouted.

"It doesn't mean us harm."

"Have you lost your mind?" Anat spat.

She glanced back again. The creature was closing the distance. It was only a hundred meters behind them now. Their speedometer read sixty kilometers per hour, so the creature had to be going eighty, or maybe even a hundred. Nothing on earth could move that fast.

"We're not going to make it," she muttered. "We need to find somewhere to make a stand."

"That would be a waste of time," Yosh said.

As if on cue, they flashed past an ornate sign that proclaimed, "Welcome to Middle Island, population 516."

"It's moving well," Yosh said. "You must not have injured it badly."

Anat could have sworn Yosh sounded pleased about that. She gritted her teeth and kept her focus on the road. What she wouldn't do for a few of her squad members. With well-trained backup and a Tavor assault rifle, she'd have been able to confront this threat head on. Running away like this felt cowardly, but she didn't have a choice.

"How close is it?" she asked, not daring to look back.

"Close," Yosh said brightly. "Nearly on top of us again."

"All right." Anat scanned both sides of the road. "Keep your eyes peeled for the gun store."

"But there's no time. Even if we find it, we need to get inside somehow."

"You're right," Anat muttered. "We'll try this instead."

She gunned the engine and swerved hard right, straight into a chain-link fence.

"Not much to it, is there?" Declan muttered.

The Yaphank Garage was just as shoddy as the facility, its

parking lot equally torn up. Old fashioned gas pumps tilted at odd angles to each other, like bowling pins poised to fall.

Still, it was the largest standing structure they'd seen so far. As they'd approached town, houses cropped up, the distance between them closing as they drove along Main Street. They'd passed a forlorn-looking shopping complex—a deli, pizza place, and beauty salon—then an old wooden house with weathered shingles that announced itself as the "Yaphank Community Center." The American version of a Galway suburb.

"Is there anything else here?" Sophie asked.

Nico shrugged, looking embarrassed. "It's a shit town," he said defensively. "Nothing like Geneva. My father only lives here because it's close to the lab."

"Not sure you'd even know if everyone suddenly went missing," Declan joked. Nico's scowl deepened, and Declan sighed. The lad had no sense of humor whatsoever.

"I hear Geneva is beautiful," Sophie said diplomatically. "How much farther to your dad's house?"

"Another few kilometers. He's at the far end of town, by Gordon Heights." Nico pointed north.

"I'm thinking we'd best switch to a different car," Declan said, shoving aside his annoyance with Nico and with Sophie for suddenly being so kindly toward him. The tire rims on their sedan had flexed into odd positions, so that the battered wheels almost formed squares. Even though he'd kept the odometer at thirty kilometers per hour, they'd taken a beating.

"Let's see what's inside the garage," Sophie suggested. "Maybe there's a car in better shape."

"Sounds grand," Declan agreed, trying to quell the irritation he felt every time he looked at her now. He could still feel the press of her lips last night, their unexpected warmth against his. He'd wanted to kiss her back, more than anything. But he wasn't like the eejits he'd grown up with. He'd never even felt tempted to cheat on Katie before.

So why was he having such a hard time getting that kiss out of his mind?

Declan shoved the thoughts away. If Sophie had set her sights on the Swiss ponce, that was her own business. He'd be back with Katie soon enough.

By unspoken agreement, they hadn't discussed the bones they passed on the outskirts of town. Why were they hanging there? A warning against entering, maybe? Well, they were here now, might as well make the best of it.

Nico was already approaching the enormous garage doors. They swung out, like barn doors. He hauled the one on the right side open, grunting as it resisted his efforts.

Declan was hit by a stench. "Jaysus," he said, gagging. "What is that?"

Coughing and choking, Nico covered his mouth with his right hand as he staggered back.

Sophie had stepped to the side. Cautiously, she peeked into the dim interior. "More food that's gone bad, maybe?"

Declan pulled his T-shirt up over the lower half of his face and tentatively approached the doors. His eyes watered as he got closer—the reek reminded him of slurry, the caustic mix of piss and manure that Irish farmers used to fertilize their fields, but much worse. It smelled like ammonia combined with wet fur, and something else, something metallic and strange . . .

It was dark inside the garage. Declan paused on the threshold, thinking that maybe he shouldn't have left that hoe back in the car. He'd grabbed it that morning, since it was pretty much the most lethal weapon in the house's gardening arsenal.

Nothing appeared to be moving, though. And he got the sense that the room was empty. It was a trait he'd honed breaking into houses; he could always tell when someone was in the next room. People were big and clumsy; their physical presence set the air molecules bouncing against each other, and those reverberations reached him through the walls.

The garage floor was covered in the same sort of mossy leaf compound they'd seen in the cafeteria. Ivy snaked up the inside walls, which was odd because he hadn't noticed any outside the building.

Incongruous shapes were scattered throughout the building, a few feet apart from each other. They were enormous, oblong things that stood shoulder high and seemed to absorb the light from the door.

The really weird thing was that they looked like eggs. Ridiculously giant eggs.

As he watched, something shifted inside one of them. The light from the door penetrated the top half of the shell. Inside, he could make out a dark silhouette. Nico and Sophie waited behind him.

"Oh my God," Sophie breathed. "What the hell are those?"

"I think we'd best be going," Declan said in a low voice. As they watched, the nearest egg rocked ever so slightly, as if whatever was inside had become aware of their presence.

"But—"

"Declan is right. Let's go," Nico said, grabbing her elbow.

"You don't have to drag me," Sophie said, snatching her arm back. "I'm going already."

They backed toward the car. As Declan drew the garage doors closed, the egg jumped again, and a small fissure appeared along the front of it. He breathed out hard. Not a good sign. He hustled back to the car. Sophie was in the front seat this time, Nico in the back. Declan struggled to get the engine turned over. *Come on, come on . . .*

On the third try, the engine caught. He ground the gas pedal down, and they jerked out of the parking lot. He didn't slow until they'd put five blocks between them and the garage.

"At the next intersection, take a right," Nico ordered from the backseat.

"Got it," Declan said.

"What were those things?" Sophie asked again. "Do you think . . . were they the creatures?"

"Their babies, maybe." His mind leapt to the henhouse at his aunt's place, the way the hens would attack anyone who got too close to their nests. Glancing back in the rearview mirror, Declan could have sworn he caught a flash of movement in the tangle of trees lining the road. After making the turn, he sped up and said, "Lots of warning before the next one, yeah?"

"Sure," Nico said. "It's a few blocks down."

"Brilliant," Declan muttered. The sooner they got to Nico's dad's place the better.

CHAPTER EIGHT

The fence bowed for a second, resisting, then gave way with a piercing shriek of shearing metal. It split around them, the ragged edges scraping along the top of the sedan. Anat winced at the sound but slammed her foot on the gas.

On the other side of the fence was a large open parking lot. She kept the pedal floored and the car lunged forward.

Another howl from behind them.

Anat glanced back. The thing was tangled up in the slashed fence, fighting to free itself. She counted three more figures in the distance, a hundred meters behind the lot.

Yosh made a strange noise. Anat glanced in the rearview mirror.

"What?" Anat demanded.

Yosh didn't say anything, but tears streamed down her cheeks. Anat couldn't worry about it now—they were far from home free. As their car approached the far end of the parking lot, it shuddered and groaned like a living thing.

"Come on," Anat hissed in Hebrew under her breath.

"You can do this." The gate at the far end was open. She tore through it and spun the wheel left. They bounced onto a long road parallel to the one they'd just escaped, past houses that looked long abandoned.

"We need to find that store," Anat said. "We need guns to fight those things."

"I know where the store is," Yosh said in a small voice.

"What?"

Yosh leaned forward. Her cheeks were wet, but she'd stopped crying. "Take a left on the next street."

Anat opened her mouth to protest, then realized they didn't have another option. No matter what, those creatures would catch up to them at any moment. She could only hope that at least one had been seriously injured.

"Turn right here," Yosh said. "It's on the other side of the street."

Anat followed her finger and saw a dimmed neon sign with a bullseye that read, MIDDLE ISLAND GUN RANGE.

She jerked the wheel left, and the car bounced violently over bumpy pavement. She drove straight to the front door, nearly crashing into it before screeching to a halt. "Come on," she said, already halfway out of the car. She threw open the back door and yanked Yosh out.

Luckily, the front door was unlocked. The plate glass windows had been boarded over, which was both good and bad. Good, in that it would help them hold off whatever was after them. Bad, in that it meant the store might already have been emptied of inventory.

Once she and Yosh were inside, she slammed the door and bolted it. It was heavy, reinforced steel and had a solid lock. With a shaky exhale, Anat leaned her forehead against it. She took a second to collect herself. Then she turned around.

It was pitch black inside. The darkness reminded her of the tunnel, and for a second she felt as if she were being smothered again, like there wasn't enough air, and the walls were closing in. She drew a few deep breaths to calm herself down. This was nothing like that. In fact, she reminded herself, *her current situation was much, much worse.*

"First we need to make sure this is the only way in," she said.

"It is," Yosh said softly.

"How do you *know* that?" Anat asked.

Nothing but the sound of soft breathing for a minute, then Yosh said, "I can't explain how. I just know."

"We'll check anyway," But Yosh was probably right—it would be unusual for a gun shop, especially one with an indoor shooting range, to have more than one entrance. Still, better to be sure. "I will try to find a flashlight."

She extended her hands out protectively so that she wouldn't smack into anything. In spite of that, a few yards into the store her hip knocked against something.

"Are you all right?" Yosh asked.

"I'm fine," she said, groping with her fingers. They slid across something that felt like well-worn wood. "I think I found the counter."

Yosh didn't respond; it didn't sound like she was moving. How had she known where the store was? And that whole thing about the exits, what was that? Something about the girl was seriously off. No matter what, she wasn't going to let Yosh handle a gun.

Anat felt her way along the hard wooden edge of the counter until she reached the end, then eased down the other side. There she felt cabinets—if this was anything like the ammunition depot at her training camp, they would be locked. She took a deep breath, said a silent prayer, then tried the first handle. The cabinet opened; Anat dug around inside. Her heart leapt: the rattle of boxes filled with ammunition. Now all she had to do was find guns, and, ideally, a flashlight. If only she hadn't dropped hers back in the tunnel, along with her backpack; she'd had a knife with a serrated edge in there, and some MREs, too. Maybe she would have made a lousy soldier. After all, she'd done exactly what her instructors had warned against, panicking and losing her supplies at the first sign of trouble.

Well, nothing to be done for it now. Anat opened a few more drawers. All were unlocked, but unfortunately most were also empty. In the last one on the left, her fingers finally closed around a hard metal object. She drew it out carefully: a flashlight, she was sure of it. She found the button halfway up the smooth case and pressed it.

Nothing.

Anat cursed under her breath, then tried again. Of course she'd have the bad luck to find a flashlight with dead batteries. Totally useless.

"What's wrong?" Yosh's disembodied voice floated out of the darkness.

"I found one, but it doesn't work," Anat said resisting the temptation to hurl it across the room.

"Of course it does," Yosh said. "Give it to me."

"Why? It won't make a difference—" She jerked away as small fingers brushed her arm. "It's just me," Yosh said in a small voice. "Please?"

Anat hesitated, then handed it over.

Yosh mumbled something under her breath. That was followed by a strange sound, like a small wheel spinning.

"What are you doing?" Anat asked, puzzled. "I told you, it doesn't—"

A cone of light illuminated Yosh's face.

Anat's jaw dropped. "How did you . . . ?"

"It has a crank here, see? In case the batteries are dead."

Anat squinted. Of course, she should have checked for something like that. Her father had a similar one in their home emergency kit.

"All right," Anat said, fighting to refocus—the Yosh mystery would have to wait. She held out her hand for the flashlight.

Yosh paused, her eyes flickering. But she handed it over.

Anat panned the beam across the walls. As she'd feared: only empty pegs in the glass cabinets where a wide assortment of firearms had probably once rested. She rifled through the drawers again. Nearly all of them contained boxes of bullets, but no guns. She did find a few novelty items: ninja throwing stars and a set of brass knuckles. Nothing that would be very useful against the thing that had landed on their car, but she tucked them in her pocket anyway.

"*Kus emek*," she finally muttered after checking the last drawer. "Bullets, but no guns. I'll have to check the range. Do you want to come?"

"I'll stay," Yosh said.

"Suit yourself."

Anat swung the beam across the store. The floor was old linoleum, so worn in places that bare concrete peeped through. She found a door in the back and pushed through.

It led to a small firing range, just four lanes divided by narrow partitions. At the far end, a few ragged targets still hung. They were pocked with holes and browning, the edges curling up.

Anat swung the flashlight across the partitions: nothing, the shelves designed to hold reserve weapons and ammo were all empty. Slowly, she ran the flashlight beam across the lanes toward the targets and back: nothing. And the section of the room she was standing in appeared empty, too.

But she wasn't about to give up; she'd been coached on being meticulous. One of her instructors talked a lot about the things your eyes were trained to miss, ordinary items that you automatically skipped over unless you took the time to examine everything carefully. Going slower on her second pass through the room, she spotted a small pistol on the floor near the far wall. Hurrying forward, she scooped it up: a standard Glock G21. Anat smiled. She'd trained on this gun; it took .45 automatic bullets. And there had been plenty of those stashed in the drawers.

Scattered on the floor around it were shell casings. Another bad sign. It looked like someone had unloaded on something, then dropped the gun.

Not her concern, Anat reminded herself. She had a real weapon now—that was the important thing.

She hurried back to the front room. Yosh was sitting on top of the counter, swinging her heels. If she was upset about having been left alone in the dark, she didn't mention it.

"Have you heard anything?" Anat asked, lowering her voice. "From outside?"

Yosh shook her head. "No, but they're still there. I can tell."

"We need to talk," Anat said, panning the flashlight up to Yosh's face. "Tell me how you know so much."

Yosh blinked in the light and shrugged. "I can't explain it. I just know." She lowered her voice and whispered. "I can hear them, in my head."

Anat's grip tightened. "What are you talking about?" Privately, she thought, *In her head? She is insane.*

"More of them are coming," Yosh continued, her voice eerily calm. "And they'll be here soon."

"Hello?" Nico called out from the front hallway. "*Vater?*"

Sophie held her breath. *Please let him be here. Please let him have a phone . . .*

"I thought his dad was American," Declan said in a low voice.

Sophie shushed him.

"Wait in there," Nico said, gesturing to a room on the left before heading for the back of the house.

She and Declan crept into the living room. Spartan was an understatement. Plain white walls, a black walnut floor, a black leather sofa, and matching chair. Everything looked spare and utilitarian—and filthy, illuminated by the bright sunlight pouring through the windows. Not a single picture hung on the walls, not so much as a magazine on the two end tables. Aside from the coating of dust, it was like a spread out of some Scandinavian furniture magazine.

"Cozy," Declan murmured in her ear.

Sophie repressed a giggle. He seemed to be warming to her again; hopefully he'd forgiven her for last night. "I'd sit, but it doesn't look like the furniture was designed for that."

"Definitely not," he agreed. "Looks like the apple didn't fall far from the tree, eh?"

Nico came back down the hall. "I'm going to check upstairs," he said, sounding choked up.

Sophie nodded, feeling a pang of empathy for him. Her family was across the country on the west coast, which in some ways made it easier. No chance of tracking them down until they found a functioning phone.

Declan was frowning as he held his cell up again. "The

battery's almost dead," he explained, catching her expression. "Maybe I should keep it off."

"Probably a good idea." Sophie didn't add what she was thinking, that if none of them had gotten a signal yet, they weren't likely to. The two of them stood in the middle of the room, listening to Nico upstairs, his voice increasingly desperate. *"Vater! Vater!"*

"Should we check for a note or something?" she asked, scanning the room. "Maybe he left something behind to tell Nico where he was going."

The footsteps and shouting stopped.

Declan frowned and called out, "Nico?"

No answer. They looked at each other. Declan's grip tightened on the hoe he'd carried in from the car.

"I'll go first. Stay back a bit, and be ready to run."

Sophie swallowed hard. The stairs were the same dark maple as the living room floor, with no runner. At the top, they hooked right into a long hallway lined with doors, two on each side. The spare motif continued: bare white walls, bare floor. Sophie repressed a shudder. It didn't feel like a house anyone had ever lived in.

"Nico?" she called out. "Are you okay?"

Still no response.

"Damn, I wish he'd answer," Declan said in a voice just above a whisper.

She stuck close as they edged down the hall, wishing she had some sort of weapon. Not that she'd be able to use it, but gripping something would probably stop her hands from shaking.

They peeked in the first door on the left: a home office with a bare black desk, black chair, white rug on the black floor. Not a single paper or framed photo in sight.

The room on the right turned out to be a bathroom, done

up in black and white tiles. A series of matching towels hung in a perfectly straight row below the sink.

"Model houses have more personality," Sophie mumbled nervously.

Declan raised a finger to his lips. They tiptoed towards the final two doors. The one on the left opened into a bedroom—Nico's, probably, since there was evidence that an actual human being had lived there. A checked bedspread on the twin bed, a few posters of sports cars pinned to the walls, a desk overflowing with papers and other paraphernalia.

But no Nico.

They exchanged a glance, then approached the final room. The master bedroom, based on its size. More of the black and white color scheme: a king-size bed that rode low to the floor, a long bench beneath picture windows, and a dresser in the corner. Nico sat on the bed, facing away from them.

Declan heaved a sigh and said, "Feckin' hell, you scared us."

Nico didn't respond. He was holding something in both hands.

Sophie approached him tentatively. From a few feet away, she could see that he was gripping a photo in one hand and some sort of official looking document in the other. "Nico?" she asked gently. "Are you all right?"

"No." He choked out.

"Can I see?" She reached out her hand.

His cheeks were wet. He wiped them as he handed her the photo: it was printed out on a plain sheet of paper rather than glossy photo stock. It showed a boy in a hospital bed, hooked up to even more machines than she'd been attached to in her last days. With a jolt, she realized it was a photo of him.

"But . . . when was this taken?" she asked.

Nico shook his head. "I've never been in the hospital. Not like this. I broke my wrist when I was twelve, but they sent me home the same day."

"So no memory of this, then?" Declan asked, peering over her shoulder.

"I said no," Nico snapped. "That's not me."

"Looks just like you," Declan pointed out. "What does the paper say?"

Nico handed it over, but didn't meet their eyes.

"Bollocks," Declan said, scanning it quickly. "Says here they were about to pull you off life support." He held it out for Sophie to see. She recognized it immediately: a standard *Do Not Resuscitate* order. At the sight of it she shuddered, remembering the awkward conversation she'd had with her parents before signing her own, six weeks ago. Her mother had sat in the chair by her hospital bed the whole time, wringing her hands while silent tears rolled down her face. Easily the worst day of her life, the day when she'd confronted the fact that no miracle was going to save her . . .

She brushed away the memory. "It must be some sort of mistake."

"No mistake," Declan said, shaking his head. "Says that you—Nico Bruder, the name's right here in black and white— were in an irreversible coma. Stony Brook Medical Center was planning on discontinuing life support on September first. Is this your mother's signature?"

Nico didn't respond.

"Your father hadn't signed it yet, though," Declan said. "So they were going to pull the plug—"

"Declan," Sophie said sharply, "stop."

"But this explains it, right? Why he doesn't remember

anything after hiking in April." He scrutinized Nico. "So maybe you took a nasty tumble and spent the next few months in a coma."

"Then how did I wake up in the lab?" Nico snapped. "Why am I here now?"

Declan shrugged. "Dunno. We could ask the same thing about you, right, Sophie?" Seeing her expression, he hastily continued, "No offense, but the both of you were deathly ill, and then you landed here, and . . . well, you're a little weak, but otherwise you feel fine, yeah?"

Sophie was thrown. This was something she'd trusted him with; she hadn't planned on sharing it with the group. Angrily, she shook her head. "That's different."

"Is it? Maybe not. Maybe Nico here had a miraculous recovery too."

"I wasn't sick," Nico protested. "And I don't feel weak."

"Right." Declan arched an eyebrow. "I'd think you'd be happy. It's not every day that you come out of a coma, yeah? So cheers on that. Maybe whatever happened cured the both of yas."

Sophie mulled it over. On the face of it, it was absurd—cancer wasn't "cured." She guessed the same held true for comas. And she didn't believe in miracles, regardless.

Of course, it was pretty absurd for a bunch of teenagers to get sucked across the planet into the infirmary beneath a research facility, too. And for whole towns to be deserted, and for weird creatures to be nesting inside auto repair shops. Absurd was the order of the day.

"I said I was never in a coma." Nico glared at Declan as he enunciated each syllable.

Sophie drew a deep breath. It would be dark soon, and she definitely didn't want to be wandering around at night, not after seeing those skeletons. "We were thinking that maybe your dad left a note or something saying where he went. Should we check?"

Nico dropped his head and rubbed his eyes. He didn't seem to have heard her.

"Nico?" she asked hesitantly. "Can you think of where he might have left something like that? Maybe—"

"Leave me alone." He spun abruptly and left the room, shoving Declan aside as he passed.

"Hey!" Declan protested.

Sophie helped him back up. He rubbed his shoulder and glowered after Nico. "Wishing I'd gone with the other group now. To hell with this bastard."

"You could have been nicer about that, you know," Sophie said in a low voice.

"Nicer?" He grimaced. "It was bloody nice of me to tag along and watch his back on this little excursion. That should've been nice enough for him."

"Still," Sophie said. "He thought his father was going to be here. Then he got this shock, that maybe he'd been about to die."

"Well, we're all a bit shocked, yeah?" Declan said. "And we just wasted a day looking for someone who probably took off with the others. We need to get back on the road. You think Anat waited for us?"

"Sure," Sophie said, although part of her strongly doubted it. "Let's just try to calm him down so we can get out of here."

"Calm my arse," Declan grumbled, but when she left the room he followed.

They found Nico in the kitchen staring at the refrigerator door with a furrowed brow. Someone had scrawled across the front of it with indelible marker: the bold black strokes stood out starkly against the gleam of stainless steel.

"What is it?" Sophie asked. It looked like something a mad scientist would have on his whiteboard, a mess of numbers and symbols. She recognized the symbol for *pi*, and a couple others from precalculus. There was no way she'd be able to make sense of it, though.

"Great, more maths," Declan muttered. "I was right, this is hell."

"Quiet!" Nico barked. "I'm trying to think." He ran his fingers lightly across the numbers, starting with the ones in the top left corner and working his way down while muttering under his breath.

"Nico, does it say anything about—"

"I said, shut up!"

Sophie glanced at Declan, who looked annoyed. They stood there waiting for nearly five minutes.

Nico finally straightened and announced, "I know where he is."

Anat sat on the floor with her back pressed against the counter, the Glock gripped in both hands. Yosh was perched on top of it a meter away. She drummed her heels against the wood in a steady rhythm.

"Stop that," Anat finally snapped.

Yosh fell still.

The adrenaline rush had dissipated, leaving Anat painfully aware of how exhausted she was. Hungry and thirsty, too, and they'd left their remaining supplies in the car outside. They wouldn't last long holed up in here. She'd tried the tap in the small bathroom—no running water. No food, either. At some point, they'd have to leave. All those creatures had to do was hang around.

The flashlight bulb started to dim again. Anat set the gun down and gave the handle a few hard cranks, channeling her frustration into the task. It flared brightly, illuminating the door. Staring at it, Anat imagined a cluster of creatures hunched on the other side, waiting. "Yosh. You said you can hear them?"

"Yes."

"How?"

"I don't know," Yosh said. "It's just something I've always been able to do."

"Do what? Hear people's thoughts?"

"Yes." Yosh nodded. "I try not to, but . . . I just can."

Anat mulled that over. It was implausible, but it wasn't the strangest thing she'd ever heard. It wasn't even the strangest thing she'd experienced this week. How was this any different from her waking up halfway across the world? Hazim's face flashed across her mind; he seemed farther away than ever. "So what are they thinking right now? Can you tell how many there are?"

"Their thoughts are . . . strange. Different," Yosh said slowly. "I can't tell exactly how many. Four, or perhaps five? Right now they're just waiting."

Just like she thought. Anat rolled her head from side to side. "Does it work the other way?"

"What do you mean?"

"I mean," Anat said impatiently, "Can you think something *at* them? To make them go away?"

"I don't know." Yosh sounded startled. "I've never tried before."

"Try," Anat aimed the flashlight directly at Yosh's face. "Because there's no other way for us to get out of here."

Yosh closed her eyes and bowed her head. Anat felt a strange prickling along the inside of her skull, like tiny ants.

"Not me," she snapped. "Get closer to the door and try to aim it at them."

Yosh slid off the counter and went to the door. Kneeling down, she pressed her cheek and both hands against it. Her eyes closed again.

Anat's heart thumped. The whole thing was insane. Maybe she should do them both a favor and end it quickly. A bullet in the head for Yosh, then one for herself. That had to be better than what would happen once they opened that door. The worst death she could conceive of involved falling prey to something else. If she was going to die, she'd prefer to do it on her own terms.

"I think it worked," Yosh whispered. "I tried to sound like one of them, ordering the others away. I think they might be like . . . bees, or something. Maybe there's a larger one in charge."

Great, Anat thought. *A larger one.* Just what they needed.

"There's only one way to be certain." Yosh reached for the handle.

Anat darted forward and pressed her palm flat against the door, holding it closed. "How about I go, since I have the gun."

"If you insist."

"I'll wait another minute," Anat said. "To make sure they're gone."

"It's better not to wait," Yosh countered. "I'm not certain how long it will work."

Girding herself, Anat said in a low voice, "Okay, open the door. If I give the signal, close and lock it fast."

"What's the signal?"

"Probably a scream," Anat said grimly, then nodded for Yosh to open the door.

Declan wasn't happy. This whole detour seemed like a terrible idea. Nico had somehow managed to convince Sophie that the jumbled mess on the fridge was a map to a specific place where they'd find his father. And for God knows what reason, Sophie had chosen to believe him. They'd voted down his suggestion to find another car and head out to meet the others.

So now they were trudging through the woods. Declan gripped his hoe firmly, keeping his eyes peeled for anything out of the ordinary. He'd never seen so many bloody trees in his entire life—it was damned claustrophobic. He'd already tripped on more tree roots than he could count, and it was still bloody hot. The bugs weren't letting up, either. How the hell had he ended up in America? He'd always wanted to come, but apparently his mates were right; it *was* overrated.

They must look a sight, he thought with sudden amusement, all clutching tools and gardening implements like a ragtag army. His mum would have a laugh if she saw him now.

Declan's eyes swam, and he quickly swiped the back of his hand against them. There was a good chance he'd never see anyone he cared about again, all thanks to some eejit in a pub. He should've known better, he chastised himself. You never take jobs from strangers. Any gig that sounded like a cakewalk would likely go arseways; this had certainly proven that. Christ, what he'd give to be back home right now, walking along the docks with Katie, his mum's Sunday roast warm in his belly.

But no. Instead he was trailing along behind a bloke he didn't trust, helping him find *his* family. It hardly seemed fair that in this godforsaken place, the biggest gobshite was the only one with someone still around who cared for him. Lucky sod had apparently survived a coma, too, and how many people could say that? If he'd ever needed further proof that life wasn't fair, well, there you go.

"How much farther?" he finally asked.

"Not far," Nico said without looking back.

Sophie shot him a thin smile. He glowered back at her, still peeved that at the first opportunity, she'd sided against him. Maybe she was just being spiteful. He'd wanted to explain that kissing her was pretty much all he'd thought of since the minute she took his hand that first day. But that more importantly, he loved Katie. Sophie should respect that, right? Even though now, he could barely picture Katie's face . . .

Well, Sophie and Nico could both stuff it. He was giving this little excursion ten more minutes, then he'd head back to the road and to hell with them both.

"We're here," Nico said, stopping in front of a towering tree.

"Where?" Declan asked, looking around. They were in a small clearing, like a dozen others they'd already passed through. The ground was heavily carpeted with pine needles. Aside from that, nothing but more trees.

Nico checked something on his watch and frowned. "A mile west, then a half mile north. This should be the spot. It's quite clear."

"Care to explain?" Declan said. "Because none of it seems clear. I thought your watch wasn't working, anyway."

"The GPS isn't, but it still records mileage," Nico insisted. "It was a gift from my dad on my last birthday. He knows that I have it, which is why he left those instructions."

Declan laughed bitterly. "Ah yes, the instructions. Clear as day, those were."

"I know that formula. We were talking about it on the day . . ." Nico's face clouded over and he cleared his throat. "Anyway, that was what we used to do on hikes, go over famous old proofs. And that one has a clear result. He added in symbols at the bottom so that I'd know which direction to follow."

"Sure, great plan," Declan said. "'Course, he could have just written, 'Nico, me boy, walk out into the woods for a bit, go stand in front of a bloody tree, and look like an arse.'"

"He wrote it in code," Nico insisted, "So that I'd be the only one who could find him."

"I believe him," Sophie chimed in. "If he says this is the spot, then it is."

"Well, that's just brilliant." Declan dropped to a crouch and rocked back on his heels. "Tell you what, I don't see any sign of the great man here. Do you?"

"We haven't looked yet." Nico kicked at the needles underfoot.

"Good luck with it, then. Wake me when you realize how nutters this is." Declan stretched out full length and crossed his hands behind his head, gazing up at the branches.

The two of them dug around the ground and tapped on tree trunks, like this was a feckin' movie and the ground would open up if they hit the right knothole. Madness. He yawned widely, inhaling the smell of dying leaves and woodsmoke and . . .

Declan bolted upright and sniffed.

Had to be his imagination. But if it wasn't . . .

Sophie and Nico were moving in tandem, kicking needles into small piles, running their hands over the bark of the closest trees.

Oh, how he hated to be wrong. Admitting it was even worse. Still, Declan gritted his teeth and said, "Either of you smell smoke?"

Nico's head snapped up. "It must be him!"

"All right then," Declan said, reluctantly getting to his feet. "Let's have a look."

It took ten minutes of scouring the forest to pinpoint the source: a lazy wisp of black wound skyward from a hollowed out stump. Nico peered inside. "Looks like it goes a long way down, then turns."

"So it's some sort of chimney?" Sophie asked.

"Yes! He must be underground," Nico said excitedly. Leaning over it, he called down, "*Vater? Sie sind da unten?*"

No response. The thin tendril of smoke curled lazily upwards, drifting past them toward the treetops.

Declan scowled. "I say we give it another minute, then—"

A grating shriek cut him off. All the hairs on his body shot up, and he froze. Whatever made that sound wasn't human, he felt it in his bones.

"I think we'd better hide," Sophie said in a low voice.

Declan wanted to agree, but he'd lost the use of his tongue. It was like one of those terrible dreams where your mind was screaming at you to run, but your feet remained stubbornly rooted to the ground. He wasn't alone. The other two had frozen in place alongside him.

"Where do we go?" Nico hissed. "Up, do you think?"

Declan managed to tilt his head toward the sky. There were plenty of climbable trees nearby, pines with thick branches that would provide good cover. But they didn't have any idea whether or not the creatures described in the diary could climb. They might turn out to be regular monkeys, and then they'd be screwed.

He examined the stump—it was too narrow for even Sophie to slip into. "Up it is." No other options.

Nico was already at the base of the nearest tree. He seized

hold of a lower branch and executed a perfect chin-up, then threw his right leg over the branch. Within seconds, he was out of sight.

Declan was about to follow when he realized Sophie couldn't reach that branch; it was too high overhead. Looking frantic, she rushed to the next tree. She jumped, arms extended, but missed entirely and landed hard on the ground. "Bollocks," he muttered before trotting over to help.

"Grab my shoulders," he instructed, clasping his hands together, "and use this as a step." He boosted her up, grunting a little as her heel ground into the palm of his hand.

"I can't quite reach," she gasped.

"Try again," he said, aiming for a patient tone. But he was all too aware of the sound of something crashing through the brush, headed their way. He pressed his hands as high as he could, straining under her weight. Again, she slipped.

"It's no use." Tears streamed down Sophie's face. "Go ahead and climb. I'll be fine."

"I haven't been carrying you everywhere just to leave you hanging about on the ground now. Now come on. Don't be such a girl about it."

Sophie pressed firmly on his shoulders. He bent both knees and said, "One . . . two . . ."

On three he thrust up with all his strength, pushing on her foot as hard as he could.

"I got it!" Sophie yelled as her flailing legs kicked him in the solar plexus. Declan looked up—her chest was on the branch, and she was struggling to swing a leg over. Panting from the effort, she made it to a seated position and flashed a thumbs up.

"Grand," he said breathlessly. "Get a little higher and I'll follow."

"Declan!" Sophie hissed. She was still perched on the lowest branch, within arms-reach of the ground. *Doesn't follow directions well*, he thought to himself. She'd blanched completely, her focus directed at something past his shoulder.

"Not to rush you, bird, but I can't exactly climb on top of you," he said. "Can we save the chat for later?"

"Behind you!"

Slowly, Declan turned. When he saw what was standing just a few yards away, he stumbled backward, scraping his hands against the rough bark of the tree trunk.

Above him, Sophie screamed.

CHAPTER NINE

Anat blinked against the sudden brightness. Dusk was falling, and late afternoon shadows crept across the shopping plaza. Her heart hammered in her chest. She swept the gun quickly in an arc, left to right. Everything was silent and still. The place looked just as abandoned as when they'd pulled in.

No creatures in sight.

She pivoted to check the roof, but an overhang above the door obstructed her view. Cautiously, Anat edged around the car until she was a few feet from the driver's side door. What she could see of the roof appeared clear, and the car itself was empty. She dropped to a squat and peered beneath it: nothing.

"*Kus emek*," she muttered. Whatever Yosh had done, it worked.

Yosh appeared at her side. "There is a grocery store a few blocks away," she said. "With metal gates. We can wait for the others there."

"Did those . . . things tell you that?" Anat asked skeptically, still unsure what to call them. Creatures? Monsters? "Maybe it's a trap."

Yosh said, "We'll be safe there."

She doesn't blink enough, Anat thought—hardly ever, in fact. "You didn't answer my question,"

"Just follow me." Without waiting for a response, Yosh started walking toward the street.

Anat hesitated. After witnessing the speed those things were capable of, she wasn't looking forward to chancing her luck against them on the road again, especially not after dark—and night was approaching fast. Yosh had gotten rid of the things, at least temporarily. Maybe she'd be able to keep them away. A grocery store would have food and water, too. She hurried to catch up.

They walked in silence. Anat gave each car they passed a cursory examination. She understood now why Ryan had commandeered the largest vehicle he could find. When they headed for the coast, she wanted to be behind the wheel of something large and impenetrable—preferably the cab of a tractor trailer, or at least the largest pickup truck she could find. Which shouldn't be too difficult. This was America, after all—and from what she understood, their passion for hot dogs and baseball was only matched by their love of obscenely large cars.

The streets were quiet and still. With dusk, a chill had set in. Anat repressed a shiver. She caught herself thinking that in spite of everything, this was a lovely, quaint little town. The majority of storefronts were set on the ground floor of historic homes, old brick buildings with wide verandas. Their window displays were crammed with old furniture, antiques, pastel-toned clothing, even an old-fashioned candy store. There was nothing like it in Tel Aviv. She'd seen this sort of setting in movies but always figured it was made up, just another part of the American propaganda machine.

Anat's eyes panned continuously, drawn by any stray flicker of movement. She'd felt like this on her first training mission: ramped up, edgy. The difference was that then, she more or less knew what to expect from the enemy.

They reached an intersection crowded with abandoned cars, where a streetlight dangled crookedly. "Straight," Yosh said softly.

Anat nodded and kept moving forward, thinking, *Yosh can't be trusted. There's something wrong with her. Something unnatural.*

"One more block," Yosh said. "There it is."

Anat followed her gaze. A hundred yards away, an old neon sign leaned sideways on a chunk of broken pavement. The dimmed letters read, STOP N' SHOP. Beyond it, another parking lot, mostly empty. As promised, the front of the store was protected by a metal gate, the kind that shopkeepers slid down nightly.

"It's unlocked," Yosh said, "And there's still food inside."

"How could you possibly know that?" Anat demanded. She was clutching the gun too hard, her knuckles had gone white. She forced herself to relax—the last thing she needed was a hand cramp at a crucial moment.

Yosh didn't answer. Anat slid from car to car, utilizing what little cover was available as they approached the doors. The gate was down, but not all the way; the bottom stopped a few centimeters shy of the ground.

Reaching the storefront, Anat bent low to examine the gate, then cupped her hands and peered inside. It looked empty, and there was still lots of food left on the shelves. But was it safe? She bit her lip, considering. They hadn't passed any other buildings that looked defensible. And she was loath to remain outside, knowing that those things could come back at any minute. She had a gun now, too, if Yosh tried anything funny.

She bent low to lift the gate. Straining and grunting, she managed to ease it up a few inches. It groaned in protest, as if the hinges hadn't been oiled in awhile. Anat winced at the noise. "I need help," she was finally forced to acknowledge.

Yosh bent over and made a great show of trying to help. The gate ground up another three inches, then jolted to a stop.

"*Kus emek*," Anat muttered. She threw her whole back into it. The gate lurched up a few precious inches at a time. Finally, they'd managed to lift it high enough for Anat to reach in and push open the door. "You first," she said, motioning with the Glock.

Yosh stood silent for a moment, staring at her with those enormous dark eyes. She smiled faintly, then ducked and scurried through the door. Anat bent low to follow, then dragged the gate back down behind them. She'd try to find something inside to latch it with, so they couldn't be followed.

It took a minute for her eyes to adjust to the dim interior. Rows of plain white shelves, most still stocked with dusty boxes and cans of food. A long counter to the left was lined with cash registers.

Her nose wrinkled. The store reeked of putrid food, though the air wasn't as foul as the inside of the cafeteria's cooler. *Better not open the freezers*, she thought, spotting them against the far wall.

Yosh had vanished into the depths of the store.

"Yosh?" Anat called out as her eyes flitted over the nearest shelves, taking a mental inventory. Hairspray in aerosol cans—that could come in handy, with a lighter she'd easily be able to turn them into flame throwers. There were probably real flashlights somewhere, too, and bottled water. Yosh suddenly reappeared and said, "Did you make a mark on the door?"

"What? Oh." Anat had completely forgotten about letting the others know where they were. She looked skeptically across the parking lot. She should have marked the sign by the street. Too risky to go back now—she'd do it on their way out in the morning.

She was about to say as much when she caught movement out of her peripheral vision. Slowly, her gaze slid up.

One of the creatures was perched on top of the metal shelving directly behind Yosh.

"Stay still." Anat whispered, tightening her grip on the Glock.

"What?" Yosh looked puzzled.

Anat waved a hand to silence her, while keeping her eyes locked on the creature. It was like nothing she'd ever seen: covered in greenish-brown fur, with a hint of iridescence at the tips, as if a giant praying mantis had mated with an alligator. A sleek, elongated head that ended in a snout. Glowing greenish-yellow eyes set on either side of a narrow ridge. Arms that ended in sharp talons. Long legs, disturbingly human looking, with clawed feet that curled over the lip of the shelf. Even hunched over, it appeared to be more than two meters tall. It stared back at her. She suddenly understood what the man in the journal had meant by "smart eyes." It seemed to be sizing her up.

While edging backward, she caught movement to her right. An even larger creature straddled the aisle between them.

"Get down!" Anat cried out, raising the gun.

Yosh had gone completely still, gazing up at the creature as it started to crawl down the shelving. Anat regained her senses and tightened her finger on the trigger, zeroing in on the spot between the creature's eyes. But she was torn. Save Yosh first, or shoot the one closest to her? There might not be time to fire on both of them.

The one above Yosh stopped moving; it clung to the shelves like a spider. Yosh was staring past her, a creepy faint smile plastered on her face. Slowly, Anat turned her head.

Five other creatures towered above her.

Anat bit her lip. She didn't have enough rounds to take out all of them. Seeing them up close, she wasn't even sure how effective the bullets would be, or what to target. For all she knew, their hearts might be in their tails.

Defeated, she turned back to Yosh. "I'm sorry. There are too many of them."

"I know." Yosh stepped forward and extended a hand. "Please give me the gun."

"What?" Anat said, startled. "Did they ask you to do that?"

"This is not a fight you can win," Yosh said softly.

Did they have control of her somehow? Anat steadied the Glock, aiming for the closest creature. She'd been trained to fight to the end. If she stayed focused, maybe she could kill a few before they tore her apart. Yosh would have a chance to get away. Her finger started to depress the trigger . . .

"Trust me, Anat. They won't hurt you." Yosh's gaze hardened as she added, "Not unless I tell them to."

Sophie couldn't stop screaming. That . . . *thing* . . . was crawling toward Declan. It looked like something out of a nightmare. As it approached, the creature made a strange clicking noise.

Declan had frozen with his back pressed against her tree. The creature was less than twenty feet away from him.

"Declan!" she cried out.

He looked up at her. All the color had left his face, and his eyes were wild with terror. Sophie's heart clenched. He'd gotten her up here and was now stuck down there fending for himself. "Jump!" she screamed.

Completely ignoring the creature that was slowly rearing up on its hind legs behind him, Declan kept his gaze locked on her. "Feckin' hell," he said in a shaky voice. "First the bear, then this. I've no luck at all lately."

"Please," Sophie pleaded. "Jump! I'll try to catch you."

He shook his head. "I wish we'd had more time to talk."

"Me, too," Sophie said hoarsely.

"Take care, Sophie. Find the others and get to the mainland. And don't let that gobshite Nico stop you."

Declan cast one final, wistful grin at her. Then he turned to face it.

The creature towered over him, nearly double his height. Its mouth yawed open, exposing two strange tentacles. They clamped together, like smacking lips. Declan drew himself up and said with strained bravado, "You might be the ugliest damned thing I ever saw, and that's saying something."

Sophie couldn't bear to watch. She turned away—and cringed as a shriek tore through the woods.

"What are you talking about?" Anat demanded. "If you can make them do what you want, just tell them to go away."

Yosh shook her head. "Not this time."

She'd lost her accent, Anat realized, and suddenly looked like a different person: confident and secure, despite being surrounded by terrifying creatures. It must have all been an act. Slowly, she asked, "What is this?"

"If you just do what I say, it will all be fine."

"So they're not going to attack us?"

"No."

But the creatures seemed poised to strike. Two were clicking their long talons together. Anat remembered something her commander always said: ninety percent of winning a standoff came down to attitude. *Don't back down or show any weakness.* The instant you did, you were done for.

Anat shifted the gun, aiming at Yosh's center mass. "Make them step back."

Yosh looked bemused, as if the gun meant nothing. She closed her eyes. The creatures shifted uneasily. Anat felt that strange tingling again, an itch on the inside of her skull. She tried not to wince.

The creatures drifted back, positioning themselves a few feet behind Yosh. "Better?" she asked.

"Not much," Anat muttered. Better would be seeing them disappear entirely, but obviously that wasn't going to happen. "What do you want?"

"The same thing you want," Yosh replied. "To go home."

"But that is what we were doing," Anat retorted. "Finding a boat to go to the military base—"

"There's no hope on the mainland," Yosh interrupted. "Or anywhere else."

"You were already here," Anat said, suddenly understanding. "You didn't come with the rest of us."

Yosh regarded her with interest, then slowly nodded. "Yes."

Anat's mind reeled as she sorted through the ramifications. "But . . . why lock yourself in the infirmary?"

"We were curious about you." Yosh said. "It was the best way to find out what you knew."

Anat cursed her own stupidity. She'd taken too much at face value, something her instructors had always warned against. "Zain never came back. What happened to him?"

"He was smart," Yosh said reflectively. "He figured it out long before the rest of you."

So Zain had realized that Yosh was a traitor. And before he could share that information . . . "Did you kill him?"

Yosh shrugged. "You'd only just met him. Why do you care?"

"Why not kill all of us, then?" Anat demanded. "Why let us out, if this was going to happen in the end?"

"I'm not going to kill you, Anat. Not unless you make me."

Anat didn't find that very comforting. Gesturing to the creatures with the Glock, she asked, "Where did they come from? I've never seen anything like them."

"No, you haven't." Yosh looked them over with apparent affection. "They didn't exist in your world before."

"What? You're talking crazy again."

Yosh sighed. "I have to say, this would all have been much easier if more intelligent people had come through."

"Come through what?"

Yosh leaned back against the shelving and crossed her arms over her chest. "You're in for a bit of a shock."

Anat gritted her teeth; Yosh was clearly enjoying drawing this out. She had to repress an overwhelming desire to march across the room and pistol-whip her. "Tell me. How'd we end up in Long Island?"

"Ah, but that's not the best part." Yosh bent forward slightly, a gleam in her eye. "The question isn't where you are. It's *when* you are."

Anat's palms felt slick against the gun. "You're talking nonsense."

"Am I?" Yosh smirked.

Anat longed to wipe that look off her face. But humoring her might provide enough time to come up with an escape plan. "*When* are we, then?"

"I really thought you'd have figured it out by now," Yosh mused, "considering the state of the roads and the cars. Not to mention the buildings."

Anat just waited, refusing to rise to the bait.

Yosh met her eyes squarely. "I'd say you've landed about twenty years in your future. Give or take."

Declan's eyes were squeezed tightly shut. His whole body had gone rigid while he awaited the moment of impact: claws ripping open his belly, teeth closing around his throat. He'd survived the bear, only to be torn to shreds by something even worse. Ironic didn't even begin to describe it.

Nothing happened.

Declan slowly opened his eyes. He was lying on his back in a pile of pine needles. Late afternoon sunlight sifted through the leaves, dappling patterns of light and dark on his bare arms. The forest around him was empty.

He blinked to make sure.

The monster was gone. He stood, brushing himself off. That . . . thing had been standing right over him. He'd been able to see strands of saliva dangling from its mouth—he cringed at the memory. *Where'd it go?*

"Declan!" Sophie wailed.

"Yeah, I'm here," he called back.

"What? You're okay?" she said incredulously.

Declan turned. She was clinging perilously to a low branch,

peering down at him. "Right as rain," he said, raising both hands in the air and suppressing the urge to laugh.

"But how . . . " her mouth gaped open.

"Guess I was too ugly for it."

"What was that noise, then?"

"Right, the noise," he said, remembering the ear-splitting shriek that rended the air as the creature towered above him. "Wasn't me."

"Wasn't me, either," Nico called sheepishly from his tree.

Kept yourself safe and sound, didn't you? Declan thought with a scowl.

"Thank God you're okay!" Sophie said, awkwardly scrambling down another branch.

"Stay up there!" he insisted. "That thing might come back."

She hesitated, but obeyed.

Declan turned in a slow circle. There was no sign of anything living in the forest surrounding him. He pivoted twice to make sure, but everything remained still, not so much as a twitching branch in sight. "Strange," he said aloud. "Do either of you remember hearing that sound before?"

A pause, then Sophie said, "At the house. Didn't Yosh scream like that, when there was something at the door?"

Right, Declan thought. At the time, he'd taken it for a cry of terror. But as soon as she screamed, whatever had been pushing against the door vanished. What if . . .

A branch snapped behind him. Declan whirled, automatically raising his fists. His throat went dry, and he chastised himself for being an eejit. He should have been halfway up the tree by now, hiding out sensibly like the others. Instead, he was down here playing detective. And now his new playmate had returned to finish him off.

A rustling noise, from the same spot.

"Declan?" Sophie said hesitantly. "What's wrong?"

"It's still out here!" he replied in a hoarse whisper. It shifted closer, sticking to the trees; which was strange, since it hadn't exactly been shy about hunting him down before. He glanced up: Sophie was staring down at him, her eyes wide with terror. "Get back!" he ordered. "I'm going to jump!"

Obediently, she moved farther along the branch.

"I'll try to distract it," Nico hissed.

"Yeah? How?"

Nico suddenly dropped down so that he was dangling from the lowest branch. He hollered, "Hey! Over here!"

"Declan! Hurry!" Sophie urged.

Declan jumped. The first time, he missed the branch by inches. The second, by nearly a foot. He heard crashing in the brush behind him. Trying to ignore it, he bent his knees and gathered himself. Drawing in a giant breath he sprung, reaching up with his fingertips fully extended.

His right hand latched onto rough bark, but barely. His arm muscles screamed at him, and he could feel his palms tearing open as he started to slip.

Just as he was about to fall, a small hand closed over his wrist.

"Gotcha!" Sophie said through gritted teeth. "Now give me your other hand. Hurry!"

Declan threw his left hand up so that she could grab that wrist, too. She grunted, straining against his weight. He slowly inched upward.

"It's coming closer!" Nico warned from the next tree.

Sophie's branch was slightly more than eight feet off the ground—not high enough, he realized. The creature that had loomed over him was easily that height; it could just reach up and grab them. "There isn't time," Declan insisted. "Let me go and start climbing."

"No!" Sophie growled. "I won't let it get you."

He opened his fingers, letting go of her wrists, but she held on. "Drop me!"

She yanked harder. Declan suddenly felt himself rise up. His shoulder crossed the branch, then his chest. He scrambled the rest of the way, facing Sophie. She'd collapsed against the tree trunk, her face flushed and sweaty.

"Thanks."

"Don't thank me yet," Sophie gasped. "Start climbing."

He waited for her to ascend a few branches before following. The whole time he kept checking for the creature. Through gaps in the greenery, he caught glimpses of Nico scaling his tree. They were fifteen feet above the ground, then twenty. That had to be high enough, right?

"Can you see it?" Declan called out.

"Can't see anything," Nico yelled back. "Too many leaves in the way."

Sophie stopped when they were about thirty feet off the ground. The branches had started to thin out; anything higher up would be too weak to bear their weight

"What now?" Nico yelled from his perch.

At least in that gear he looks like he belongs up a tree, Declan thought. Meanwhile, he and Sophie looked like hapless flood victims. The sheer absurdity of the situation struck him, and he almost laughed. Declan Murphy was halfway up a tree in Long Island, with some B-movie monster chasing after him. His mates would be pissing themselves if they could see this. Katie, too . . .

It was silent down below. Declan strained his ears, listening for movement.

"Where'd it go?" Sophie whispered.

Motioning for her to be quiet, he inched out along the branch. The leaf cover was too thick, he couldn't get a clear view of the ground. He wasn't sure what kind of tree this was—oak? Sycamore? They didn't have anything like it in Ireland. Leastways, not in Galway. Then he caught a flash of something below. "I think—"

In the next tree, Nico suddenly yelped.

"What is it?" Sophie called frantically. "Do you see it?"

"There's something on my tree . . . it's climbing!" Nico cried out. "I think—oh my God."

Nico fell silent. Declan squinted through the canopy of leaves and branches. Nico was no longer visible.

"Nico?"

No response.

Declan and Sophie looked at each other.

"What do we do?" she asked.

"I don't know," Declan admitted, avoiding her eyes. "If these things can climb, well . . ."

Sophie stared at him, a look of utter defeat on her face. He scooted over until he was sitting beside her and took her hand. For what seemed like a very long time, they both listened. From this high up, all he could discern was scuffled movement in the brush—likely the sounds of Nico being eaten alive. He shuddered.

"Declan?" Sophie said quietly.

"Yeah?"

"So many times when I was lying in that hospital bed, I wished that I'd done something earlier, when I still had the chance. Having my family sit around, waiting for it to happen, well . . . it was horrible. For them, and for me." She examined her hand in his. Without looking up, she continued, "I don't want to watch you die."

"We're not going to die," he said forcefully. "I'll think of something."

"Yeah?"

"Sure," he said with false bravado. "It's times like this I'm at my best."

Her lip trembled, and a tear rolled down her cheek. But she nodded. "I bet you are."

"Seriously. This is nothing compared to a few days ago. Russian bastard had a gun pointed at my head."

"Right, but wasn't that how you ended up here?"

"Got away from him, though, didn't I?"

Sophie smiled through her tears. "Any way you can make it happen again?"

"Trust me, I've been trying since we got here. No luck yet, though." He squeezed her hand and added, "The odd thing is, meeting you . . . I didn't expect that. It almost makes it worth it."

Sophie sniffled. "Really?"

"Well, I could live without the giant man-eating lizards, but . . . yeah." He brushed a strand of hair out of her eyes. They were lovely, green with yellow flecks around the irises. *A man could drown in those eyes*, he thought. The dark circles beneath them were gone, and the sun had tinted her skin the same honey-brown as her hair. Gently, he wiped her tears away with the back of his free hand.

Sophie started trembling as he ran his thumb along her jawline. Softly, she asked, "What about Katie?"

Declan bit his lip. Katie felt so far away right now, he was having a hard time even remembering her face. What did that say about him? They'd been together nearly a year, and after just a few days she seemed intangible as a dream. And the worst part was that he hardly even felt badly about it. Something about Sophie just felt . . . right. And they were about to die, anyway. Whatever happened, Katie would never know.

"Right now, I can only see you." Leaning forward, Declan pressed his lips to hers. Sophie kissed him back, and for a moment he forgot about the danger they were in, forgot about Nico, forgot everything but the warmth of her face in his hands.

She pulled back first and said, "Wow."

Declan couldn't speak. He could barely breathe.

"Was it okay?" Sophie asked hesitantly.

"Okay?" he laughed weakly. "Bloody hell, that was—"

"Hey!" someone hollered from below.

Declan nearly fell off the branch. "Nico? That you?"

"Yeah, it's me."

Declan leaned over and peered down. Nico was standing at the base of their tree. Weirder still, he was grinning widely. "What happened?"

"Is he all right?" Sophie asked incredulously, gripping Declan's elbow for stability as she jutted her head out to see.

"You can come down now, it's safe," Nico yelled up. "But hurry!"

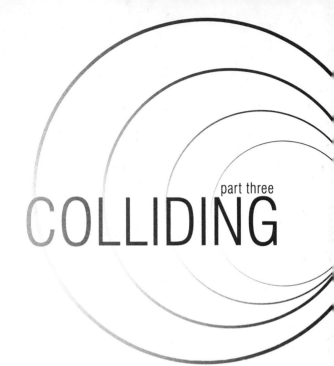

part three

COLLIDING

Sophie carefully descended, following Declan from branch to branch. Halfway down, her breath caught and she stopped dead—Nico wasn't alone. A sinewy old man stood at the base of their tree. His hair and beard were long, matted, and streaked with gray. There was a longbow strapped across his back, and he wore a strange mix of clothing: threadbare jeans, a frayed flannel shirt, and a thick wool coat despite the heat. He was easily in his sixties, yet carried himself ramrod straight.

She and Declan exchanged a look.

"It's okay!" Nico called up. "This is my father!"

"Bloody hell," Declan muttered. "The man himself."

They proceeded more slowly. Based on what little Nico had said about his father, she'd pictured a tweedy geek, with glasses and maybe a pocket protector. This guy looked like he could kill someone with his bare hands. Plus every time she glanced down, he was glaring at her from beneath heavy brows. Self-conscious, she let go of the bottom branch too quickly and landed hard, stumbling before righting herself.

"All right?" Declan asked with concern.

"I'm fine," she mumbled, embarrassed.

Declan extended a grubby hand. "Declan Murphy. Nice to meet you, Mr. Bruder."

Mr. Bruder's glower deepened. He turned and said something to Nico in German. Nico's face went dark, and they started arguing. After a moment, his father waved for silence. "We leave now," he said in a gravelly voice. "They'll be back."

Without waiting for a response, he turned and started walking through the forest. Nico threw them an apologetic look, then fell in behind him.

"So much for nice to meet yas," Declan muttered as they hurried to catch up.

Sophie managed a thin smile. She was seriously regretting the decision to help Nico find his father. So far, the guy seemed almost as creepy and dangerous as the creatures chasing them.

Declan's thoughts were apparently running along similar lines, because he called out, "Was it you who scared that thing off, then? How?"

Without breaking stride, Bruder held up a small flute. It was rough looking, clearly hand-carved. "I made this to mimic their signals. Very effective." He tucked it back in his pocket. "It won't fool them for long, though. Walk quietly. No talking."

He threaded sure-footedly through the trees, with Nico right behind him. Sophie exchanged another glance with Declan, but they followed in silence. Night was falling fast, and the sky above the treetops was already tinged dark blue. No matter what, she didn't want to be out here if that thing came back.

Bruder suddenly stopped so abruptly Nico nearly crashed into him. "*Vater*? What is it?" he asked.

Without replying, Bruder stalked back to where Declan and Sophie had frozen in their tracks. Looming over them, he demanded, "Nico said you all woke up in the infirmary together a few days ago. Is that correct?"

Sophie shrank under his glare. It sounded like a test, as if he suspected they were lying. "Yes," she stammered. "The day before yesterday."

"Not sure how we all ended up there, though," Declan added, his voice strained. "Nico said you worked there. Any chance you can explain it?"

Bruder stared at them for another long moment. Sophie shifted under his gaze. It was oddly predatory, like he was trying to figure out which part of them to eat first. Nico said something in German and touched his arm. Bruder jerked away, admonishing, "I said, be quiet! The thrinaxes have formidable hearing."

He spun on his heels and marched ahead. After a beat, Nico followed sullenly.

"Thrinaxes?" Sophie asked Declan in a low voice.

"Should've known Nico's dad would turn out to be a nutter," he murmured back.

"Shh," Sophie said. "He'll hear you."

"You think he has *formidable hearing,* too?" he asked, aping Bruder's grave tone.

Sophie nearly laughed out loud but caught herself in time. The two of them scurried to catch up.

Nico and his dad had reached a small clearing. At the far end stood a jumble of enormous boulders; the largest was the size of a shed. Bruder weaved between them, then abruptly vanished from view.

"What the . . . ?" Declan muttered.

There was a space in between the boulders, just large

enough for a person to squeeze through. And in the center, a hole led down into the ground. Nico stopped beside it.

"See?" he said triumphantly. "I told you he was probably underground."

"Bloody hell," Declan muttered.

"At the bottom of the ladder, turn left," Nico instructed. "The last person has to pull those branches over the top." His head dropped down into the hole.

"Ladies first," Declan said, waving elaborately.

"Thanks a lot," Sophie muttered.

"You'd rather be the one dragging over the branches?" He cocked an eyebrow.

Sophie glanced at the heavy looking pile of brush stacked beside the opening. "Nope. That's all you."

"See you down there." He squeezed her shoulder reassuringly.

Sophie felt herself flush. To cover, she ducked her head and carefully lowered herself into the hole. After a moment's groping, her feet found the rungs of a ladder. She descended carefully, fighting back claustrophobia as the darkness swallowed her.

She paused at the base. It was damp and musty down here, pungent with the smell of earth. She wondered how Nico's dad knew about this tunnel—could he actually have dug it himself? Seemed like a strange thing for a scientist to do, especially one whose home décor suggested a total neat freak.

Declan dropped down beside her. "All right?"

"I guess." Sophie swallowed hard.

"Dark as a tomb down here," Declan noted cheerfully, taking her hand in the dark. "This way, bird."

Sophie followed him down a narrow tunnel not much wider than her shoulders. There was a faint gleam of light up ahead. Despite the cold, a small part of her was panicking over the possibility that her hands might be sweaty. She tried to force it aside—she was underground, with monsters after her, and all she could focus on was the fact that a cute boy was holding her hand? It was ridiculous.

After about twenty feet, the tunnel opened into a small room. The ceiling was so low that Nico had hunched over to avoid knocking his head. His father moved around the room, lighting rough-hewn candles. A tiny fire sent a thin stream of smoke up to a narrow hole above.

"The bees survived, thank God," Bruder said cheerfully, waving a candle. "Actually, they're probably enjoying better numbers than they've seen in a century. The cataclysm was a true boon for the insect kingdom. Not so much for the animal one, unfortunately," he muttered as he bent to light another wick.

"The cataclysm?" Sophie asked, taking in the room. Yup, this pretty much completed the portrait of a mad scientist. The packed earthen walls were covered in scrawlings and for-mulas. There was a pile of blankets in one corner and stacks of books everywhere. No chairs or a table in sight.

"Right, you know nothing." Bruder straightened and scratched his beard. "Hard to know where to begin, really."

"Do you have anything to eat, Dad?" Nico interrupted.

His face split in a wide grin—which, if anything, made him look even more alarming. "Of course! Sorry, you must all be starving." He rummaged around in a plastic bin at the far end of the room, finally withdrawing a small plastic packet.

"What is it?" Sophie asked as he ripped it open and handed her something long and brown.

"Turkey jerky," Bruder said reverently. "Probably the last package left on Long Island."

"Oh," Sophie said. "Thanks."

"Never had jerky before," Declan said dubiously, examining it. "You're sure it's edible?"

"Long past the expiration date, but with jerky, that shouldn't matter." Bruder flashed another rotten yellow smile. "It doesn't really go bad. That's its chief merit."

"It's certainly not the taste," Declan said, grimacing as he chewed it.

Sophie had never been a big fan of jerky either, but after the cobbled-together meals of the past few days, she wasn't feeling picky. She devoured hers in a few bites.

"Don't suppose there's any more?" Declan asked, echoing her thoughts.

"That's the last of the jerky," Bruder said mournfully. "I had hoped it would last the winter, but . . . well, I wasn't expecting company. I do have some nuts left over. Tomorrow we can fish. The fish have done well, too." He had a faraway look in his eyes, as if he was actually seeing through the walls to some healthy-looking fish.

Sophie cleared her throat. "Mr. Bruder, we have a lot of questions—"

"Dr. Bruder," he grunted. "Sit." At a glance from Nico, he added, "Please."

Following his lead, Sophie settled on the floor. It was bare earth, and the cold pressed through the thin material of her borrowed jeans. Despite what waited for them outside, she found herself shuddering at the thought of spending much time down in this dark, creepy hole. It smelled terrible, stale air mingled with body odor and dying leaves and smoke. And she didn't like the way Bruder kept glancing over at her.

Declan cleared his throat and said, "So—"

"Silence!" Bruder thundered.

They all froze. Even Nico appeared taken aback. Bruder tugged at his beard. "I just . . . it's been a long time since I've spoken to anyone. I need to figure out how to explain it. Have you all studied physics?"

Sophie shook her head.

Declan shrugged. "A bit. But not much," he amended when Nico threw him a skeptical look.

Bruder sighed. "That would have been too much to hope for." He abruptly lunged forward. Sophie reared back as he stopped inches from her face.

"Hey!" Declan protested, grabbing Bruder's arm. "Stay back, you nutter."

"*Vater*, what are you doing?" Nico said, sounding horrified.

"I won't hurt her." Bruder shook off Declan's hand and stared at Sophie, giving her the kind of once-over she used to get in doctors' offices. After a second, he sat back. "Doesn't appear to be anything remarkable about you. Probably just a fluke that you were caught in an eddy."

"An eddy?" Nico asked.

Sophie's pulse was still racing. She swallowed hard. Bruder had moved alarmingly fast, like a snake. She had to fight the urge to run back down the tunnel and scramble up the ladder.

"Nico, you should know all about this," Bruder said reproachfully. He picked up a small piece of wood and started carving it with a nasty-looking knife. "We've spoken many times about how Kolmogorov's theory could be applied to quantum physics."

Nico shifted uncomfortably. "Was that the one about chiral perturbation theory?"

Bruder sighed and shook his head. "I blame your mother. She was never serious enough about your education."

Nico's brow darkened. His hands closed into fists in his lap. Sophie felt sorry for him. He'd gone to a lot of trouble to find a dad who turned out to be a bizarre jerk. Now she was really wishing they'd stuck with Anat and Yosh. They'd probably be on a boat right now, instead of cloistered underground with a maniac.

"I'll do my best to break it down into layman's terms," Bruder continued, lapsing into a professorial tone. "There was an accident at the place where I worked. It created a rift, of sorts, that kicked off a chain reaction. Strangelets, mini black holes . . ." He tapped the wood against his palm as he ticked off each point. "Anyway, you were all caught in a sort of eddy, just like one in a river."

"We were in a river?" Declan asked. "That doesn't make any sense. And what are strangelets?"

"An eddy in the *space time* continuum, not a river," Bruder said laboriously. "Strangelets are a kind of matter containing an almost equal number of particles: up, down, and strange quarks. Although it's a good term for you, now," he added with a small laugh, shaking his head. "A bunch of strange-lets."

"But how did we get here?" Sophie asked, fighting back a wave of vertigo; none of this made any sense. She almost preferred Nico's nuclear accident explanation.

"That's the question, isn't it?" Bruder held up his hands, gesturing around them. "Odd that you were all consolidated in one location. Fascinating, really." He jumped to his feet and started to pace. "This turns several theories on their heads. If only Fitzgerald was still alive, I could run it past him, he might have some thoughts—"

"I'm sorry," Sophie interrupted. "What are you saying exactly? We time traveled?"

"Well, yes, in a manner of speaking," he said impatiently. "Although that's not really how it works."

"So what year is it?" Declan asked.

"Twenty thirty-three," Nico muttered.

"What?" Declan spun on him. "You knew?"

"He told me," Nico said defensively. "When I first saw him he looked so much older, I almost didn't recognize him."

"And you didn't tell us?" Sophie said.

Nico shrugged avoiding her eyes. "There wasn't time."

"All right, then." Declan ran a hand through his hair. "Bloody hell. So what are those creatures? Some sort of new animal? Because from what I remember about evolution, it takes a lot longer than twenty years for nature to come up with something like that."

"The thrinaxes? Oh, they've been evolving for millennia," Bruder said breezily. "Just not here."

"What do you mean, not here?" Sophie asked. A cold ball of fear had formed in her belly. None of this could be true. If it was twenty years later, that meant . . . what? Her sister was now thirty-three? And her parents were in their sixties? No, Bruder had to be insane. Maybe he'd suffered a breakdown when Nico fell into a coma, and this was all a fantasy he'd concocted.

But even as she thought it, Sophie couldn't repress the sense that this answered a lot of questions. "So where did they come from? The thrinaxes?"

"You don't seriously believe this?" Declan challenged her.

"I don't know," she said honestly. "But . . . we haven't really come up with a better explanation for how strange everything is, right? I mean, that could be why the roads and buildings are such a mess. And why the houses are so dusty."

"Where's everyone else, then?" Declan demanded.

"It was hard to come up with exact numbers without accurate data sampling, but I've estimated that about eighty percent of the world's population was lost to the cataclysm." Bruder's tone was off-handed, like he was talking about the weather.

Sophie shivered involuntarily. "Eighty percent of the people died?"

"I didn't say died," Bruder grumbled. "You really must pay attention. They were lost."

"Lost to what?" Sophie asked, her ire rising at his condescending tone. "You still haven't explained what the cataclysm was. Was it an earthquake? A volcanic eruption?"

"I told you," he said impatiently. "It was a rift in the space time continuum."

"And what started the cataclysm in the first place?"

"That's a bit complicated." Bruder tugged at his collar. Sophie got a sudden flash of what he must have looked like twenty years ago. "You see, there was an accident, of sorts."

"The Collider," Nico said suddenly. "It was the Collider, wasn't it?"

"Yes." Bruder got that faraway look again, like he could see it unfolding before him. "There was an . . . experiment." He hesitated, then continued, "It didn't go as expected."

"So basically," Declan said softly. "Almost everyone on the planet is gone, but not dead?"

"Exactly," Bruder said, jabbing the air with the knife before returning to his whittling. "They're just someplace else. Although almost everyone who withstood the cataclysm has been killed by the thrinaxes," he amended. "Vicious predators, they jumped right to the top of the food chain. It's been years since I've seen another person, in fact. Although I suppose there are probably more on the mainland."

"So where did everyone go?" Declan demanded. "The eighty percent who were lost in the cataclysm?"

Bruder shrugged. "Your guess is as good as mine. There are potentially infinite alternate universes out there. They're probably scattered across them."

"The many-worlds theory," Nico said in a hushed voice.

"Exactly." Bruder looked pleased. "So you retained something, at least."

"English, please!" Declan said with exasperation.

"It's a quantum theory," Nico's gaze flitted from his father to the bare earth floor. "It's really not that complicated. Basically, a guy named DeWitt figured out that every possible outcome of every event exists in its own world. So everything that could possibly have happened, but didn't, might be happening somewhere else."

"I saw a show about this once," Sophie suddenly remembered. "It said that there might be an alternate universe where Germany won World War II."

"Exactly," Nico said. "Or even smaller things, like say that one morning you decided to take the train instead of the bus. Theoretically, there might be another you who took the bus, and that might have led to a whole series of other events that changed the rest of your life. So there's a version of you living an alternate life in a different dimension."

"That's completely nutters," Declan said, but his face had gone pale again.

"So the . . ." Sophie began.

"Thrinaxes," Bruder supplied helpfully.

"Right, them," Sophie said, working it through in her mind. "You're saying that when everyone else got sucked through these little black holes—"

"Mini black holes, technically," Bruder corrected. "Strangelets."

"The thrinaxes got sucked here, from somewhere else?"

"Precisely!" Bruder clapped his hands together. "So you're not all cretins. Other things came through too, of course, though most weren't quite as deadly."

"What are they? The thrinaxes, I mean," Sophie asked. "We found . . . bones. And what looked like a nest."

"My guess is that they're related to modern-day alligators. It's possible that in their dimension, there was never a great extinction."

"Hang on," Declan protested. "Are you saying those things are bloody dinosaurs?"

"In a manner of speaking, yes." Bruder added, "Their world must be fascinating. Just imagine what we could learn by studying it. Shame we couldn't replicate the event."

"Yes, such a shame," Declan said. "Unless, of course, that might bring everything back to the way it was."

"Impossible." Bruder furrowed his brow. "Don't you think I already would have tried? Even if I managed to restart the Collider—which, by the way, is an extraordinarily complicated piece of equipment that requires a significant energy source—we could end up in any of an infinite number of realities. And there's almost no chance of bringing anyone back to this one, in the past or otherwise."

"No chance?" Sophie said faintly. "So you're saying . . . we're stuck here?"

"Most definitely," Bruder said. After a beat, he added, "Sorry."

Sophie saw her own shock and horror reflected in Declan's eyes as the true magnitude of the situation hit them. There would be no calling home. No families left to return to. No school, she realized, no government. Just this . . . a hole in the ground, and monsters everywhere.

The thought made her feel faint. The ceiling was too close overhead. The walls pressed inward. She was suddenly convinced that there wasn't enough air down here, and they were all slowly suffocating.

"But *Vater*," Nico said, looking perplexed. "No one would have survived entry into a mini black hole."

"Jaysus, you're focused on *that*?" Declan barked.

Sophie felt his hand lightly stroking her back. It grounded her, and her breathing slowed. Panicking wouldn't solve anything.

"Excellent, Nico." Bruder beamed at him. "Your mother was wrong; you do possess a scientific mind. There's a process called spaghettification, where the gravity at your feet is much greater than that at your head. So theoretically, if you were drawn into a mini black hole, you'd be stretched as if on a rack, until you finally splintered into atoms."

"Brilliant," Declan muttered, "Well, last I checked, we don't all look like piles of atoms."

"Precisely," Bruder said. "Which is why all of this is impossible to explain. It completely defies the laws of physics. If you really had slipped through a rift, none of you should have survived. Including the thrinaxes."

"So how do you explain it, then?" Declan demanded.

Bruder shrugged. "Obviously the original theories were wrong. You're living proof of that."

After a long beat, Declan said, "So to sum up, you're saying that we're twenty years in the future, all the people are basically gone, and there are monsters running around?"

Bruder shifted uncomfortably for a minute. Then he shrugged again. "Yes. I suppose you could say that."

CHAPTER ELEVEN

"Twenty years?" Anat said incredulously. The Glock was still pointed directly at Yosh's sternum.

"Or so," Yosh said. "Based on what we've learned from your culture, that seems a fair estimate."

"What do you mean, what you learned from our culture?" Anat demanded. "You can't possibly have been here for twenty years."

Yosh smiled. "No, I was born here. My parents arrived twenty years ago."

"That's insane," Anat argued as she checked her peripheral vision. The creatures were holding their positions, staring down at her with slitted yellow eyes. The metal gate to the outside was down, and she had no idea if there were any other exits. She had to keep stalling for time, and hope that an escape opportunity arose. Yosh was smiling at her, as if guessing her thoughts. Anat wondered just how extensive her mind reading skills were.

"It makes sense when you think about it, though, doesn't it?"

"Maybe Long Island is always like this," Anat grumbled.

Yosh laughed out loud. "You're actually very funny, Anat, even though you don't think so."

"I have no reason to believe you," Anat snarled. Yosh was clearly mocking her, and she hated that more than anything. Her finger depressed the trigger a fraction; she could picture a hole forming right in the center of the girl's forehead. That would wipe the irritating grin from her face.

"I have no reason to lie to you. Not anymore, at least."

Anat mulled that over. She caught herself fervently hoping that this was all just a terrible dream. Maybe she'd hit her head in the tunnel and was actually unconscious right now. Any moment now she'd awaken in her bed back home. Or better yet, in the hotel room with Hazim. She tried to picture his arms around her, his mouth against her ear, murmuring all the things he'd promised time and again. His hands clasping hers, their rings shining . . .

"All right," she finally said. "So if you're right, and we're twenty years in the future, where is everyone else?"

"Dead, mostly," Yosh said impassively. "Although there weren't many left when we came. At least, that's what my parents told me."

"Where are your parents?"

"They fell ill a few years ago," Yosh said, her voice flat and emotionless. "They're dead now, too."

"So how did you end up with us?"

"We live near the facility. A few of my parents' friends realized early on that the Collider had something to do with how we came to be here. We've been experimenting with it for years. The last test was a few days ago; that's probably how you all ended up here."

"So you decided to pretend to be one of us?" Anat asked.

"Yes, because we need help," Yosh admitted. "There's not enough food here anymore. We need to go home."

"What are you talking about?" Anat jerked her head toward the shelves. "There's plenty of food around."

"For us, maybe, but not for the cynogs. They're dying off." Yosh sounded genuinely sad about it. "The fresh meat ran out quickly. We've tried to feed them other food, but it makes them sick."

Anat eyed the creatures surrounding Yosh. They stared back, their eyes flat and menacing. "So what do they eat?"

"Anything large," Yosh said dismissively. "They started with the bigger animals."

Anat didn't really want to know, but she forced herself to ask anyway. "They ate the people?"

"Yes," Yosh said. "But there aren't enough left now, and there are too many of us. We need to find another food source. This planet . . ." She looked around the grocery store and wrinkled her nose. "It's not right for us. I hate it here. The stories my parents told me, about our world . . . it sounds like a better place." She murmured something soothing to the creature beside her.

It was such a weird scene that Anat was having trouble processing it. She forced herself to focus and asked, "I still don't understand what you want from us. Why are you keeping us alive?"

"I was curious. I've never met one of you before."

Shifting uncomfortably under her gaze, Anat asked, "How many of you are there?"

Yosh smiled. "Still trying to figure out a plan, Anat? I have to say, in many ways, you're the most interesting of all. So different from what I've read about girls."

"If all the girls hadn't been eaten, you wouldn't have had to read about them in books," Anat muttered.

Yosh casually leaned against the creature beside her and stroked its nose. It shifted, nuzzling against her side like a cat. *A giant, terrifying, lizard cat*, Anat thought.

"Don't blame me," Yosh said airily. "Most of the people were gone before I was even born."

Anat watched, fascinated in spite of herself, as the creature emitted clicking sounds as if it was . . . purring? "Can you really get these things to do what you tell them to?"

"That's the way it's always been," Yosh said. "We speak the same language. They're kind of like . . . what's the word for the small animals you kept in your houses?"

"Pets?" Anat said dubiously.

"Yes, pets. I should have liked to have seen a dog," Yosh said wistfully. "There are some wonderful books about them."

After several deep breaths, Anat lowered the Glock. She'd keep it in reserve for later; it was no good to her at the moment anyway. And much as she longed to put a hole in Yosh, the creatures would probably set upon her immediately. "So what do you want me to do?"

"We're going for a drive," Yosh announced. "Back the way we came."

Anat's heart sank. Every mile she traveled only seemed to take her farther away from Hazim. "And if I say no?"

"Then . . ." Yosh shrugged. "I suppose we won't have any more use for you."

Declan was dreaming. Katie was in his arms, and he was stroking her hair. She shifted closer to him, and he wrapped his arms more tightly around her.

"That feels nice," a sleepy voice said.

He started awake. He was embracing Sophie, not Katie. Her eyes were still closed, and she had a small smile on her lips. He drew away carefully, and she adjusted in her sleep.

She was a pretty girl—and so different from Katie, but not in a bad way. He felt guilty for even having such thoughts. Katie was the only girl he'd ever dated, the girl he'd had a crush on since they were both in primary school. But right now, she seemed very far away. And Sophie . . . well, she was something. The way she'd saved him yesterday, pulling him up that tree. She exuded a sense of calm strength, iron at her core. He felt safe with her. It was strange and unsettling, but true. Being with her felt like home, even in this foreign place.

Sophie's eyes opened. She covered her mouth as she yawned and blinked sleepily at him. "We still in the crazy house?" she whispered after a second.

"'Fraid so," he said, resisting the urge to brush her cheek with his hand. "You sleep all right?"

"Really well," she said, looking around. "I need to get me one of these ground mattresses."

Declan repressed a chuckle. They were curled up on one side of the cave, with Nico and his dad at the other. The fire had gone out, so the only light came from the small hole in the ceiling. It was hard to tell what time they'd fallen asleep, but he felt well rested for the first time since arriving here.

"Now what?" she asked in a low voice.

"I don't know." After everything Bruder had told them last night, their original plan seemed like a bad idea. Was it really possible that most of the world's population was gone, and that they'd only find similar devastation on the mainland? Bruder claimed to have made forays there over the years, encountering only a handful of survivors. More important, Katie was now in her mid-thirties, and he was still just a kid. If she'd survived the thrinaxes and hadn't been whisked off to some strange alternate dimension, that is.

Sophie must have been thinking along similar lines. In a low voice she asked, "Do you believe him?"

"Nico said his dad was quite a bit older, yeah?" he responded. "And it explains why everything is such a mess out there."

"He's got to be at least sixty," Sophie agreed. "But then, we don't know if Nico is telling the truth. Maybe his dad was old to start with."

"I know. Odd thing to lie about though, yeah?"

"I suppose. But it's all odd."

They both fell silent. Declan realized that he couldn't necessarily trust what any of the others had claimed about themselves. Except for Sophie, he amended—he could tell that she was honest to the core. But he'd been suspicious of Nico from the start.

Still, Bruder's story explained a lot of things. And why would he and Nico have set all this up? The bit about the coma, and the lizard things . . . if this was a long con, they were certainly outdoing themselves for a bunch of penniless kids. Of every explanation they'd come up with so far, Bruder's crazy ramblings made the most sense. And at least it meant they were still alive and not in purgatory. Which was kind of comforting. Plus he had a lovely girl in his arms, so all things considered, it could be worse. He looked into Sophie's enormous eyes and asked, "What do you want to do?"

"We need to find the others," Sophie said decisively. "We can decide together."

"Grand. Hopefully they didn't meet up with any of those tri-things."

"Thrinaxes," Sophie said.

"Right." The whole concept made Declan's head hurt. *Dinosaurs*, of all things. *Jaysus*.

"Maybe it can be fixed," Sophie said quietly.

A twig or something was poking his side; Declan shifted off it, which moved him farther back from Sophie. She frowned slightly but didn't say anything. "He said there was no way, remember? An infinite number of realities, and all that."

"Right, but maybe's he's lying. Like you said, we don't know if we can trust him."

"True enough. But why would he want things to stay like this?"

"He has Nico now," Sophie pointed out. "Alive, and not in a coma. Maybe he wouldn't want to risk losing that."

"Maybe," Declan admitted. Everything Bruder had said last night was jumbled in his brain, something about spaghetti and strangelets. "So what are you proposing? We march him back to the lab and demand that he give it a whirl?"

"Maybe Nico can convince him," Sophie said. "I'll try to talk to him alone, see if I can get him to listen."

Declan wasn't thrilled by that idea. For one thing, he didn't like the idea of Sophie owing Nico any favors. And the way Bruder kept eyeing Sophie was enough to make him want to punch the bastard.

But then, what was the alternative? For the two of them to set up camp in the woods, trying to live off roots and berries? He really didn't want to spend the rest of his life holed up underground, trying not to be devoured by a dinosaur while mastering a dozen ways to prepare worms and acorns.

In truth, he hadn't a clue what to do.

"You're awake," Bruder growled from across the room.

They both started. Sophie gave Declan a wary look, then they both sat up. Bruder hunched across from them, hands crossed over his knees, eyes cloaked. He bent forward and lit one of the small homemade candles. The wick was nearly at the base; it guttered, sending a stream of oily black smoke upward.

"Looks like it's morning," Sophie said. "We should probably go find our friends and explain everything that's happened to them."

"I'm staying here," Nico declared from the shadows. "With my dad."

"Your choice, mate," Declan said, secretly relieved. One problem solved.

"Do we need wood or anything?" Sophie said tentatively. "Maybe Nico and I could go gather it."

"Don't bother," Bruder said airily. "There is more than enough for the two of us."

"Water, then?"

"We're fine," Nico said with finality.

"All righty then." Declan stood and clapped his hands together, ignoring the pointed looks Sophie was throwing his way. "Guess we'll be off."

"Tell Anat . . . " Nico paused, then said, "Just tell her that if she ever needs anything, she can come stay with us."

Based on the few days they'd spent together, Declan knew that the chances of Anat admitting she needed anything from anyone was about as likely as him sprouting a pair of wings, but he nodded. "Sure, mate. See yas."

"Hang on," Sophie said, a slight edge of panic undercutting her voice. She turned to Bruder. "So that's it, then? You're just sending us out there on our own?"

Bruder shrugged, looking puzzled. "Would you like a whistle? I have an extra one."

"No, I don't want a damn whistle," Sophie snapped. "I just can't believe you're not offering to help us more."

"Why would I help you?" Bruder sounded genuinely bewildered.

"Because we came back here with your son, even though we could have gone with our friends!" Sophie was practically shouting now, and her eyes seemed to be throwing off sparks. "Instead, we helped Nico find *you*, and all you offer us is a whistle? God, we're just a couple of kids! What's wrong with you?"

Bruder blinked rapidly and shook his head. "I . . . I guess I hadn't really . . ."

"And you!" She spun to face Nico. "You're even worse. Great, you found your dad. Well, the rest of us just found out that everyone we know might be dead or gone, and we're all on our own in a really dangerous place. And you're just going to stay here with him, while we go back out there? What about Anat and Yosh?"

Nico swallowed. He glanced at his father. "I guess . . . you could stay if you want. Right, *Vater*?"

"Of course," Bruder said, recovering. "Stay as long as you like."

"Now hang on," Declan protested. This wasn't going at all the way he'd hoped. "I say we head back to the infirmary, hole up there . . ."

"No," Sophie said firmly. "We're all going together to find Anat and Yosh. Then we're going back to the Collider—"

"It's much safer here," Bruder interrupted. "I'm surprised that you didn't encounter the others at the facility. The area is usually swarming with them."

The others? Declan thought. Was he talking about the dinosaurs again? "Well, there was something—"

"I want you to try and restart the Collider," Sophie stated firmly.

"I told you, that's impossible." Bruder said. "It's not as if I can simply plug in a date and time and send us back there."

"But you could try to replicate what happened last time. I mean, you were there, right?"

"Yes. I was there." His tone was flat.

"So maybe you could just do what they did," Sophie offered. "I mean, it certainly couldn't make things any worse."

"Of course it could! I have my son with me now. If I retrigger the cataclysm, we could all be swept into another dimension. One without air, or water. One where the chance of human survival would be negligible." He shook his head. "It's simply not worth the risk."

"The risk?" Now Declan was angry. He pictured his mum and Katie, living in a hole like this for a couple decades. "Doesn't seem like you thought much about risk when you turned that machine on in the first place."

"It was a controlled experiment," Bruder said. "All the necessary precautions were taken."

It was too dark for Declan to clearly see his eyes, but it was hard to shake the sense that the bastard was lying. Something about his tone whenever he mentioned the experiment indicated there was more to the story than he was saying.

"I'm truly sorry. I know this has all been a shock," Bruder said. "But you'll learn to make the best of things. This world isn't so bad, once you get used to it."

They stood in silence for a minute.

"So that's it, then," Sophie said. Her voice was laden with defeat. Declan stepped close and wrapped an arm around her shoulder, but she stayed stiff and resistant. "We're stuck here."

"Nico and I can help you find the others," Bruder offered. "If you'd like."

"No. Just stay here in your hole and hide." She turned and marched toward the dark corridor. Declan had to hurry to catch her.

"You're sure about this?" he asked in a low voice.

"I'm sure. Screw them," she said firmly. "We'll be fine without them."

Declan wasn't as confident about that, but he didn't say anything. Now that they were going topside, he was having a hard time blocking out the image of the creature from yesterday. Much as he disliked the Bruders, Nico's dad had managed to survive out here for a good long time. Probably not a bad idea to have him as a tour guide, at least for a bit. And his stomach was rumbling again; he really wished Sophie could have saved the whole storming off thing until after breakfast. He sighed. Apparently that strong will he so admired had its drawbacks.

The base of the ladder was faintly haloed by light filtering down from overhead. As he helped her onto the bottom rung, footsteps echoed down the tunnel behind them.

"Sophie! Declan!" Nico called out. "Wait!"

Declan turned, hoping that Nico was holding a plate of eggs and bangers. No such luck, though; he had the same water bottle they'd taken from the facility and a small rucksack on his back.

"I'm coming with you," Nico said, panting slightly.

"Yeah?" Declan asked. "You sure?"

"I'm sure."

"What about your father?" Sophie asked warily.

"He's not happy about it," Nico admitted. "But I told him you were right." He examined the floor. "I owe you two for coming with me. I can't let you go out there alone."

"And a fat lot of help you were," Declan grumbled, but

Sophie jabbed him in the rib cage with her elbow to shut him up.

"Just until you find the others," Nico clarified. "Then I'm coming back."

"Fine," Sophie said. "You can help explain everything."

"Better you than me," Declan said. "I can just imagine how well Anat will take the news. You'll be lucky if she doesn't take your head off."

They all fell silent. Declan figured they were thinking the same thing he was, wondering if Anat was even still alive.

"Well, let's go," Sophie said with forced bravado. "They're probably already at the meet spot."

Nico went first up the ladder, shoving aside the concealing branches at the top. Sophie followed a minute later. Declan glanced back down the tunnel. Bruder hovered silently at the far end, his stooped form cast in silhouette.

Declan turned away and started climbing. He pulled himself over the dirt lip surrounding the hole and squeezed out the gap between boulders. Sophie and Nico stood there waiting for him. It was cooler than yesterday, a crispness in the air hinted at autumn. *Lovely weather for 2033*, he thought to himself.

"Let's head back to the car," Nico said. "Keep your eyes open for thrinaxes. My dad gave me a flute just in case, but I'm not sure how to use it."

"Right," Declan agreed. They collected the weapons they'd stashed the night before. *Not that a hoe will be much use against a dinosaur, but what the hell*, Declan thought. Worst case scenario, it could double as a walking stick.

Sophie shuffled ahead of him, her head bowed. Something occurred to him.

"Hey," he said, scurrying to catch up. "If we went back to how things were, you might be sick again, right?"

"Probably." Sophie's eyes darted up to meet his, then focused back on the path in front of her.

"So why would you want that?"

She shrugged. "I was ready to die. But everyone else on the planet probably didn't feel that way. Especially my parents, and Nora. Knowing that they'd be fine made it easier for me to let go."

"So you'd give up your life, then? For people you've never even met?"

She gave him a curious look. "Of course," she said. "Wouldn't you?"

Declan thought it over. Going back, the worst thing he'd have to face would be that Russian in the alley. Funny, after confronting an honest-to-God dinosaur, that bastard didn't seem nearly as frightening. But if he knew that returning would guarantee a bullet in his head, although other people would survive . . . tough choice. "Maybe. If I knew for certain that my mum and . . . other people I care about would be safe," he finished lamely. It was hard for him to say Katie's name out loud. He was still having a hard time letting go of the guilt, although if Bruder was telling the truth, he and Katie had technically been broken up for decades.

Sophie grazed her finger along a tree trunk as she walked past it. After a minute, she said ruefully, "When I woke up here and realized I was still alive, I was pretty angry about it."

"Really? Because you've been fighting awfully hard to stay alive," he pointed out.

She laughed at that.

Nico turned and scowled at them. "We need to be quiet," he warned.

"You're right. Sorry," Sophie whispered. She turned back to Declan and said, "I got a chance to *feel* alive again. That part has been kind of fun. Among other things," she added with a small smile, avoiding his eyes.

Declan could feel a grin tugging at the corners of his mouth. She was right; in spite of everything, parts of it had been bloody fantastic. "Remind me to never go on holiday with you."

"Oh, but you already are," Sophie said with a smile. "This is as close as I've come to a vacation in years."

"Bad lot, then. You should complain to your travel agent when you get back."

Sophie was opening her mouth to reply when a yell cut her off. They both froze. Nico turned back toward them, a puzzled expression on his face.

"Is it one of them?" Sophie asked in a hushed voice.

There was rapid movement, closing in. A second later, Bruder crashed through the undergrowth.

"Dad?" Nico said uncertainly. "Did you—"

"Run!" Bruder screamed, his eyes wild. "They're coming!"

CHAPTER TWELVE

Anat's fingers gripped the steering wheel. Unlike yesterday, she drove slowly, carefully swerving to avoid cars and potholes.

As before, Yosh sat in the back staring passively through the windshield.

It was all contributing to a strange sense of déjà vu. She kept her eyes focused forward to avoid looking at their unlikely escorts.

A phalanx of Yosh's "pets" kept pace with their car. Eight of them had emerged from the dark recesses of the grocery store last night. Under instructions from Yosh, Anat had eaten some of the stale food from the shelves; crackers, mostly, and a few cans of pears. Then she'd tried to sleep.

Every time Anat opened her eyes, she found one of the creatures standing watch over her. She'd kept the Glock clutched in both hands—they'd made no effort to retrieve it from her. Not that it would be much use. Under that smelly fur, their bodies were covered in thick, armor-like scales. She'd spent most of the night rigid with terror, her mind racing, trying to come up with an escape plan.

But right before they left the store, Yosh took the Glock from her. For a moment Anat had considered fighting, but she was surrounded by the creatures—*keep watching and waiting*, she thought grudgingly. She still had other weapons anyway; less effective ones, but the throwing stars were tucked away in her pocket. Yosh didn't know about those.

After finding a car in the parking lot that started on the fourth try, they set off. Yosh had instructed her to drive back the way they came. "I'll tell you when to turn," she'd said as she settled into the center of the backseat.

So here they were, retracing their steps. All of her questions about the other three kids had been dismissed.

"They'll be there," Yosh assured her. "It's been taken care of."

Anat tried not to think about what she meant by that. From the sound of it, Yosh somehow knew that the others were alive. Maybe when they were all together again, there would be an opportunity to craft a plan. *But to what end?* she reminded herself. If any of this was true, Hazim was long gone.

Even if he had survived, he would be twenty years older and half a planet away, in a world without any functioning transportation systems. He might as well be on the moon. He'd probably married someone else. He might even have children. The thought made her feel physically ill.

"I can drive if you like," Yosh offered placidly. "My father taught me."

"They have cars where you come from?"

"No. But we figured yours out soon after getting here," Yosh said. "In general we don't use them, though. The penalties for venturing outside your own territory are severe."

"Who sets the boundaries?" Anat asked. In her personal experience, confining people to "territories" never worked out well.

"We have leaders, just like you did," Yosh said. "But generally, we're left to manage on our own."

"Are the other territories having trouble with their . . . food supply, too?" she asked.

"That's what I've heard," Yosh said. "Although we don't get information as regularly as those on the mainland."

"So your people are everywhere on the planet, then?" Anat had no idea if the information would prove helpful but figured it couldn't hurt to find out as much as possible. According to her instructors, intelligence gathering always provided an edge. Of course, they probably hadn't been referring to this type of situation.

"I have no idea," Yosh said, sounding bored. "Maybe."

Anat mulled that over. It didn't sound like there was much communication available, even though Yosh had that mind reading ability. There were probably limits to it, maybe related to distance. She filed that away. "And these . . . pets of yours—"

"We call them cynogs," Yosh supplied helpfully.

"Right. Aside from them, and you, nothing else from your world came through?"

"A few smaller things, like dumas and yoris," Yosh said. "They ate up a lot of the smaller wildlife. But my parents said we were pretty much the dominant creatures in our world."

Top of the food chain, like us, Anat thought.

"Some of my people studied your books to find out more about the animals. But most of them disappeared in the first few years. The cynogs require a lot of food. By the time they realized we might be here permanently, it was too late to start farming them."

"That was stupid."

Yosh met her eyes in the rearview mirror. "It was. I agree."

Anat's eyes flicked toward the creature outside her window. It turned its head a fraction of an inch; yellow snake-eyes bored into her own. She repressed a shudder. "Where am I driving us, anyway?"

"Back to the facility."

"The facility?" Anat said, surprised. "Why there?"

"You'll see. No more questions."

Sophie was exhausted. It felt like she'd been running for hours, although it had probably only been thirty minutes or so. Every time she fell against a tree, trying to catch her breath, another thrinax appeared and she was forced to dash headlong through the woods again.

She'd lost sight of the others, although occasionally a high-pitched scream tore through the trees. It was hard to tell if it was a cry of terror, or one of *them*. Her feet throbbed, blisters rising where the ill-fitting shoes chafed her heels. She was hot and sweaty and thirsty. What little strength she'd regained over the past few days had entirely dissipated.

Declan, she thought. *Please be okay.*

When Bruder had suddenly appeared, she'd frozen. Declan spurred her into motion, yelling in her ear, "You heard the man—run! I'll draw them away."

Then he raced past Bruder, sprinting *toward* those things.

And like a coward, she'd done exactly what he'd told her to do. She'd run the other way.

She couldn't stop picturing him on the ground with a

group of those creatures hunched over him, tearing at his flesh with their long, nasty claws . . . She wiped away tears with the back of her hand and tried to get her bearings. The sun was still low over the trees, it was probably late morning.

Sophie had a terrible sense of direction to start with. She had no idea how far she was from the underground cave and doubted she'd be able to find it again.

Movement in the bushes behind her. Fighting panic, Sophie scrambled to a rotted fallen tree and crawled underneath, wedging herself in the gap between it and the ground. Rough bark scraped her cheek, and she could feel her T-shirt and jeans absorbing dampness from the mud below. She wasn't completely concealed, but maybe they wouldn't spot her.

Leaves crunched on the far side of the clearing. Sophie peeked out. Two thrinaxes had emerged from the woods. One was bent nearly double by the weight of something slung over its shoulder. Their heads turned from side to side, scanning the clearing. Sophie held her breath and squeezed her eyes shut, praying they wouldn't see her. Seconds later, the sound of retreating footsteps. Sophie opened her eyes: they were moving past; she hadn't been discovered. She'd remain hidden until they were definitely gone, then try to figure out where she was.

The thrinax in the lead shifted right, and she caught a glimpse of what it was carrying: Declan. His arms dangled lifelessly, and blood stained the back of his hands. He looked dead.

Sophie gasped involuntarily.

It wasn't a loud noise, but the forest was so silent she might as well have screamed. The creatures stopped and turned back toward her. Their eyes flickered as they approached. One bent low and reached long talons under the log, latching on to her leg. She kicked and clawed at the ground as it dragged her out, tearing up clumps of dirt as she fought to get free.

The thrinax was too strong. Sophie cried out as it gave her leg a sharp tug; she slid into the sunlight. As it bent low over her, a claw raked open a narrow seam along the length of her arm. The last thing Sophie saw before losing consciousness was a horrible mouth gaping open to reveal dangling tentacles and rows of teeth.

CHAPTER THIRTEEN

Declan blinked a few times—the room seemed awfully bright. His tongue felt too big for his mouth, too, and he was terribly thirsty. Clearly he'd had too much to drink last night. His head throbbed. This was worse than a hangover; he must have gotten into a fight, as well . . .

"He's waking up," someone said. "Declan? How do you feel?"

"Like shite," he said truthfully. Sophie and Anat swam into focus; they were bent over him, looking concerned. He groaned. The memory of where he was flooded back; and *when* it was.

"Are you hurt?" Sophie asked anxiously.

"I don't know. Am I? I feel wrecked." He tried to take a physical inventory, but everything felt sore.

"Minor cuts on your hands," Sophie said. "Maybe a blow to your head. Do you remember what day it is?"

"Never figured that out, did we?"

"Nope." Sophie sounded relieved. "But you remember that, so you're probably fine."

"I'm a long way from fine," he grumbled. "Since apparently we're still trapped in this bloody nightmare." He managed to raise himself up on one elbow. "Where are we now?"

"Back at the Collider." Anat stood over Sophie's shoulder. She didn't look pleased to see him, but then she never looked pleased about anything. He, on the other hand, had to admit that he was pretty feckin' happy she was alive.

"Hallo, Anat. Did you have as much fun as we did out in the great unknown?"

She made a disparaging noise. "No fun. You?"

"Could've been better." He eased up to sitting, wincing as the movement caused his head to throb with pain. "So we're at the facility again? How the hell did we all get here?"

"They carried us," Sophie said grimly. "Be glad you were unconscious for most of it."

Now that she mentioned it, Declan remembered bouncing along as the ground below moved swiftly past, his nostrils full of the stench of matted fur. "Carried us? Why?"

"Yosh was born here." Anat's face was smeared with dirt and her hair was tangled, but other than that she appeared none the worse for wear. "She's with them."

"What do you mean, with them? Christ, I really must've hit my head," he muttered. "Neither of you is making any sense at all."

Sophie glanced at Anat, then said, "I guess that Yosh grew up here, after the cataclysm thing that Bruder described. She's not really from Japan."

"Not *our* Japan," Anat added.

"Right, many worlds and all that." Declan rubbed his forehead with one hand. What he'd give for an aspirin right about now. "So you're saying she knew what was going on all along."

"Right. And she can control those thrinax things. You were right, about her stopping them when she screamed. They're kind of like pets, right?" Sophie looked to Anat for confirmation.

"Pets," Anat spat. "Nasty killer pets that eat people."

"Right," Sophie said faintly. "Anyway, they dumped us in here."

"Where's Nico and his dad? Did they get away?" he asked, taking in the rest of the room. It was a small space, just a few meters wide, empty save for a table pushed up against the wall. Some sort of utility closet, maybe?

"No, they were captured, too," Sophie admitted. "But, they separated us when we got here. Anat arrived about an hour ago."

"Huh." He ducked his head between his knees, mainly because if he didn't, he'd either start vomiting or pass out. "So what happens to us now, then?"

"They'll probably kill us," Anat said matter-of-factly. "The cynogs will eat us."

"Cynogs?"

"That's what Yosh calls the thrinaxes," Sophie explained.

"That's just grand." Declan rubbed his eyes. "Don't suppose I could trouble one of you to knock me out again? This is all a bit much."

"We're getting out," Anat said, crossing her arms in front of her chest.

"Oh, yeah? And how will we be doing that?"

"You broke out of your room, right?" Sophie said. "Do you think you can get us out of here?"

Declan fought off a wave of wooziness. *Right. Time to get it together.* "No vents?"

"Not in this room. We already checked."

Declan lifted his head and squinted at the door. The thought of standing up was overwhelming. But the two girls were staring expectantly at him. Sophie's enormous green eyes were filled with anxiety and fear.

"Let's have a look." His first attempt to get to his feet failed miserably—he swayed and dropped immediately back to his knees.

"Let me help," Sophie said, rushing forward.

"Suppose you do owe me a bit of carrying around, eh?" he said weakly.

She smiled as she helped him up. By leaning heavily on her shoulder, he managed to get to his feet. She walked him to the door. His legs felt funny, they kept trying to step across each other. "Must've taken a pretty solid knock," he remarked as the room spun.

"You have a big lump on your head," Anat announced. "Probably a concussion."

"Lovely."

He planted both hands against the door and leaned over, examining the bolt. It was almost identical to the one in the room he'd first woken up in, which was a stroke of luck.

"Can you pick it?" Sophie asked anxiously.

"Sure." Declan fumbled in his pocket for his kit. His fingers felt clumsy too, and he hoped he hadn't spoken too soon. The last lock had taken hours, and he'd been in top form then. He kind of doubted they had that much time on their hands. Still, he declared, "Won't take a minute." He dropped to one knee and took a deep breath. Digging through his kit, he removed the two picks he'd used last time. One was slightly bent, but hopefully that wouldn't matter. He felt Sophie and Anat hovering at his shoulder.

"Bit tough with an audience," he grumbled.

"Sorry," Sophie said. "We'll just wait over here."

They stepped toward the back of the room and started talking in low murmurs. On the plus side, the two of them were finally getting along. He tuned them out, focusing solely on the lock.

Time slipped away as he concentrated. Even the throbbing in his head dissipated as he fell into the familiar zone. His field of vision narrowed to the bolt and the picks. He pressed his ear to the door, listening for the sound of tumblers shifting, jimmying the picks slightly in one direction, then another. After each failed attempt he started over, silently praying that the picks wouldn't snap off in the lock. Finally, after what felt like an eternity, the tumblers responded and he heard an audible *click*.

"You did it!" Sophie exclaimed, rushing forward to wrap her arms around him.

"Always knew God gave me this gift for a reason," Declan said, swiping a hand across his forehead as he sank back on his heels. He felt shaky, exhausted. "Not exactly eager to see what's there, though."

"I wish they hadn't taken Nico," Sophie said. "He might know more about this place."

"Well, they did," Anat stated bluntly. "And we have no weapons. Be quiet and stay behind me." She stepped past him and grabbed the door handle. "Ready?"

"As I'll ever be," Declan muttered. He leaned on Sophie as they followed Anat out of the room, trying to muffle his footsteps.

They found themselves in what looked like an employee break room: a dusty vending machine against the far wall, assorted tables and chairs.

"No dinosaurs yet," he said in a low voice. "That's encouraging."

Anat shushed him with a frown. They eased across the room to the opposite door. She pressed her ear against it, then pulled it open. Declan peered over her shoulder down a long, narrow hallway similar to the one they'd first used to leave the building. Bare concrete floors and walls were cast in an eerie red light by shoulder-height emergency bulbs. There were metal doors off either side of it, all unmarked. Anat moved forward stealthily, silent as a cat. He and Sophie tried to match her furtiveness, but in spite of their efforts footsteps echoed and reverberated.

Suddenly, he heard voices approaching.

"Someone's coming!" Sophie hissed.

Anat jerked her head toward a door on the right. She opened it a crack and peeped around it, then flung it wide and darted inside. He and Sophie barely managed to follow before it closed behind them. Pitch blackness. Vertigo. He stumbled and nearly fell, but Sophie caught his arm, bracing him. Together they leaned against the wall, breathing hard.

The sound of people entering the hallway they'd just come from.

"If you don't do it, we'll kill your son."

"Is that Yosh?" Sophie whispered in his ear.

It was hard to tell; the voice sounded familiar, but different. Not that Yosh had been much of a talker to begin with, so he couldn't say either way. "Maybe."

"Shh!" Anat hissed.

"If I activate the Collider, there's a chance we all die. Besides, there's no guarantee it will even start. The power demands alone are well beyond what's available."

That voice he *did* recognize—Bruder. So they wanted him

to start the machine again. Funny that they all seemed to have the same idea.

Yet even when faced with monsters, Bruder still refused to give in. Declan couldn't help but be impressed. The bastard had a set of stones on him, he'd give him that. If their circumstances were reversed, Declan would be doing pretty much anything they asked.

"We've already taken care of that," Yosh said impatiently. "The solar panels will provide all the power you need."

"And you know this because you're a trained physicist?" Bruder's voice was filled with disdain. Declan suppressed a grin. He was liking Nico's dad more by the minute.

"So we'll kill you and your son," Yosh said in a hard voice. "Is that what you want?"

A pause, then Bruder replied, "Even if we could precisely recreate the circumstances of the cataclysm, there's no guarantee that will send you back to your point of origin. We could all be swept into an entirely different dimension. You might die if I do this."

"We're willing to take that chance."

Their footsteps receded down the hall, the voices fading with them.

"They're trying to do it again," Sophie said after the last echo had disappeared. She sounded just as scared as he felt.

"Grand idea," Declan said stonily. "Wonder what exciting place we'll land in this time."

"What if it works?" Anat asked quietly.

The room was too dark for him to see, but he discerned a note of something unexpected in her voice: hope.

"Bruder doesn't seem to think so, and he'd know, yeah?" Declan didn't add what he thought: *if Bruder was so reluctant even when his son's life was being threatened, the chances of something truly awful happening must be extreme.* But at the moment, he was having a hard time mustering the strength to care whether or not they restarted the Collider. His head was pounding, and his throat ached from thirst. "I say we focus on getting out."

"Agreed. See if you can find the lights," Anat said. "We need weapons."

"So no luck with the gun store, then?"

"I found a Glock there," Anat said, her voice more forlorn than he'd ever heard it. "But that *bat zona* took it from me."

"Shame, that," he muttered. "A gun would've come in handy."

Sophie's hands brushed lightly across his chest as she fumbled across the wall. "Sorry," she apologized.

"No problem," Declan said, but her touch had sent a small electric current through him. He swallowed again.

Suddenly, the lights flicked on; the glare made him wince. After his eyes adjusted, he could see that they were in another storage closet. This one had an industrial bucket in the corner with a mop jutting out of it and a metal shelving unit stacked with cleaning supplies. Everything was coated with a thick layer of dust.

"What's that?" Sophie asked.

He followed her pointing finger. Bits of cloth were piled in the corner.

"Looks like a stack of rags," he said. "Probably for cleaning."

Anat stepped closer and peered down at them. She nudged them with her toe, then recoiled as they shifted sideways before sliding to the ground. "Not rags," she said in a low voice.

"But what . . ."

Sophie sucked in air sharply at the same instant that Declan made the connection in his mind.

A faded T-shirt and a pair of filthy shorts . . . and stacked beneath them was a small pile of mottled bones.

"Oh, Christ," he breathed out. "Zain."

We're all going to die, Nico thought, looking up as his father and Yosh reappeared. He was back in the enormous room they'd first encountered when they left the infirmary; was that just two days ago? It felt like forever. Four of those thrinax creatures surrounded him. His guards, he was assuming. They'd carried him here, then dumped him on the floor before taking up these positions. The perimeter was filled with a couple dozen more thrinaxes. Scattered among them were men and women of all ages. No kids, though. They looked surprisingly normal: dressed mainly in polyester, their hair universally cut in the same no-nonsense bob as Yosh. Some were scratching the thrinaxes on the heads or backs. There was an odd, low murmur everywhere, kind of a buzzing noise. It was hard to tell if he was really hearing it. Oddly, it seemed to emanate from *inside* his head, as if he was wearing invisible headphones. The thrinaxes made occasional clicking noises, like giant crickets.

Ten minutes after he'd arrived, Sophie had been carried in kicking and screaming. Minutes later Declan showed up draped over the shoulder of another thrinax; he hadn't been moving at all and was either unconscious or dead. Nico's dad had been last, but they hadn't gotten a chance to talk. The minute he was dropped to the floor, Yosh came out of nowhere and led him away.

She hadn't even glanced at him. When he saw her, his heart sank because it meant they'd been attacked, too; Anat would

never have left the slight girl out there on her own, defense-
less. *And Anat wouldn't have been taken easily*, he thought
grimly. *She must have fought hard, and the outcome had
probably not been good.*

Nico squeezed his eyes shut at the thought. He'd really
liked her. Anat was beautiful and strong, the only member
of the group he'd cared much about, to be honest. He'd been
an idiot. They should have stuck together. At least then they
might have made it to the mainland.

Yosh and his father stopped fifty yards away from him,
whispering furiously at each other. Six thrinaxes encircled
them, but they maintained a slight distance. It made no sense.
The same bloodthirsty creatures that had chased him through
the woods were now calm, controlled. He wished his father
had explained more about them, or that he'd thought to ask.
My own fault, Nico thought, *for not having what his dad
termed an "inquisitive mind."*

Why had Yosh and his dad been singled out? Who
were the rest of these people? And where were Sophie and
Declan? Had they already been eaten? He shuddered at
the thought. Maybe they were going to ration the group
out slowly, keeping a few of them alive for a couple days.
He had no idea how much food these things ate. He wondered how many thrinaxes would be sharing bits and
pieces of *him*.

His father's voice suddenly rose to a shout, "Threaten all
you want, I won't do it!"

Yosh crossed her arms. "Get the son," she commanded.

Nico furrowed his brow. *What was she doing?* Light
dawned as two thrinaxes swiveled their heads toward him.
Yosh is in charge, he realized. She'd betrayed them all.
He struggled as the creatures grabbed his arms and began

dragging him toward Yosh. His father's whole body went rigid, but he didn't say anything.

Claws dug into his biceps. "Stop! I'll walk!" he sputtered. But they lifted him up, dragging him forward until he was toe-to-toe with Yosh.

"Hello, Nico," she said.

"Tell them to let me go." He fought to keep the quaver from his voice.

Yosh cocked her head to the side, then glanced at the thrinaxes. They simultaneously released him; he stumbled and nearly fell before righting himself. Nico shook his arms to get some feeling back. Then he drew up to his full height and demanded, "What do you want?"

Yosh glanced at the creature on his left.

Without warning, a claw lashed out. Nico felt a sharp stabbing sensation along his right side. Startled, he looked down. Blood was streaming through a new hole in his shirt.

"No!" his father yelled.

"Again," Yosh said in a low voice.

The animal on the other side of him struck so swiftly that Nico registered the movement at the same time something sliced into the back of his right leg. His knees buckled, and he dropped to the floor. A spreading pool of red encircled him. *That's my blood*, he tried to say, but his tongue seemed to have stopped working.

"Stop!" his father begged. He reached for Nico, but two of the creatures restrained him. "I'll do anything you want. Just stop hurting him!"

Yosh gazed down at him coldly.

"You're killing me," he managed to say.

"You can still be saved," she said. "If your father helps us."

"*Vater*," he said faintly.

"Nico, son, just hang in there. It'll be okay, I promise." His dad's face was twisted with anguish; Nico wondered if this was how he'd looked while he lay in a coma. *Shame that I'm only seeing it now*, he thought in a small, faraway part of his brain. Maybe things could have been different between them, if his father hadn't always come across as so cold and unfeeling.

The room was starting to waver. He closed his eyes against the pain, and Anat's face flashed across his mind. What would she do? She'd be brave. She wouldn't let them win.

"Don't do it," Nico managed to say. "Whatever they're trying to make you do . . ." He choked on something coppery and swiped a hand across his mouth—it came away bloody. He struggled to get the words out, gasping, "Don't help them."

"Nico . . ." His father spun toward Yosh. "Fix this and I'll do whatever you want."

"There's only one way to fix it."

They sounded distant now, like they were drifting away from him. Nico tried to focus, but his eyes refused to listen to the orders his brain was sending. They flickered like bulbs going dim.

"Nico!" his dad called out. But the voice was faint and rapidly receding.

Darkness came swimming up to meet him, and he smiled.

So this is what they were all talking about, Nico thought as he let it guide him away.

Sophie crouched down on the floor beside Declan, with Anat hunched over her shoulder. The three of them were hidden behind one of the large computer towers on the catwalk above the main floor. She could see a circle of thrinaxes in the center of the room but couldn't tell what they were doing.

"Well, this isn't good," Declan murmured.

"We have to find another way out," Anat said in a low voice.

"We already tried that. All the hallways led here," Sophie whispered. They'd spent the past quarter hour investigating every corner of the building. Luckily, they hadn't run into any more of those thrinaxes, or cynogs, or whatever the hell they were. Not so luckily, there appeared to be no way out except through the huge room below. There were a couple dozen people ensconced in the shadows along the walls, with even more of the creatures with them. Sophie had stopped counting at thirty. And the only weapon they'd managed to come up with was the mop from the closet where they'd found Zain.

She shuddered. *Poor Zain.* He'd never had a chance. The worst part was that there was so little left of him. The bones had been picked clean, as scoured of flesh as the ones they'd seen hanging from trees yesterday. At the thought, a wave of bile rose in her throat.

"Maybe they'll leave in a bit," Declan said. "We can just wait them out."

His face was still pale, speech slightly slurred from the concussion. A faint sheen of sweat covered his forehead. She brushed the hair back from his eyes and forced a smile as she said, "Maybe. How do you feel?"

"Oh, just grand," he said. "Aside from the worst feckin' headache of my life. How about you?"

"Terrified," she confessed.

"Have a bit of faith. Got you this far, didn't I?"

"Pretty sure this is where we started," she said wryly. "More or less."

"But look at all the lovely new people you've had a chance to meet." Declan nodded toward the dark shapes that lurked in the shadows. "How many girls get up close and personal with real live dinosaurs, eh?"

"We need to create a distraction," Anat interjected, scanning the room. "Something to draw them away from the door."

"Brilliant," Declan said. "What're you thinking? Pipe bomb? Or perhaps we announce that there's free cake in the infirmary, first come, first serve?"

"This is not the time for jokes," Anat scowled.

"I doubt we'll be able to draw them all away," Sophie said doubtfully. "Don't you think they'll leave a few to guard the door?" She eyed the thrinaxes. The thought of confronting just one of them was terrifying enough. They'd never have a shot against this many.

"You prefer to stay here and die?"

"No," Sophie retorted. "But I'd rather come up with a plan where dying wasn't guaranteed."

"What's that they're standing around?" Declan asked.

Sophie chanced another glance around the machine. The thrinaxes had moved back; now she could see that they'd been encircling Yosh and Bruder. The two of them were standing over something lying in a puddle.

Anat leaned farther over her shoulder to see. Suddenly she stiffened and swore under her breath.

"What?" Sophie asked.

"It's Nico," Anat said bluntly. "They've killed him."

Sophie stared in horror at the figure on the floor. He wasn't moving. The liquid surrounding him was dark, and still spreading. She sucked in a breath. "Oh my God."

"Well, that settles it." Declan's voice hardened. "I'm not waiting around to be next."

Anat yanked him down as he started to shift back the way they came. "They're coming!"

Sophie risked another glance; Anat was right. Yosh was walking purposefully in their direction. Bruder followed her, his shoulders slumped. He looked utterly defeated. They all ducked behind the computer tower.

". . . your only chance to save him," Yosh said, her voice carrying clearly to where they were huddled.

Bruder's response was muted. The group started to ascend the catwalk.

"Quickly!" Declan whispered urgently in her ear. "This way!"

Anat was already racing down the hallway to the utility closet. Sophie followed, keeping her eyes averted from what was left of Zain as they settled inside, breathing heavily.

"Bollocks," Declan spat. "Those bloody bastards."

Sophie blinked back tears. Poor Nico; poor Zain. They were all going to die here. At the thought, she felt a familiar wave of hopelessness. It was the same emotion she'd experienced as they'd wheeled her into the hospice. When the doors swung shut behind her, blocking out the trees surrounding the parking lot, she'd been hit by the realization that she'd never be outside again.

Only this was worse. At least then, she didn't have to worry about getting eaten.

"We have to do something," Anat growled, pacing the room like a caged cat.

"Let's offer to help them."

"What?" Sophie turned to Declan, startled.

He shrugged. "No other way out of here, yeah? Maybe Bruder can convince them that he needs us to start the machine."

"But he said it wouldn't work," Sophie said faintly.

"Maybe not, but could anywhere be more god-awful than

where we are right now?" He gestured to the pile of bones on the floor.

"Bruder seemed to think so," Sophie countered.

"Yeah, but that was back when he had his son with him." His brow furrowed. "This morning you were the one trying to convince me, remember?"

Sophie's heart clenched in her chest as they stared at each other. He was right, she had been in favor of restarting the Collider just a few hours ago. But that was before she'd seen Declan dangling from that monster's back, looking dead. Now, the thought of trying to carve out some sort of a life in this new world didn't seem as frightening—not as long as he was doing it with her.

But if it worked . . . then Declan would be back home with his mom and Katie. And Anat might end up with her fiancé. She was the only one who wouldn't benefit. Sophie took in Declan's square jaw, the cowlick on his forehead. She was being selfish, putting her own newfound happiness above everything else.

And what did she care, really? She'd be dead either way. At least this would give the others a chance.

Sophie turned away so Declan couldn't read her face. "You're right," she said in a low voice. "We should offer to help them."

"Grand," he said, although his voice lacked its usual bravado. "So how do you propose we do it? I mean, without getting killed?"

"They kept us alive this long," Anat said. "They must want something from us."

"We do," a voice chimed in.

Sophie slowly turned.

Yosh was standing in the doorway, framed by a pair of thrinaxes.

Anat lunged forward and demanded, "Why did you kill Nico?"

"We must have struck an artery accidentally," Yosh said dismissively. She reached out and stroked the nearest thrinax on the snout. It closed its eyes like a cat; Sophie could practically hear it purring. "It was unfortunate, but Dr. Bruder is being much more cooperative now."

"After you killed his son? Why?" Declan asked.

"The only way to save Nico now is to do what we want."

"You want the Collider restarted," Sophie stated. "To send us back. Then Nico will be alive again."

"Yes." Yosh smiled slightly. "So you *are* smarter than I gave you credit for."

Sophie shuddered as the cynog Yosh had been petting suddenly snapped its eyes open and stared at her. It emitted a high pitched clicking noise, and Yosh tapped it playfully. "You'll eat soon enough. Of course, if it takes a long time to get the equipment ready, I might have to reconsider."

"What makes you think it'll bloody work?" Declan asked. "I've seen *Dr. Who*. What if you end up shooting us into the center of the sun or something?"

"Then we all die," Yosh said flatly.

"Brilliant." Declan ran a hand through his hair. "Until then?"

"Until then, you can help him." Yosh stepped aside and motioned for them to go ahead of her.

Sophie stepped warily past her into the hallway, doing her best to avoid the creatures, which wasn't easy since they pretty much filled the small space. She walked back toward the main room.

Bruder was on the catwalk staring blankly at a computer monitor. The decades seemed to have abruptly caught up with him. He'd transformed into a broken, stooped shell of a human being.

"Are you all right?" Sophie asked hesitantly. She was half-tempted to lay a comforting hand on his shoulder but still found him too frightening to touch.

He didn't seem to hear her. He was muttering to himself as he played with the array of buttons and dials. "Fairly simple, really. Throw the switch, and the linear particle accelerator feeds into the proton synchotron booster. But the calculations, how am I supposed to—"

"So we're meant to lend a hand, yeah?" Declan interrupted. "Anything we can do that doesn't involve actual science?"

"What?" Bruder looked up at them and blinked. His eyes were red-rimmed and shot through with burst blood vessels. Sophie bit her lip. The expression on his face was nearly identical to the one her parents wore that final afternoon by her deathbed.

"We're so sorry about Nico," she said gently.

"Nico . . ." Bruder stared past them. "They killed him. After all that, he died anyway."

"I know. It's awful." Sophie bit her lip. The words seemed horribly insufficient. "Is there something we can do to help?"

"You know, I never wanted children." His rheumy gaze softened. "But that all changed when he was born."

That seemed like an odd thing to say in light of the circumstances, but maybe he was in shock. "He knew that you loved him," Sophie offered.

"No, he didn't," Bruder scoffed, the old insolence back in his voice. "He thought I looked down on him. I told him he was a fool, that he'd never make his mark on the scientific community. I never got a chance to fully explain what I'd done for him." Bruder turned his palms upward and examined them helplessly. "If it wasn't for my selfishness, none of you would be here."

"What do you mean, selfishness?" Anat asked, her eyes narrowing. "What did you do?"

"I always end up making things worse for you, Nico," Bruder continued as if she hadn't spoken. "Your mother claimed that I put my work first, that I was never there. Don't you see?" He stared past Sophie at Declan. "That was why I did it. This time, I put you above everyone else, above an entire world. More than one world, although that part wasn't intentional. Surely that counts for something."

Sophie took a step back. Bruder had fixated on Declan in a way that seriously spooked her. He'd seemed unbalanced before, but he was rapidly veering off into scary crazy.

Bruder's voice rose as he continued, "All this. The cataclysm. That was me, trying to save you."

Declan held up both hands and said, "Easy there, mate. Let's just take a moment—"

"You were in a coma." Bruder strode forward and grabbed Declan's shoulders. "For months. Your condition wasn't improving. And your mother," he spat, "was about to terminate life support. She claimed that since there was no activity in your cerebral cortex it was cruel to keep you alive any longer. She said you were already gone."

"Listen," Declan said, his voice tinged with desperation. He looked helplessly at Sophie, but she was frozen. Her legs seemed to have turned to jelly. "Just take a few breaths—"

Bruder's words tumbled out in a rush, as if Declan hadn't spoken at all. "We were hiking, and your foot slipped. You fell into a gully—not a deep one, but you hit your head on a rock. Your mother kept saying it was my fault, that the trail was wet and slippery, that I wasn't close enough to catch you. I don't know." He rubbed his eyes with his thumb and forefinger. "Maybe she was right. But she was the one who was going to kill you, Nico. Not me. I couldn't let her do it."

Sophie suddenly realized what he was saying. "You started the Collider by yourself. It wasn't an official test."

"A previous experiment had produced some astonishing results," Bruder said. "Proof that we'd shifted time. By just a few seconds, but I calculated that if I recalibrated the machine and increased the strength, I just might be able to take us back far enough."

"To before the accident," Sophie said softly.

"But instead . . ." Bruder looked around. "All this. I couldn't stop the reaction. There was a power surge, and it rapidly started feeding on itself. I finally managed to shut it down, but by then it was too late."

"Bloody hell," Declan muttered. "You destroyed the world? You, alone?"

"I was trying to save you!" Bruder shouted. "I knew we didn't have much time. Once you were dead, it wouldn't work. And I took every precaution. I tried to calibrate the Collider to only detect you, Nico."

"How?" Sophie asked.

Bruder turned to her. She thought she caught a glimmer of sanity in his eyes, the faintest flicker of recognition. But all too quickly his pupils darted away again, refocusing on some inner stretch of memory. Still, she had to try. It was the only question left that mattered.

"How did you set it to only detect Nico?" she pressed.

"Oh." He rubbed both hands through his hair, shaping it into ragged tufts. "Once I removed you from the machines, it was only a matter of time before . . . well, before . . ."

"Before Nico died," Sophie said softly.

"Yes, yes, before that happened. There was a special set of calculations, I spent weeks on them . . ." Bruder gazed blankly down at the desk he'd been sitting at. "Special . . . so that I'd know at precisely which moment to activate the machine."

He fell silent, still glowering at the desk.

"So you set it to detect someone who was about to die," Sophie said slowly, working through the implications in her mind.

"It's hardly that simple," Bruder growled. "And of course I didn't want to affect everyone who was about to expire. That would have been senseless, affecting hundreds of thousands of people, possibly even more. But a very distinct energy signature appears right at the moment of death, and it's particularly pronounced with late adolescents . . ."

His voice trailed off and he stared at her. Sophie saw that he suddenly understood, too.

"That's why we came through," she said in a low voice. "Not just Nico. Declan was right. It's because we're all around the same age. And we were all about to die."

"That would explain it." Bruder's voice dropped to a cracked whisper. "I'm sorry. I'm so very sorry."

Declan pushed past her and shoved Bruder hard, making him fall back into the chair. He shouted, "What of my mum, eh? And my girlfriend? What about everyone else on the planet?"

Behind them, Sophie could hear the crowd shifting. "Declan," she warned. "Don't let Yosh hear this."

"What, she doesn't have a right to know?" he said wildly. "Is that why they got sucked in, too? Were her parents about to croak? What about all these lovely dinosaurs?"

"I don't know," Bruder muttered. "None of this could have been predicted. I can't explain why it all went wrong.

Believe me, I've tried. For decades, I've worked on unraveling what happened, but it . . . it's beyond me." He dropped his head into his hands.

The thrinaxes started shifting and clacking their claws together in an unsettling way. Sophie glanced back and saw that they'd been joined on the platform by Yosh, flanked by two of the creatures.

"What's going on?" Yosh demanded suspiciously.

"Nothing," Sophie said. "Mr. Bruder is just a little upset—"

"And a lot feckin' insane," Declan said. "Plus, it's his fault we're all here in the first place. So there's that."

Yosh's eyes flickered. "What do you mean, his fault?"

"He performed his own bloody little experiment, yeah? Only he mucked it up, and boom!" Declan clapped his hands together. "You, me, and all your little pets landed here."

"Is this true?" Yosh demanded, turning to Bruder.

"Nico," Bruder reached a hand out toward Declan. "I was only trying to save you."

"Well done on that." Declan slapped his hand aside. "You're as much of an eejit as your son."

Bruder's face suddenly darkened. He lunged forward and grabbed Declan's throat, clamping his hands around it.

"Let him go!" Sophie yelled. She tugged at Bruder's wrist, trying to pull him off, but he was too strong. He banged her with his hip, sending her flying. Sophie slammed hard into the nearest computer tower, the wind knocked out of her. Anat pulled on Bruder from behind, but he barely seemed to notice.

Sophie pushed off the machine and lurched back toward them. Declan frantically pushed against Bruder's chest, trying to shove him away. His face was rapidly turning purple.

"Stop him!" Sophie screamed, turning to Yosh.

Yosh made a small noise and suddenly the thrinaxes were

on Bruder. He gasped and sputtered curses as they held him aloft in front of her.

Declan dropped to the floor.

"Declan!" Sophie raced to his side. "Are you okay?"

He was still gasping, but the color in his face was returning to normal. Angry red fingerprints encircled his throat. He wheezed, "I've had a knock on the head, and nearly been strangled. So not really okay, no."

Sophie's fingers stopped an inch shy of his throat; if only she had some ice, or ibuprofen. He had to be in a lot of pain. Her concern must have shown on her face, because Declan forced a smile and said, "Honestly, I wanted to choke the hell out of that bastard, too."

With effort, she kept her tone light as she replied, "It's good you showed some restraint, then."

Declan made a strangled sound—after a second she realized it was a laugh. "Isn't it, though?"

Sophie glanced back. Bruder was still in the grip of the thrinaxes. His chest heaved as he repeated Nico's name over and over again. She realized with a sinking feeling that he'd lost whatever small shred of sanity he had left.

"So," Yosh said. "It looks like we waited too long."

"Maybe you shouldn't have murdered his son right in front of him," Sophie snapped. "That pushed him over the edge."

"As I said, it was an accident."

"What now?" Anat asked.

Yosh's eyes flicked over each of them in turn. "Did Bruder enter the calculations?"

Sophie hesitated. He'd moved dials and knobs on the panel, but had he finished? It hadn't sounded like it, from what she'd heard. "I'm not sure," she admitted. "Maybe not entirely."

"Then it's too much of a risk." Yosh's shoulders sagged.

"We were so close." There was a depth of sorrow in her voice that almost inspired sympathy. Almost.

Sophie was secretly relieved. As she took in the tiny freckles dotting the bridge of Declan's nose, she couldn't help but think that this wasn't the worst possible outcome. Anat seemed to know a lot about survival. Maybe the three of them would be okay. They'd get as far away from Yosh and the thrinaxes as possible and find some other survivors; they had to be out there somewhere. Maybe things were more normal on the mainland, in spite of what Bruder had said. He could've just been trying to discourage them from checking it out.

A small seed of hope sprouted again. They could build some sort of life here.

As she was thinking it, Yosh flicked a hand in their direction.

"Kill them."

"Wait, what?" Declan protested. He struggled to his feet. Yosh was already descending the stairs from the catwalk. The people who had been standing against the walls started drifting toward the center of the room to meet her.

"I'm doing you a favor," Yosh called back over her shoulder. "Trust me, you wouldn't last long out there. This way, at least you'll be of some value to us."

"As what, food?" Sophie cried. Her small hand gripped his elbow, although he wasn't sure whether that was to steady him or to support herself.

"Yes," Yosh replied curtly. "The cynogs are hungry."

"You can't do this!" Sophie shouted. "Yosh, please!"

But Yosh acted as if she didn't hear them, walking purposefully toward the rest of her people.

Anat made a noise somewhere between a growl and a

curse. The two thrinaxes were advancing slowly. The buzzing and clicking sounds had started up again, much louder this time.

Sophie said in a low voice, "Declan, I'm sorry."

"Sorry for what?" he asked, puzzled, turning toward her. Sophie had a strange expression on her face, and her eyes glistened with tears. She leaned forward and pressed her lips to his. His hand instinctively went to the back of her head, but before he could really kiss her back she'd already drawn away. She ran a hand lightly over his cheek and said, "I'll miss you."

"You'll what?" Declan chanced a glance back over his shoulder. The thrinaxes were just a few feet away. He swallowed hard. Odd that just a few days ago, he'd been afraid of being shot by a Russian. He'd take that over this fate any day of the week. "Sophie, wait—"

But she'd already slipped away.

Anat bit her lip, wishing she still had the Glock. The creatures were advancing. They'd be on her in seconds. Well, she wasn't going down without a fight. She clamped down hard on the pieces of metal she held in each hand, feeling them pinch her skin as she debated where to aim. The creatures had thick plates covering most of their bodies. But the bridge of the nose, between the eyes . . . that was where Yosh touched them. So there were probably unprotected nerve endings there. She drew a deep breath, gathering herself.

Without warning, she released the first throwing star. It caught the creature on the right squarely between the eyes. Its shrieks echoed off the walls as it fumbled for the chunk of metal embedded in its snout. Shouting from down below, and the sound of people running toward them, Anat released the other star. The hit wasn't quite as accurate, but it lodged in the other thrinax's eye.

"Come on!" she yelled to the others.

Declan had frozen, jaw agape as he stared at the injured creatures. Sophie was racing in the wrong direction, headed back toward the machines. Anat snarled with frustration. Did she really have to do everything? "We need to go now!"

Neither of them responded. In fact, Declan headed the other way too, yelling something as he ran. *What were they doing?* This was their only chance to escape, and they were squandering it. The creatures had dropped to the ground and were clawing at their snouts, mewling pitiably. Footsteps raced up the metal stairs, heading straight for them.

She'd done all she could. Sophie and Declan were on their own. Anat spun and tore back down the hallway.

"What are you doing!" Declan yelled in Sophie's ear. "Anat hurt them! We need to go!"

She forced herself to tune him out as she focused on the panel in front of her. There wasn't time to explain. She'd had a moment of clarity as the creatures advanced, the sudden realization that only one option remained. They knew exactly how they'd die if they stayed here. But she could give them one last shot at life.

One large, red switch stood out from the rest—she recalled that Bruder had taken care not to touch it when he was fiddling with the controls. Maybe that didn't mean anything, but it was all she had to go on.

Drawing a deep breath, Sophie flicked the switch.

Nothing happened for a few seconds. Then a low hum started. Sophie could feel the pulse of it deep in her bones, riding through the metal of the catwalk beneath her feet. It slowly and steadily grew louder, until it sounded like a wind turbine spinning faster and faster . . .

"Jaysus," Delcan said, his eyes wide with shock. "What did you do?"

"It's our only chance," she said breathlessly. "Maybe this way you'll get to see your mom and Katie again."

"But Bruder hadn't finished setting it up."

"I know." Sophie bit her lip. "Better to go out with a bang than a whimper, right?"

Declan stared at her for a second, then he grabbed her hands and peered intently into her eyes. "You're bloody nutters, you know that?"

Sophie managed a weak laugh. "Yeah, I know. With our luck, we'll end up on the moon or something."

"Or something," he agreed.

The thrumming noise grew louder. Pressure mounted in Sophie's eardrums until it felt like they were about to pop. The room suddenly seemed to expand and contract, as if it was taking a giant breath. Sophie gasped, remembering how it had been the first time. Suddenly seized by panic, she squeezed Declan's hands hard and said. "If we don't make it—"

"It'll be okay," he said reassuringly, squeezing back. "Either way, this beats getting eaten."

"But if we don't . . ." She leaned in and pressed her mouth to his again.

His lips were warm and solid and reassuring. It was an amazing kiss, filled with frustration and longing and apology and sorrow. Sophie pulled back slightly to catch her breath. Before she could kiss him again, there was a large thwacking sound, like a rubber band being snapped, and the floor abruptly vanished beneath her feet.

CHAPTER FOURTEEN

Anat stumbled and fell. But instead of landing on rough concrete, her fingernails dug into loamy soil. Confused, she jerked her head up.

She was outside. Nighttime. The air smelled oddly familiar. She blinked, trying to orient herself. Spun in a slow circle. Her eyes alit on the nearest building, and she suddenly realized where she was . . .

Training camp. She was on the hill above it, looking down at the low-slung barracks at the rear of the compound. *But how?* She thought over the past few minutes, Sophie rushing over to the machine . . . she must have started it. It must have worked!

Anat felt a surge of elation. She wanted to laugh and cry and start screaming, all at the same time. Something struck her, and she dug in her pocket, hoping to find her cell phone. It was there! She took a deep breath and said a silent prayer before clicking the screen.

It read *August 31ˢᵗ*. Hot tears pressed against her eyelids. Anat pressed the phone to her lips and kissed the screen.

"Put that away!" a voice hissed behind her.

Startled, Anat nearly dropped the phone. She spun around. It took her eyes a second to adjust from the screen's glare. A figure was crouched behind a low stone wall a few meters away.

Night exercises, Anat suddenly realized as she felt the familiar weight of a Tavor rifle slung across her shoulder. She must still be in training. Obediently, she put the cell phone away and crept toward her squad mate. It was Lev, the leader of her unit. He frowned at her, his face tight beneath night vision goggles. "What were you thinking?"

"Sorry," she said in a whisper. "I . . . got distracted." It was such a relief to be speaking Hebrew again. Her eyes still smarted; forcefully, she blinked back the tears. "What are we doing?"

Lev yanked up the goggles and glared at her. "Get your head out of your ass, Erez," he snapped. "You've been briefed."

Anat swallowed hard. She'd just have to play along until she figured out what was going on. Something was off, she could tell. She'd already finished her training, she wasn't even supposed to be here on August thirty-first. *Hazim*, she thought suddenly; *where is he*? Why wasn't she at the hotel in Egypt with him?

She fought back a momentary twinge of panic. It would be okay. She was home now, and as soon as they finished whatever bullshit maneuver this turned out to be, she could call him. They'd be together soon enough.

Drawing a deep breath, she hunkered down beside Lev. He'd pulled his night vision goggles back on. She felt for hers; they were seated across the front of her helmet. She drew them down over her eyes, and the world suddenly sprang into relief, varying shades of green and black.

"There!" Lev whispered, exhilaration in his voice.

Anat followed his pointing finger and frowned. A few hundred meters away, a couple of figures were moving stealthily toward the training facility. But they didn't seem to be wearing military gear.

Lev muttered something disparaging about Arabs and waved for her to follow. Anat trailed at his heels, trying to process what was happening. Was this not an exercise?

The two figures they'd been tracking hunched down behind a bush. They were talking in low voices, the tones sharper than Hebrew. *Arabic*, Anat realized. She watched through the goggles as they struggled with something large. When they reached a point a half-dozen meters away, she suddenly recognized it: a mortar launcher. *What the hell?* she thought. How could their enemies have infiltrated so close to camp? It was unheard of.

"Stop!" Lev yelled, suddenly straightening and leveling his rifle at them.

The two figures froze, then broke into a run, tearing toward the trees on their right. Lev tracked one with his rifle. A loud *crack!* and the figure dropped to the ground.

"*Kus emek*," Anat breathed.

They'd always shot blanks during training, but that had sounded like a live round. Which meant that whatever was happening was real.

The thought had barely registered when she was suddenly shoved hard. She landed on her back, a sharp rock gouging her left shoulder blade. Anat yelped, struggling to get a grip on her rifle, but whoever had jumped her was fighting for control of it. It was a man, about her size, but fortunately not very strong. The two of them gasped and panted. Anat drew her knee up hard and felt it connect. The guy yelped but continued struggling.

A *crack!* and he suddenly went limp, dropping on top of her. Anat shoved him away, fighting against the dead weight. Lev grinned down at her as he flipped his Tavor back around; the stock was smeared with fresh blood from clubbing the guy over the head.

"New boyfriend, Erez?" he teased.

"Help me up," she muttered

The Arab was unconscious, but that probably wouldn't last long. She cocked her rifle; the temptation to pull the trigger was almost overwhelming. Her whole back felt bruised and sore. She'd barely been back five minutes, and already she'd sustained more abuse than in three days on Long Island with man-eating monsters.

"Don't shoot him," Lev warned, laying a restraining hand on the barrel of her gun. "We need to find out what the bastard knows."

"Right." Anat steadied her breathing. She kept sighting along the rifle just in case; there was no way she'd be taken by surprise again.

"Shall we get a look at our new friend?" Lev drew out his Maglite.

Anat kicked the guy's shoulder so that he rolled onto his back. Lev shone the flashlight beam down on his face.

Anat gasped and staggered back. The Tavor dropped from her hands, dangling from her shoulder strap.

"You okay?" Lev asked with concern.

Anat couldn't answer. She stared down at the terrorist who had been mounting an attack on their compound.

It was Hazim.

Her eyes immediately darted to his right hand, which had fallen limply across his chest. She blinked back tears, then knelt for a closer look.

"What is it?" Lev asked.

Anat choked back a sob. His finger was bare—Hazim wasn't wearing the ring she'd given him. Her mind spun as she considered what that meant. "It's August thirty-first," she said in a low voice.

"Erez, did you hit your head when you fell?"

Lev moved toward her, but she shied back. "I'm not even supposed to be here," she said, feeling dazed. "Why am I here?"

"Let's get you to the medics," Lev said firmly.

Anat ignored him, sinking to her heels and setting her head in her hands while she tried to work through what was happening. She was home, back the same day she'd left. But she wasn't supposed to be *here*. She was supposed to be with her family in Tel Aviv on August thirty-first, on her final leave before reporting for duty. Which meant something had changed. And if she was somewhere different . . .

Then maybe this was a different Hazim, too.

"Declan! Supper won't keep all night!"

Declan blinked a few times, disoriented. "Sophie?" he said tentatively. He could still feel the pressure of her hands in his, the warmth of her lips . . .

No, he realized. He was sitting alone in his bedroom. The Clash and The Fratellis posters on the walls, clothes strewn about the floor, and the smell of his mum's roast drifting up the stairs. Declan jumped up and ran a hand through his hair. They'd done it. They'd bloody done it! They weren't going to be eaten by giant lizard creatures, or forced to spend the rest of their lives in a hole in the ground. He let out a whoop of elation.

"Holy Mother of God, Declan, you nearly gave me an attack!" his mum called up the stairs. "Quiet down or you'll have the neighbors phoning the guards!"

Declan turned in a circle, amped up. He wanted to do a thousand things simultaneously: run down the stairs and throw his arms around his mum, scream out the window, call . . . *Sophie*, he thought with a sudden pang. Had she saved them, only to end up back on the brink of death?

There had to be a way to find out. She lived in . . . Palo Alto, he remembered. Near San Francisco. Right, he'd just get on the Internet and find her. He dug his mobile out of his pocket and tried to turn it on, but the battery was still dead. '*Course it is*, he thought, cursing silently. Couldn't use the damn thing even when he was back in the land of mobile towers. His computer was buried under a pile of clothing and papers on his desk. While digging it out, he hit the edge of something hard. Declan's brow furrowed. Using both hands, he swept everything away.

It was the box. The one he'd stolen from the house in Salthill. The one the Russians had taken from him.

But that didn't make any sense. "Mum!" he yelled. "What day is it?"

She grumbled something about him yelling, then shouted up, "As if you don't remember missing mass. Sunday. Now get your arse downstairs, the roast is going cold."

"No, I mean, what's the date?"

She didn't answer, plainly refusing to carry on a conversation up a flight of stairs. Declan ran a hand through his hair. On an impulse, he reached out and opened the box.

What he saw inside made him fall back into the chair. "Bloody hell," he breathed.

It was a claw: long, yellow, and all too familiar. A thrinax claw, here in Galway.

What the hell was going on?

• • •

Sophie opened her eyes. She was lying in a hospital bed. She recognized the pale-puce colored walls and tacky oil paintings immediately; she'd spent over a month staring at them. The bed was familiar, too, as was the view of Stanford University's spires. She was back in the hospice. For a second, she wondered if the past few days had all been a crazy, morphine-induced dream: Declan, Anat, the thrinaxes, everything.

Then she felt a throbbing in her arm. She lifted it up to inspect it: a long, narrow cut where the thrinax had sliced her with its claw.

Sophie let her arm drop back down on the covers. Not a dream, then. She'd done it; she'd hit the reset button. Hopefully they'd all gotten back home.

Of course, that meant she was still on her deathbed.

Oh well, she told herself, trying to repress a surge of disappointment. The others might be okay. And she'd had a decent couple of days, barring that whole narrowly escaping death thing. At least she'd been moving around again. And she'd visited Long Island, for the first and last time. *Too bad we never made it to the Hamptons*, she thought with a slight smile.

Sighing, Sophie took a physical inventory. She ached all over and felt like she could sleep for a week. Still, she was alive. For the moment, at least.

Her room was empty, which was odd but kind of a blessing, since she'd prefer a few minutes alone before facing her family. An IV line jutted from her left hand, the cord led to a hanging stand. The nurse call button was right where it should be, resting on the covers.

She hesitated for a second, then tapped it.

A minute later, a middle-aged nurse with close-cropped

hair and kindly eyes bustled into the room. It was Betsy, one of her favorites.

"Miss Sophie," she said brightly. "What can I do for you?"

"Um, well . . ." Sophie's head swam, there were a dozen different things she wanted to know. Like, what day was it? Hell, what year? And were there dinosaurs running around outside? She decided to start with an easy one, though. "Where are my parents? And Nora?"

"They went out for lunch."

"Lunch?" Sophie said dubiously. Kind of weird that they'd left her all alone at death's door. "Um, did they say when they'd be back?"

"They mentioned something about swinging by the house to grab a few of your things." Betsy moved adroitly around the bed, double-checking the saline drip and monitors. There were fewer than usual, Sophie noticed. And the morphine drip was inexplicably gone, it usually hung right next to the saline.

"Great," she grumbled, digging her head into the pillows. "Hopefully I won't die before they get back."

"Die?" Betsy's forehead crinkled. "Is that a joke?"

"A joke?"

"I thought . . . oh my, are you feeling disoriented?" Betsy leaned in, checking her pupils.

"No," Sophie said, resisting the urge to push her away. "I feel fine." And she did, she realized suddenly. Sore and achy, but basically fine.

"Well, I'm not surprised that it would take some getting used to." Betsy stepped back and smiled broadly at her. "I mean, it's not every day we send someone home, you know."

Sophie blinked, trying to process what she was saying. "I'm going home?"

"This afternoon. That's why they're getting your clothes. You don't want to walk out of here in that thing, do you?" Betsy eyed her nightgown reprovingly.

Sophie followed her gaze; she was still wearing the smiley face one with the bullet hole in the forehead. "I don't understand," she said. "What about the lymphoma?"

Betsy swept her hands in a wide arc. "Gone."

"Gone?" Sophie was dumbfounded. "But . . . it can't just be gone."

"That's what Dr. Zimmerman thinks, too," Betsy said smugly. "But they've run every test. Of course, you'll still need to come in for regular check-ups. But with any luck, it'll stay in remission." Unexpectedly, Betsy leaned down and planted a kiss on her forehead. "I'm so happy for you, dear," she said, her voice thick. "Miracles don't happen much around here."

And with that, she swept out of the room.

Sophie lay back on the pillows, stunned. Was it possible? If anything, this was even more surreal than waking up at the facility.

Declan, she thought.

She had to find a way to get in touch with him. Of course, he was probably back home now . . . which meant back with Katie. She bit her lip, wondering if he'd even want to talk to her. Would it only make things more complicated? Maybe she should pretend it was all a dream . . .

But just because she'd ended up back in the same place, didn't mean he had. There was no harm in checking to make sure he was okay, right? Deciding, she grappled for the call button and pushed it repeatedly.

Betsy scrambled back into the room. "Sophie? Are you okay?" Her eyes darted reflexively to the machines that recorded her stats. "What happened?"

"Can you access the Internet on your cell phone, Betsy?"

"What?" Betsy's forehead wrinkled, and she crossed her arms sternly over her chest. "You called me in here for my telephone?"

"Please, Betsy. It's really, really important. I swear."

Betsy eyed her for a minute longer, then drew an iPhone out of her pocket as she grumbled under her breath. Sophie quickly thumbed open the browser. An Internet search for Declan Murphy produced thousands of results.

She swore, and Betsy threw her a sharp look. Why couldn't he have a more unique name, like Aloysius or something? Sophie chewed her lip, then narrowed the results by "Galway City" and "seventeen."

Still dozens of websites. She scanned through them quickly, until a Facebook page caught her eye. There was a small jpeg next to it. She hit the button to enlarge it, and Declan's face stared back at her from the small screen. It was a typical teenage photo: his arms flung around two other boys, mouth open as if the camera had captured him mid-yell. He was wearing jeans and a ragged T-shirt and he looked absolutely incredible.

"Betsy, can I use this for another minute? I need to get on Facebook," Sophie asked, suddenly feeling breathless.

"Facebook?" Betsy looked bewildered. "Sophie, what on earth—"

"It really is important, Betsy. Life or death."

More grumbling, mostly about what teenagers considered to be life or death, and how Sophie of all people should know better. But seeing the expression on her face, Betsy softened. "I'll be back in five minutes," she warned. "And I'll want it then. No calling China, hear?"

What about Ireland? Sophie thought, but she nodded meekly in response. After Betsy left the room, she logged into Facebook and navigated to Declan's page. Her breath caught at one of the photos on his timeline—the kind people take by holding the camera above themselves, super close-up. Declan was cheek-to-cheek with a gorgeous red-haired girl, both smiling like they'd never been so happy. Sophie's gut wrenched. Maybe she should just leave Declan to his normal life. He might not want anything to do with her now, anyway. He probably just wanted to forget any of it had ever happened.

She was about to log off when an alert flashed: *Declan Murphy wants to chat with you. Accept?*

Heart thudding in her chest, she clicked the *yes* button.

After a brief pause, words streamed onscreen.

Never so happy to see stinking Galway. U make it home all right?

Yes, she wrote back, heaving a sigh of relief. So Declan had made it home too. She wanted to pour out everything she'd experienced since the moment she opened her eyes . . . including how anguished she'd felt when his hands slipped from her grasp. But she hardly knew where to begin. Finally, feeling totally lame, she wrote, *U ok?*

Still got a knot on my head, but yeah. Another beat, then he wrote, *R u sick?*

Nope, I'm fine.

A dancing emoticon with a goofy grin appeared.

Sophie smiled in response. She was sorely tempted to ask for his number, but Betsy would kill her if she made an international call. For now, they should stick to IM'ing.

Sophie rubbed her forehead, debating what to write next. She was exhausted, it still felt like she'd spent the day tearing through a forest, fleeing down dark hallways . . . of course, she had. Although that had all really happened . . . what, two days from now? Or twenty years? Just thinking about it made her head hurt.

Still there?

Yes, she typed back. *Have u checked for Anat yet?*

Was going to do that next. Wanted to find out if u were ok first.

Thanks, she wrote, feeling her cheeks flush. He'd thought of her first—that was good, right? *I'll check too. Do they even have Facebook in Israel?*

They have FB everywhere, you nutter. Americans. Always think you're so special.

Reading it, Sophie could practically hear his voice. She didn't know what to write next, her hands hovered over the screen. There were so many things she wanted to say, but she wasn't sure if any of them were a good idea.

I'd like to talk to you, he wrote. *I miss you already.*

Sophie bit her lower lip. Her eyes misted over as she typed, *Miss you too.*

Good. Send me your # and I'll call tomorrow. Night, love.

"Good night," she said out loud, even though it was late morning in California.

Commotion in the hall. Sophie looked up, her parents and sister crowded through the doorway. All three of them beamed at her.

"Hi, sweetheart. Ready to come home?" her mother asked, rushing to her bedside.

Sophie threw her arms around her and squeezed. "Oh, Mom. I missed you."

"It's only been a few hours." Her mother laughed and touched her cheek. "But I missed you too."

Sophie didn't think she'd ever felt so happy. "I've had enough of hospitals for pretty much ever," she said. "Let's get out of here."

"You could just audit a class, you know," Sophie said, nudging Declan with her elbow.

"Already checked the catalog." He bit into his roll, talking around it as he continued, "Read it through twice, didn't see anything on safe-cracking. And here I thought university was supposed to teach some useful skills."

Sophie furrowed her brow. "You said you were done with all that."

"Have a sense of humor, lass." Declan reached over to tuck a lock of hair behind her ear. "I'm kidding."

She smiled. Every time he touched her she still got chills. "Sure you are."

She kept having to remind herself that this was real: the two of them, sitting at a café right off campus in the center of Dublin. Sophie tilted her head back, drinking in the sun. Declan kept warning her that this wasn't typical Irish weather—in the two weeks she'd been here, it hadn't rained once. He kept joking that she must've brought the California sun with her. She didn't care if it poured every day. After nearly a year apart, all their plans had finally come true. She was enrolled as a first year student at Trinity College in Dublin. And Declan had moved in with friends from Galway: it was a raucous apartment filled with five guys, all of whom regarded watching soccer to be a competitive sport. Not that he'd spent much time there lately. She smiled at him across her mug of coffee.

"Y'know, a proper Irish girl would be drinking tea," he pointed out.

Sophie grimaced. "Ugh. I still can't stand the stuff."

"It's an acquired taste," he acknowledged.

"Good thing I've got four years to acquire it, then."

Declan expression turned serious. He leaned in closer and said, "Listen, I heard from Anat the other day."

"Really?" Sophie repressed a twinge. Apparently Anat's contempt hadn't faded over the past year. Not that they'd become close in 2033 Long Island, exactly, but it still hurt that Anat had reached out to Declan, not her. "How's she doing?"

"Eh." Declan shook his head. "Not good. Hazim is still locked up, and hasn't a clue who she is."

"Poor Anat," Sophie said, half to herself. She couldn't even imagine how awful that would be. It had become apparent over the past year that the place where they'd landed was slightly different from the one they'd left. Most of the inconsistencies were small and insignificant, at least for her. But Anat wasn't having the same experience in Israel.

"Anyway, I invited her to come for holiday. She probably won't," he added, taking in her expression. "But I figured I'd offer."

"That was sweet of you." Sophie reached out and took his

hand. He was right; it was unlikely that Anat would come. But maybe being asked had made her feel better.

"Anat's the toughest bird I know," he said. "She'll be fine, yeah?"

"Sure," Sophie said, gnawing her lip.

"What's wrong?"

"I just . . ." Sophie shook her head and looked down. "It's just strange that we never found any sign of Nico or Bruder here. I mean, it's like they never existed at all."

Declan shrugged. "We've talked about this. Maybe they didn't. Many worlds and all that, right?" He squeezed her hand. "Might be for the best, don't you think?"

"Maybe," Sophie acknowledged. "Still, I can't help but wonder . . ."

"Wonder what?" Declan pressed gently when she didn't continue. They'd come to an unspoken agreement long ago not to dwell on the fates of Nico or Zain.

"I wonder if there's another version of us out there somewhere . . . a dimension where we both died," she said softly.

Declan took her face in his hands, leaned forward, and kissed her. Sophie closed her eyes, giving in to the rush of emotions. "It doesn't matter if there is," he said, pulling away. "We're here now. Together. And nothing is going to change that."

"Okay." She managed a slight smile, but it felt forced. Survivor's guilt, probably. Over time, that would fade.

"Grand. Now that's settled, let's get out of here. Plans tonight, you know." He winked.

"Oh, really?" She cocked an eyebrow. "What sort of plans?"

"There's a Godzilla double feature playing," he said gravely. "Not to be missed."

Sophie burst into laughter. Linking arms with him, she leaned her head against his shoulder as they walked away from the café. Music and laughter spilled out the open doors of pubs as they strolled past. The sun hung low in the sky; the streets were packed with people. She felt light, clean, happy. A year ago, she was at death's door. Declan was right. Maybe there were thousands of versions of them out there somewhere, but for now, she was right here. And it was as close to perfect as she'd ever known.

Michelle Gagnon is an International Mystery Book Association bestseller whose books have sold worldwide. Her first YA thriller, *Don't Turn Around*, was published by Harper Teen in August 2012. Michelle has also been a modern dancer, a dog walker, a bartender, a freelance journalist, a personal trainer, and a model. She lives in San Francisco. Visit her on the web at www.michellegagnon.com.